FIRE LINES

CARA THURLBOURN

Bewick Press Ltd.
Unit 1, Hall Barn Road, Isleham
Cambridge, CB7 5RJ

This edition was published in the UK by
Bewick Press Ltd in 2017.

ISBN: 978 0 9957266 1 1

For Mum and Dad

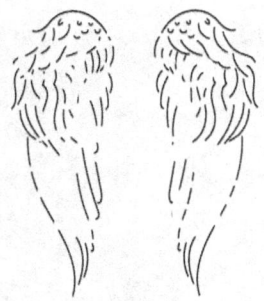

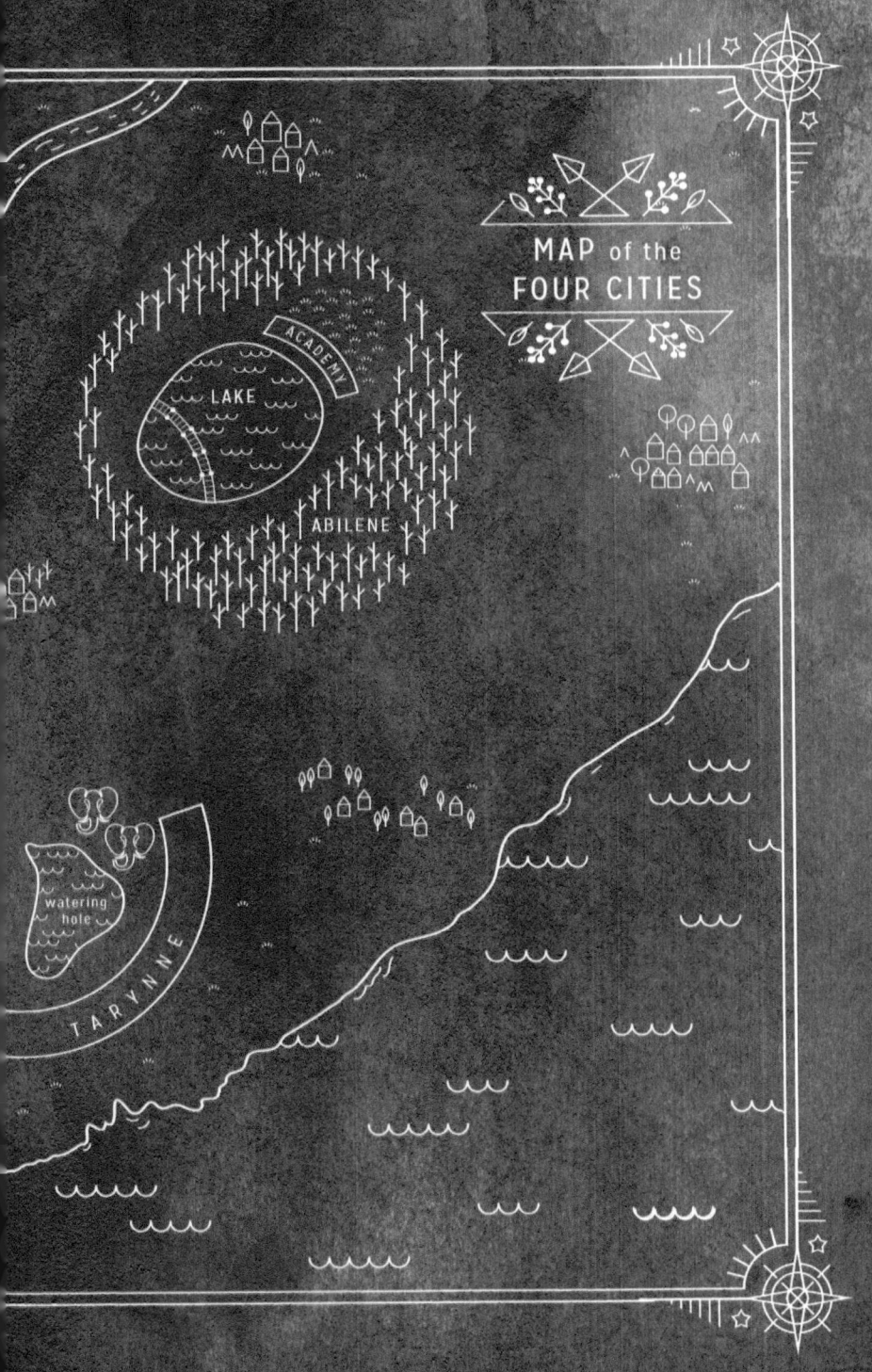

MAP of the
FOUR CITIES

ACADEMY

LAKE

ABILENE

watering
hole

TARYNNE

ONE

O n the other side of the door, my mother's shallow footsteps drift across the living room. No one in the Red Quarter sleeps through the night, but she doesn't even try. She spends the hours between sunset and sunrise rearranging our meagre possessions, moving them this way and that, until they're just right. Sometimes I want to burst out of the bedroom and scream at her to be still. Other times, I'd like to wrap my arms around her bony frame and whisper in her ear:

"Everything will be alright."

Tonight, as with most nights, I do neither. I lie in the dark and listen. Outside, the congealed night-time air squeezes all signs of life out of the Quarter. The streets are motionless. The lamps have been extinguished. Everyone is waiting. Everyone is wondering if it's their turn to suffer an inspection.

In the three years we have lived in Red, we've endured twenty-eight inspections. At first, I tried to spot a pattern. I kept track of when the Cadets visited our neighbours, how long they stayed, how many there were. But I know now that there's no way to predict when they will knock; the Council instructs them to vary the times, the streets, the order, so there is never even a glimmer of complacency.

It's different in the upper quarters, of course. When we were Greens we would receive a polite tap on the door, usually in the middle of the afternoon, and the Cadets would be in and out within minutes. Here, inspections take place largely at night. The Cadets slip silently through the shadows in their neatly pressed uniforms. They wait until they're right outside your door, then they hammer their fists and blow their whistles and everything quakes as though the world is ending.

Ma says the relentless anticipation of this skull-splitting noise has shredded her nerves. I can't remember a time when her nerves were un-shredded, even from before we were down-graded, but I've never said this to her. My father was always the strong one – the one who took care of things. At least, that's the way I remember it.

The summer months here are the worst. Even with the windows open, there is no breeze. The congested streets trap the heat, encouraging it to swell until, eventually, a bone-rattling storm shatters the tension and it starts all over again. I've become quite prophetic at forecasting the rain; the day before it comes, the air shifts and my skin begins to tingle. It's a useful talent to have, but not one you want to shout about – there's a fine line between intuition and *magick*.

We've always had to be careful. Even in the upper quarters you learn to edit your actions so that no one can accuse you of harbouring hidden abilities, or yearning for the days before the wall. But, like the weather, everything is amplified when you're a Red. So I don't tell anyone about the tingling.

The day we left the Green Quarter we dragged our trunk down to the canal, where a huddle of Reds waited to board the ferry back home. A rotund woman in a short-sleeved tunic and long brown waistcoat helped us up onto the deck.

"Call me Nor," she told us, wiping beads of sweat from her brow. "You two have a place to stay?" My mother simply shook her head, unable to stop worrying at the scarlet sash that now pinched her upper arm. Nor pretended not to notice. "My brother Junas has a flat. I'll take you there but he'll want to see what's in the trunk – he won't want any trouble."

That was when I knew things would be different.

From the ferry station, Nor marched us through side streets teeming with noise and smoke and people. She warned us to keep our heads down and move quickly. Ma did as she was told, fixed her nervous gaze on her feet and hurried as close to Nor as she could. But I couldn't help staring. At school, the Red Quarter was used as a cautionary tale to keep us on track and out of trouble – but I never imagined it would be so different. In Green, everything was neat and ordered. Here in Red, sprawling streets are crammed with flats, taverns, stores and rubbish. At first, I thought it was rain water running in miniature streams down the pavements, but I soon realised it was sewage. For the first two weeks, I refused to empty our bucket into the street. Each day, I carried it to the patch of scrubland behind the flats. But eventually, like everyone else, I gave in.

Junas's flat turned out to be the top floor of what had once been his parents' house. When my mother realised it was comprised of just two rooms, with no kitchen and no bathroom, she pinched my arm and whispered, "Émi, we can't live here." I told her we should take it for the night and look for something better the next morning. As it turns out, there wasn't anything better. I was fourteen then. Next month, I'll be seventeen and here we are – still living in our two concrete rooms. Ma has promised she'll find regular work to help me pay the rent, but the upper quarters won't hire the wife of a convict and she can't bring herself to work in a tavern or a laundrette. So, for now, my wages are all we have.

I turn over, away from the door, and try to find a spot on the mattress where the coils don't dig into my side. A persistent drip, drip, drip is coming from outside the open window. The guttering is probably clogged with something dead or dying because the dripping is beginning to smell, but Junas won't even contemplate investigating it until we've paid him the rent we owe. Reluctantly, I unfold my creaky limbs and climb up onto the window ledge. In our old house, we could open the shutters on nights like this and calming whispers of air would soothe the walls, and the floors, and lull us to sleep. Here in Red, as I lean my upper body out into the street, the heat seems to magnify. Instantly, a film of sweat springs out on my forehead and I have to resist the urge to wipe it away for fear of losing my balance. I use one hand to grip the top of the window frame and, with the other, reach up into the guttering. My fingers squelch into something moist that sends a shiver of nausea down into my throat. I move my hand through the sludge until I come across something a little more solid. I stretch upwards and pull it loose; flies and stench and blood come with it. As I suspected, a dead rat. It probably got stuck and drowned in the last rain storm. Poor thing. For a brief, horrendous moment I find myself turning the rat over in my hand and wondering whether it is too far decayed to be edible. Then I come to my senses and toss it down to the street below.

At the very same moment the rat hits the ground, the knocking starts. The block of tenements on the opposite side of the street has been chosen. Sometimes the Cadets inspect just one, but tonight they are descending ruthlessly on the entire building. I step back so that I'm hidden from view as men, women and children are herded out onto the street. At least ten Cadets have entered the building. As they light their lanterns and begin to search, their silhouettes jerk up and down like vicious shadow puppets. Outside, the remaining Cadets are dividing the Reds by family group and lining them up in order of age – youngest first. Barefoot, and in the mandatory grey tunics we are forced to wear as pyjamas, the Reds stare blankly ahead, waiting for it to be over.

Callous laughter booms out from the open windows of the tenements; the soundtrack of the inspection is reaching its crescendo. Drawers and wardrobes are emptied, possessions clatter to the ground. The entire episode lasts just minutes, but feels like hours. The first time I saw an inspection like this, I cried. Tears streamed down my cheeks and I shook uncontrollably long after the Cadets had gone. Tonight, I clench my fists so tight that my nails draw blood from my palms. I hate that they are all just standing there, letting this happen. I hate that, if it was my turn, I'd do the same thing. And I hate that for so much of my life I had no idea what it was like here.

When the noise stops, the Cadets who inspected the building file back onto the pavement and I shudder as I notice who's in charge: Falk, a blonde from the Silver Quarter who has mottled acne scars on his cheeks and thick cabbagey breath. At least once a week I have to avoid him on my late-night walks back from the ferry. Falk clears his throat and orders the Reds to present their paperwork. One by one, he studies their permits and ensures their red sashes are tied correctly, forcing them to present their left arms so that he can scrutinise every minute detail, from the knot to the position above the elbow. I hold my breath until he reaches the very last person, and then slowly unclench my fists. It's over. The Reds turn back to their dismantled homes. Then:

"I'd like to speak to Jennyfer Kray... Jennyfer?"

Falk is smiling. My skin begins to prickle. From the back of the crowd, a middle-aged woman with tendrils of matted brown hair steps forwards.

"I'm Jennyfer," she croaks.

Falk bobs down to Jennyfer's level, forcing her to meet his eyes.

"I found something of yours, Jenny, and I wanted to return it to you – in person."

He reaches out his hand, offering her something small and round. I grip the windowsill, begging under my breath, "Don't take it, don't take it."

For a moment, Jennyfer hesitates. She glances over her shoulder at the crowd but everyone is looking at the floor instead of at her. She doesn't know what to do. Falk is still smiling at her, so she returns a crooked, grimy smile and hastily takes the object from him.

"Thank you, sir."

"Ha!" Falk shouts, jabbing a finger into the air. Jennyfer stares wide-eyed at whatever she's holding. "So, it is yours?" he demands, planting his hands on her shoulders and giving her a shake.

"I... no, sir... I..."

"But you accepted it from me. It must be yours? Otherwise you would have said, 'I'm sorry, sir, you're mistaken...' Would you not?" His words come out quickly, blurring into one another. She doesn't have the chance to keep up.

Jennyfer looks wildly from Falk to the object and back to Falk. "Please, sir, I never seen it before. I promise."

Falk grimaces, as though he is finding all of this very upsetting. "Oh, Jenny. I would love to believe you – I would. But you know that magick is banned here in the City of Nhatu, don't you?"

Jennyfer nods. I feel my stomach tighten.

"And you know that when the wall was built to keep Mahg and the evil forces at bay, the Council decreed that anyone caught with magickal paraphernalia should be punished?"

Jennyfer begins to tremble. I am gripping the windowsill so hard it feels like it might crack.

"And when I showed you this object, this forbidden object, you accepted it from me willingly. Didn't you? So what am I supposed to do? The law says you must be punished. There is no way around it. We cannot allow magick within the City walls."

Falk clicks his fingers and stands aside. Two green-banded Cadets take Jennyfer by the arms. She starts to buck against them. Still, no one looks up. No one helps. The Cadets are trying to drag her down the street but she is digging her feet into the ground.

"No, you can't take me, you can't!"

Falk strides after his colleagues. When he reaches them, he grabs Jennyfer's hair and tugs. Her head snaps backwards and she releases a throaty groan. Then he drives his steel-toed boot into the middle of her back and she crumples like a rag doll.

Standing above them, a complicit observer, my hands begin to shake. The tightness in my stomach has turned to heat and it's spreading through my chest, into my throat and down my arms. Suddenly, there is a crack, and a pop, and sparks of light jump from my window into the street. My heart is thundering. Was that me? It can't have been me? What was that?

From below, Falk is shouting. "You! Up there! What are you doing?"

Too late, I duck down to the floor, staring at my hands. Was that me? It can't have been...?

Falk yells at his Cadets, "Get over there... A girl... Find her!"

The window ledge is singed black. My mind is whirring and my hands sting. Quickly, I grab the lantern and lighter fluid from my bedside table. I soak the wick, spill a little fluid on the floor and wrap the lantern in a blanket to muffle any sounds. Then, I jab at the lantern until the panes of glass break into splinters.

Footsteps are charging up the stairs. The Cadets are pounding on the door.

"Émi... Émi, what's happening?" Ma's trembling voice calls from the other room.

Working quickly, I shake the glass loose, scatter it onto the windowsill and the floor, and set the lantern on top of the burn mark, on its side. Then, my mother lets them in.

Three silver-banded Cadets charge into my room, the force of their urgency almost prising the door from its hinges. A Cadet I don't recognise grabs my shoulders and shoves me away from the window so that I'm standing beside the bed. The other two return to the living room and I hear my mother pleading with them to tell her what's happening. I wish she would be quiet. I wish she had refused to let them in and barricaded the door. I wish she was like my father, and then I hate myself for wishing it. If she was like him, she'd be gone too.

Falk saunters through the smashed-open door as though he's walking into a tavern. His steely eyes graze all the way from my collarbones down to my spindly legs, and back again. The Cadet who shoved me gestures to the windowsill and Falk swipes his gnarly index finger across it. He turns to me and raises an eyebrow.

"Miss Fae. Would you care to explain what happened here?"

"I must have used too much fluid," I reply, gesturing to the shards of glass.

"The lamp?"

"Just went..." I fling my fingers outwards into star shapes to indicate an explosion.

Falk moves his gaze to the street below. The Reds are back

inside. Jennyfer is nowhere to be seen. He makes an *mmm* noise with the back of his throat. "And you were lighting your lamp in the middle of the night, because...?"

I step away from my bed and point to the small, battered writing desk in the corner of the room. "I couldn't sleep, so I thought I'd use the time to do some work."

Falk stares at me, unblinking. I force myself to add, "Sir."

He moves over to the desk and beckons for his colleague to bring him a light. He sifts through my papers, deliberately sending my charcoals and paints clattering to the floor. He studies the pictures, then scrunches them violently in his fist and whirls around to face me. "This is work?"

I nod. "Yes, sir."

"Last time we spoke you didn't mention you were an artist, Miss Fae. You told me you worked in..." He rifles through his memory. "A cafe in the Green Quarter. Isn't that right?"

"I do both. I waitress at The Emerald but I do some sketches for the Council too – for the posters." I glance out of the window at the billboards on the building opposite, as though Falk wouldn't know instantly which posters I am referring to. Slowly, he pulls the stool from underneath my desk and sits down, legs spread, elbows on his knees. I hate that he is here, in my room. I couldn't give a jot about the drawings. He can tear them into a thousand pieces and throw them down there with the rat for all I care, but I hate that he is making me talk to him. When we're inspected, we usually wait outside. We don't have to interact. My skin burns with irritation, but when the same heat that caused the sparks begins to swirl in the bottom of my stomach, I force myself to breathe deeply. If I created that flash of light, and if Falk finds out...

"So, Miss Fae. You woke up, you couldn't sleep, you thought you'd do a little night-time sketching, and when you went to light your lantern, it exploded – poof! – just like that. Am I right?"

I nod a little quicker this time, and try to widen my eyes. He likes it when we're scared of him. In my most genteel voice I add, "I'm so sorry if I alarmed you, sir. I didn't mean to interrupt..."

Falk's eyes flicker as his mind flashes back to Jennyfer. He is still pleased with himself. Perhaps this is why he suddenly stands, abandons the stool in the centre of the room and announces, "Very well. I accept your apology."

I half-curtsy and dip my head. "Thank you, sir."

Falk motions for his lamp-holding colleague to leave, and we descend into an eerie half-light. My ears begin to throb. I want to scrape my fingernails down his pockmarked face and kick him like he kicked Jennyfer. I'm using every fibre of willpower in my body to keep my breath steady and my hands still but the swirl in my gut is pulling harder and harder. Falk is so close now that I can feel his acrid breath on my cheek.

"I'll be watching you, Émi," he whispers. "I know who your father is. I know what he did. And I don't trust you."

TWO

F alk and his Cadets charge back downstairs. I don't need to watch to know they're heading for the nearest tavern. In the living room, my mother is no longer pacing. Despite the heat, I shiver and wrap my arms around myself. My insides are returning to normal and I'm starting to wonder whether maybe it was the lamp that caused the sparks. But it wasn't. I know it wasn't.

I find Ma sitting on the edge of our hand-me-down sofa, rubbing the back of her neck and twisting an unlit cigarette between her fingers. She looks at me as though she has forgotten I live here. "Émi? What happened? What did they want?"

I sit down next to her. "It was nothing, Ma. I'm sorry. The lantern exploded." I try to laugh, to make her see it's funny really, something so silly causing such a fuss. "I explained. It's fine."

She looks down, taps her hand nervously on her thigh and nods. "The lantern, I see, the lantern."

"Did you see what happened to the woman opposite?" I ask. She ignores my question. "We can't afford a new lantern."

I tell her it's alright, I'm sure Nor can find us one, and ask if she'd like a cup of tea. We don't have a stove, so our water is heated in a little metal bucket, suspended over a hot flame. It only ever reaches tepid, never hot. I pour us two cups of black tea, each with half a teaspoon of sugar. When I return to the sofa, my mother is staring at the trinity of copper-coloured bands that encircle her ring finger. She looks up at me and begins to slide them off, one by one. "I need you to take these down to the shop."

"Pa gave you those."

"I'll get them back at the end of the month," she says, forcing a smile.

"Are you sure?"

Her forehead sharpens into a frown. "Just do as you're told, Émi. We owe Junas two weeks' rent, and the lantern…"

She's right. The Quarter tax went up again last month so, even with the cafe and the posters, my wages simply aren't enough any more. But pawning her wedding rings? I swallow the urge to tell her that sooner or later we'll run out of things to pawn and she'll have to consider taking one of those tavern jobs she despises. I want to say this, but I don't. Whenever I lose my temper her porcelain fingers start to tremble, and her lips quiver, and I regret it. So, I say nothing and take the rings.

We sip our tea in silence for a few minutes, but when she goes back to fiddling with the picture frames on the sideboard I take my mug and return to my room. Really, it's our room. In the beginning, we shared the bed. Despite the heat, we lay next to one another and I tried not to notice when the pillow became wet with her tears. Then, slowly, night by night she spent more time in the living room. Now, I think of it as my room.

I rest my mug on top of the pictures Falk mauled with his ugly fingers. I despise those pictures. It was a job I never imagined I would take – creating dastardly images for the Council to use on their posters and flyers. In Green, they're more discreet, but here they are plastered on every spare piece of wall and forced through doors on a daily basis. I didn't think they would give me the job. When Nor saw my sketches and suggested I apply, I told her there was no way the Council would allow the daughter of a traitor to work for them. But I was wrong. They say I have an 'uncanny talent' for visualising the horrors beyond the wall. They say it's unusual in someone so young. Nor thinks they are using it as a way to keep a closer watch on me but I don't much care why, the important thing is that they pay me ten crowns for each new drawing I take them. Usually I produce two each week, but with the tax increase I may have to raise my output to three or four.

I don't want to confront the blackened mark on the windowsill, but I can't leave the splinters of glass; Ma might come in here and cut her feet. Carefully, I pick the fragments from the floor. I move the broken lamp back to the bedside table and fold the blanket so I can return it to its place under the bed... The blanket! Did Falk see the blanket? It was here, out in the open, the entire time. Tiny splinters of glass have fixed themselves between its scratchy fibres. Did he see them? A shudder runs from my stomach to my knees and I sit down, hard, on the edge of the bed. I'm trying to remember his eyes, where did he look? Did he see? Did he know I was lying? I glance out of the window. Above the rooftops of the tenements, the dawn sky is glowing pink. There is no time to worry about the blanket, or think about the sparks of light that burst from my fingers. I shove the blanket back and gather my things. As I leave, I call goodbye but Ma doesn't reply.

Because we have no bathroom, every morning I take our wooden, urine-filled bucket down to the shed in Junas's back yard. Inside, there is a trough full of grainy-looking water that we are supposed to wash with. When I'm finished washing, I ladle some of the water into the pee bucket to dilute it a little, then empty it into the street behind the back gate. Thankfully our street is on a slope, so the sewage creeps off towards the corrugated huts down near the river.

When I've emptied the bucket, I use the reflection in the trough to pin my unruly hair into a bun at the base of my neck and make sure my red sash is tied neatly and prominently around my upper arm. The sticky heat of the shed is making my face damp and my cheeks flushed, so I exit quickly and pad down the gated alleyway that leads past Junas's living room and out onto the street. My sandals sit waiting by the gate and I have barely finished lacing them up my calves when Junas unbolts his back door and bellows, "Émi!"

I force a smile. "Morning, Junas."

"What in The Four Cities was all that commotion?"

"The tenements were inspected," I say.

Junas waddles forward, rests a hand on his stomach and leans against the door frame. "Don't get cocky with me, Émi."

"Sorry, Junas. I had an accident with one of the lanterns. They came to see what happened, that's all."

Junas narrows his podgy eyes at me then waggles his finger. "Now listen, I don't want any trouble. I've been good to you, and your Ma. There's folk in this Quarter who'd give their last crown to live in a nice place like this."

I am nodding, I have heard this speech before.

"Even when I found out about your Pa, what he done. Even then, I let you stay because Nor said you're a good'un. But I don't want any trouble!"

I shake my head. "Of course not. I'm sorry, Junas, it won't happen again."

"It better not, Émi... and if I don't get the money I'm owed by the end of the week, well I'm sorry, but you're out. I need paying tenants." Junas's voice is stern but his eyes say that he really would be sorry if he was forced to evict us. I promise him

I'll have the rent by the end of the day and he makes a tutting sound and closes the door.

When I step outside, Rygour Street, which cuts a jagged line through the centre of the Red Quarter, is already swarming with people. Now it's daylight, and everyone is going about their business, I wonder whether Jennyfer's arrest and my tiny fireworks were nothing more than a vivid nightmare. But when I see a boy of eight or nine retrieving the remains of the rat that I pulled from the guttering and shoving it into his pocket, I know I wasn't dreaming.

The sun is already creeping higher in the sky, so I merge with the crowd and weave down towards the market. I pass Nor's house and the turning that leads to the ferry but, instead of following it, I exit down a narrow alleyway on the opposite side of the road. At the far end, a couple of emaciated stray dogs and a scraggy black crow are fighting over a sack of rubbish. I wave my arms but they ignore me. Midway down the alley, Garvey's pawn shop is shuttered closed and I'm the first in the queue so I must stand and wait.

Like the main street, the alley is lined with posters. The smaller ones are mainly text – reminders that we should be watchful of our friends and neighbours, rewards for those who report suspicious behaviour. They carry the Council's slogan: *Strive, Thrive, Survive.* The larger ones, however, are designed to remind us what lies beyond the wall. The biggest is one of mine – an enormous reconstruction of Mahg The Dissenter, his face twisted with rage, his soulless eyes staring straight ahead. Watching, waiting. In the background, his immense, coal-black wings block out the sun and the land below is decimated with shadow. When I handed this one in, the clerk behind the desk looked like he was afraid to even touch it. His supervisor was more discerning, examining it over the top of his gold-rimmed glasses and asking me to add some mangled corpses to the ground below Mahg. "Remember," he said, waggling the drawing at me, "these posters must convey the danger beyond the wall. They must show people what Mahg's evil magick did to The Four Cities. They must..." I nodded and quickly sketched in some bodies, tongues hanging out, blood on the floor. The clerk looked away. The supervisor smiled. "Better. Much better."

As it approaches six o'clock, others join the queue to trade their goods for cash. Immediately behind me, an old man holds tight to a paper bag that rattles as he shuffles forwards. Behind him, a couple with pale greasy skin and dark cropped hair complain loudly about the potholes near the market, agreeing that the Council would be quicker to fix them in any other Quarter but ours. And the line continues to grow. Eventually, one of Garvey's dishevelled employees flips the sign on the door to 'open' and ushers us inside. I tell the old man he can go first and he nods appreciatively, emptying a bag of knick-knacks onto the counter. He receives a few crowns in exchange for his goods and swiftly secures the money in a purse attached to his belt. He nods goodbye to me as he leaves.

The employee who opened the shop is called Duke. He often does the early shifts. When the old man has gone, he asks me how my mother is, glancing over my head as though he expects to see her there.

"She's well, thank you," I reply, hand still in my pocket. Duke straightens some paperwork and raises his thick, wiry eyebrows. "I..." The words catch in my throat. The chatting couple from outside sigh impatiently. Finally, I pass Duke the rings. "I'd like to leave these with you, to buy back at the end of the month."

Duke hums and turns the three bands over in his hand.

They clatter sharply as he drops them onto a scale next to the cash register. He hums again and gives them back to me. "I'm afraid I can't take these from you, Émi. They're not worth anything."

My face reddens and I feel the couple inch closer to the counter, eager for me to finish my turn and leave. "Is there anyone else who could take a look?" I ask.

Duke drums his fingers on the counter. "I'll call the boss down. Wait over there."

When Garvey appears from the back room, he is tall and angular, with a pair of dark brown glasses balanced precariously on the end of his nose. He shifts the glasses a little higher and pinches his eyes at me. "Are you seventeen?"

"Yes," I lie. "Duke knows me."

Duke, who I suspect has a soft spot for my mother, nods and calls, "It's fine, Guv."

Garvey folds his arms. "My colleague tells me you're not happy with his valuation?"

"He said they're not worth anything," I reply, handing over the rings.

Garvey glances at the jewellery, weighing the rings in his palm. "Sorry, Duke's right. There's nothing of value here. Anything else with you?"

I shake my head and I'm about to turn around when Garvey points to my throat. "What about that?"

He's seen my necklace. The chain is copper but the pendant is made of four intertwined squares of metal that are coated in gold, silver, green and red: one for each of the Quarters. I was given it as a prize when I was eleven years old because I recited the entire history of Nhatu, word perfect, at the Autumn Parade. A Council official in golden robes presented me with the coveted Quarter necklace at the end of my reading. He shook my hand and my mother was so proud that she whooped, and waved, and didn't care whether her behaviour was inappropriate. I don't remember my father whooping.

I remove my necklace and hand it over. Garvey slides the squares off their chain and rests them on the countertop, then takes a magnifying glass from inside his jacket. The corner of his mouth twitches and he mutters something under his breath. He looks up at me and smiles. His voice is now silky smooth. "I could stretch to one hundred and fifty crowns for the necklace." When I don't answer he repeats himself, more firmly. "One-fifty. You can buy it back at the end of the month for two hundred." The empty spot on my chest where the pendant usually rests already feels cold. But Junas's warning rings in my ears. One hundred and fifty crowns is enough for six weeks' rent. I can't afford to turn them down. So I sign the paperwork, stuff the crowns into my pocket and push past the couple, leaving before I change my mind.

THREE

The queue outside Garvey's now stretches to the end of the alley. The morning ferry to the Green Quarter leaves in fifteen minutes and, by now, the line at the check point will be more than twenty Reds long, so I quicken my pace and rejoin Rygour Street. When I reach the check point, there are at least thirty people ahead of me and the Cadets seem to be working particularly slowly this morning. The crowd is becoming restless. A woman who has an infant swaddled against her chest is turning her permit over and over in her hands. I tap her gently on her shoulder. "Are you alright?"

She turns around sharply, clutching the child closer, her eyes wide. "What do you want?"

I gesture to her permit. "Are you late for something?"

She nods and a swathe of dirty blonde hair falls across her face. "The baby. He's sick. My sister cleans for a medic in the Silver Quarter. He told her if I brought the baby before opening time he'd take a look. He's going in early – special – as a favour. If I miss this ferry…"

Up ahead, I can see Nor's stocky frame standing about three people away from the check point. She looks around at just the right moment and I motion towards the baby. Nor rolls her eyes but waves for us to join her so I take the woman's hand and hurry her past the waiting Reds. The line grumbles and swears under its breath but a Cadet shouts, "Settle down!"

Nor pulls us into the line in front of her and smiles at the Cadet checking the permits. Avery, a Green who was a couple of years above me at school, takes the woman's permit and nods, ushering her and the baby onto the ferry. Then he turns to me.

"Well, hello, Red," he chuckles. He used to call me Red because of my fiery auburn hair, but now I have the armband to match he enjoys it even more. "You know I'm not supposed to allow queue jumping – even for my favourites." I can smell last night's ale on his breath. I wonder whether he was among the Cadets who raided Jennyfer's building and force myself to stand a little straighter.

I tuck a loose wave of hair behind my ear. "You can make an exception, just this once, can't you?"

Behind me, Nor stifles a coughing sound and my freckles blush. I hope Avery assumes it's because of him. "Oh, go on then. As you asked so nicely," he drawls, offering a cursory glance to my permit and turning to watch me climb on board the ferry. I expect Avery to chastise Nor for encouraging disorder but he simply waves her past, too.

"You always fall for a sob story," she says, joining me to sit on deck.

"I know," I sigh. The mother has disappeared.

"Not like you to be late. What happened?"

"Had to go to Garvey's," I say, resting my fingers on the spot where my necklace usually sits.

"Oh, you didn't?" Nor folds her arms across her protruding chest. "What's Patti been up to? Sitting on her sorry behind as usual, letting you work yourself into the ground." I feel as though I should come to my mother's defence, but I can't think of one so I turn away, leaning against the side of the ferry to watch the spray that spits from beneath as we chug away from the Red Quarter. Nor pats my leg. "You're a good girl, Émi."

As the boat trundles forward, we pass under the bridge that connects the Green Quarter with the Red Quarter. Corrugated roofs and gnarly flats turn to houses and, eventually, the canal is lined by grass instead of dirt. Usually, the ferry is close to silent at this point of the journey but this morning hushed chatter fills the deck. From the corner of her mouth, Nor whispers, "Is it true? They arrested someone?"

"A woman. About my mother's age, I think."

"Hard to tell with some of them."

"Mm."

"They find something? Or was it..." She tails off, glancing at Avery, who is watching us closely.

"She said it wasn't hers, but they all say that." I roll my eyes, but Nor knows my disdain is for the benefit of our audience.

"Silly, silly woman," she sighs.

I wonder whether any of the people on the ferry are talking about the girl whose window lit up. I desperately want to tell Nor what happened, but it's too dangerous, especially here. I am transfixed by the spray beneath the boat, lost in my thoughts, when Avery's whistle cuts through the chatter and the ferry falls silent. I sit up straighter and place my hands palm down in my lap.

"Good morning, Red Quarter citizens," says Avery, disarmingly upbeat. "Another glorious day is upon us here in the city of Nhatu and it is time for the daily lesson." It's always the same greeting, no matter the weather: another glorious day.

Avery continues. He begins to walk up and down the deck, his hands clasped behind his back. He is too young to be intimidating, and too eager. It isn't long before he comes to a halt in front of Nor and I. He's chosen Nor. He makes her stand and her cheeks start to pink.

"Today's lesson," Avery proclaims, "will be read by..." He pauses and looks at Nor. She mutters her name through gritted teeth and he continues. "By Noreen Dyot." He pats her on the shoulder, a little too hard, and ushers her to the front of the deck. "Make your Council proud, Noreen."

Nor takes a deep breath. I mouth, "Sorry," but she offers me a gentle shake of her head. Avery chose her because she let me jump in with the woman and the baby but Nor isn't angry. She's been through this many times before. She plants her feet square and looks straight ahead. Then she begins.

For forty-five minutes, Nor recites the history of Nhatu. It is similar to the speech that won me the necklace, but less eloquent and more jittery. It is the story we have been told ever since the wall was sealed; a tale carefully crafted to convince us we are lucky to be here, protected from the dangers of the outside world.

Nor begins with the time before the wall, when Nhatu was still one of The Four Cities. She tells us that The Four Cities were powered by the Fire Stone. A mystical amulet from the First City, Abilene, the stone formed deep in a lake that fed water and life to the other cities. And for hundreds of years The Four Cities lived in peace, with the Fire Stone carefully guarded by the Watchers of Abilene.

Nor doesn't elaborate about the Watchers, not the way my father used to when he told me stories by candlelight, late in the evening. She doesn't mention the Watchers' wings or their silvery hair. She doesn't tell us that they live in trees surrounding the lake, or that they can perform somersaults in the air and glide like eagles in the sky. Instead, she moves swiftly on and describes the Second City, Tarynne, with its rocky dwellings and its elephant riders. She talks about the Third

City, Esyllt, which was home to the sorcerers and magicks. And all the while, she is careful not to make anything in the first three cities sound exotic or exciting. She throws in words like 'primitive' and 'chaotic,' because the Council likes those words, and then she comes to Nhatu. Nhatu was known as the Fourth City, and it was always different from its neighbours – 'progressive', 'ambitious', 'wise'. Nhatu was stifled by the ways of the other three cities, held back, denied its true potential.

Nor steadies herself before she reaches the most crucial part of the lesson. The early morning heat is beating down on her thinning hair. A bead of perspiration trickles from her temple to her jaw. Avery and his colleagues watch her, scrutinising every word.

"Fifty-one years ago, in the city of Abilene, the Watcher known as Mahg was born..." As Nor says Mahg's name, fear ripples through the deck. Avery fixes his gaze on his shoes and scrapes his fingers through his hair. He'll never be promoted to silver, not with a delicate constitution like that.

Nor swallows hard. She explains that Mahg was different from the other Watchers – an outsider who developed a troubling obsession with magick. He delved deeper and deeper into the magickal arts until, one day, he performed a spell so evil it turned his wings as black as his soul.

"Mahg fled to the lawless Islands on the west coast. There, he discovered the ways of the dark magick. His powers grew. He vowed to take revenge on Abilene and become ruler of The Four Cities. There was just one thing he needed – the Fire Stone."

We have heard this story hundreds of times before yet, still, every Red on the ferry holds their breath.

"Mahg brought an army of savage followers to Abilene and he tried to take the Fire Stone for himself. He failed, but many Watchers were killed and, with their numbers weakened, they knew they must take drastic action to stop him capturing the Stone.

"The Elders of Abilene summoned a sorcerer from Esyllt and asked him to divide the Fire Stone. Each of The Four Cities was given a piece, and one last piece was hidden by the Elders. But while Abilene, Tarynne and Esyllt were content to wait, praying Mahg wouldn't return, the Council of Nhatu grew restless.

"The wise and ingenious Council cared deeply for their citizens and were determined to protect them. So, the Council consulted Nhatu's most prominent historians, scientists and philosophers..." Nor pauses to wipe her forehead with her sleeve. She mumbles under her breath as she tries to recover where she was, "and philosophers..."

Avery marches over and waves his hand dismissively; he enjoys telling the final part of the lesson himself. Nor returns to her seat and leans back against the side of the boat. Avery opens his arms and channels his reedy voice into something deeper. "By studying the history of The Four Cities, the wise and wonderful Council learned that magick was the cause of all evil, and they knew what they must do to keep their people safe. They knew they must build a wall, and seal it tight to keep the darkness at bay. And they didn't stop there! After the wall, the Council created the Quarters, which empowered the people of Nhatu to *strive, thrive, survive*. It's true – for a while, the citizens of Nhatu pined for the ways of their ancestors. But five years after the wall was built the Council was proved right." Avery clears his throat, trying not to waver when he says, "Mahg returned and he destroyed Abilene, Tarynne and Esyllt. The world beyond the wall became dark and lawless, devoid of life, full of carnage and chaos, and death. But safe within our majestic flint walls, with the Council watching over us, the people of Nhatu remained unharmed. And we became The

One City." Avery stands with his feet together and his arms straight at his sides. We all rise to our feet. "Today," he shouts, "the people of Nhatu are safe and happy, protected by the benevolent Council and the high city walls. And so, The Four Cities have become The One City."

This is it.

On cue, we recite as one: "All hail The One City – The Only City – The Metropolis of Nhatu!"

We repeat the chant three times in unison, then we stand and wait until Avery tells us we can sit down. He scratches his chin and paces up and down between our lines. The blonde woman's baby starts to cry. We are nearing our stop. Finally, he nods and we fold back into our seats, breathing a collective sigh of relief.

The first time I rode the ferry with Nor, I was astounded that they forced the Reds to perform, or listen to, this speech every single day. For months, I found myself longing for the forbidden details that my father used to tell me. But then I learned to nod in the right places and say, "Mmm," in the right places, and let it wash over me. Perhaps there was a time when people questioned the Council's motives for blocking up the walls, but not now. Nearly fifteen years have passed since they sealed the gates and anyone who remembers what life was like before is too afraid or too tired to care. The visions they have shown us, the scenes I draw on my posters, of what lies beyond the wall – dark magick, decimated landscapes and ruthless scavengers – they have crushed peoples' curiosity. I wish mine was crushed. You'd think that after everything that happened, with my father, it would be. But it's not. Every night, in the few moments of sleep I manage to snatch before sunrise, I dream of Abilene. I see Watchers gliding through the sky and a lake so blue it is imprinted on the backs of my eyes when I wake...

Nor nudges me out of my daydream. "We're here."

When we disembark at the Green Quarter jetty, we go through the permit-checking process in reverse. Out on the street, Nor turns left and waddles towards the hotel where she works as a cook. I cross the road and veer right, away from the canal but towards the wide fast-moving river that flows from the Green Quarter, down through Silver and Gold, under the city walls, and out into the ocean.

The journey to The Emerald Cafe takes me past our old house. Usually, I avoid looking at it. Its neatly manicured hedges and pretty green door sting my eyes. Today, though, I find myself coming to a stop on the pavement. I look at my hands and then up at the house, as if it might know the answer to the questions that are swarming in my head: *What happened last night? Did those sparks come from me? Did I...* I don't even want to think the word because it is blasphemous and if the Council knew... *Did I do magick?*

As though it has heard me, the house blinks as sunlight bounces off its windows and onto a sign next to the door: *For Sale, Vacant.* Just a few weeks ago, I overheard the new owner telling someone in The Emerald that her husband, a bank clerk like my father, had been promoted. They must have already moved to the Silver Quarter. I look over my shoulder. No one is watching me, they are all too busy with their own lives and thoughts and troubles. I inhale sharply and steal my way to the front door. I peer through the glass at the empty hallway and try the handle. Locked, of course. Turning towards the hedge, I make my way down the side of the house.

In the short time since the new owners left, the garden has become horrifically overgrown. Ma would hate it. Weeds and unruly grasses have taken over her flowerbeds; Nhatu's potent combination of vicious rainstorms and blazing sunshine proving a cocktail for growth. I feel beneath the deep crevice below the kitchen window. Is it still there? Yes! My fingers close around cold metal and I pull out the spare key I forgot to hand over when we left.

I unlock the back door and gingerly step inside. A floorboard creaks and my heart flutters. Memories of my childhood dance from room to room. I want to go upstairs, but my feet refuse to carry me any further so I sit down in the middle of the hall and lean my forehead against the coolness of the creamy wall my father so painstakingly painted. I look down at my palms and my insides swirl. I remember the sparks, and Jennyfer, and the dead rat that I so nearly wanted to eat.

For the first time in three years I let myself cry.

FOUR

I'm late. When I arrive at The Emerald, the owner, Amin, is already in the kitchen. I shout an apologetic good morning and move from window to window, throwing open the shutters. Then I join him in the kitchen.

From beneath his long ashen beard, Amin smiles and tosses a scone in my direction.

"Not happy with the first batch, what d'you reckon?" he asks, turning back to his dough. He often finds excuses to feed me, and I never refuse. My stomach lurches into a growl as I sniff the gently spiced crust. I can't remember the last time I ate.

"Tastes okay to me," I say, mouth already full. Amin laughs and tells me I've never had a very discerning palate.

"I'll bag up the rest of that batch. You can take 'em," he says. I must be looking especially scrawny around the edges today because he's never offered me this much food before. But I learned a long time ago that pride doesn't get you very far when you're a Red, so I nod my thanks and start shaping the remaining dough into balls.

Three large urns of coffee are on the go, the scones are baked and displayed in neat wicker trays, and we're almost ready to open up, when Amin reminds me it's the first Saturday of July. My insides somersault. Already? I glance up at the calendar – he's right.

"Is he definitely coming?" I ask.

Amin beams and his eyes twinkle. "He wouldn't miss this one, not so close to your birthday."

I brush my floury hands on my apron and go to freshen up before it gets too busy. In the cramped but clean customer bathroom, I splash water on my face and onto the back of my neck. My hair is already doing its best to escape its pins, and my eyes are grey from lack of sleep. I haven't seen Amin's son, Tsam, for a little over four years. I can't imagine the changes he will notice when he looks at me. That is, if he actually visits us this time. When we were younger, Tsam and I spent hours playing in the treehouse at the back of the cafe. He was like the brother I never had, but when he turned eleven he won a coveted place at an academy in the Gold Quarter, and he left. Amin threw him a going away party and I remember feeling horribly jealous when he ceremoniously switched Tsam's green sash for a gold one. Now, we barely see him. Scholars are allowed to visit their families for just two days, once every six months, but Tsam doesn't always make it. I used to write him letters, which Amin posted alongside his own, but after everything that happened with my father I ran out of things to say.

When I emerge from the bathroom, the first morning customers are filtering in to buy scones and coffee. I join Amin at the counter and we flit around one another, serving and pouring, until the rush dies down and the urns need refilling. Our day continues in much the same fashion – customers buy coffees, and scones and biscuits all day long. Mostly, they eat outside, although a few choose the coolness of the seats just inside the door. As evening rolls closer, Amin looks more and more frequently at his pocket watch. Each time, he mutters, "He'll be here," and I nod, although I am doubtful.

At nine o'clock, the sun begins to set and Amin releases a deep, frustrated sigh. He unties his apron and tugs at his beard, shaking his head. I'm about to tell him there is still time for Tsam to make an appearance, but he speaks first.

"Stay for dinner, Émi? There's plenty..." Sensing my reluctance, he continues, "I'll make sure you don't miss your ferry." So, I agree.

When the last customer has packed up and gone home, Amin hands me a bowl of stew and suggests we eat down by the river. I frown at him but he says, "It's just the two of us, Émi. The Cadets won't take any notice."

I hesitate, holding my bowl in front of me. I'm desperate to sit in the long grass, to feel it tickling my calves and smell the freshness of the river.

Amin wrinkles his eyes at me and grabs a hunk of bread from the counter. "Come on..."

Down by the water's edge, the night breeze kisses my skin and it's hard to believe that when I return to the Red Quarter I'll be swelteringly hot.

"It was one of the first things they stopped, you know," says Amin.

"What was?"

"Nocturnal gatherings... That's what they called them. No 'nocturnal gatherings' in open green spaces." He waves his hand at our surroundings. "All out of bounds after sunset."

I shift uncomfortably and glance over my shoulder, half expecting a Cadet to leap out from the grass and arrest us. Amin has never spoken this way before.

"No one talks about it," I say, lowering my voice. "About the time before the wall..."

Amin balances his bowl on his lap. "They're scared."

"You're not?"

Amin looks at me and his eyes twinkle. "Not particularly," he says. "Although I wouldn't want to get you in trouble, so maybe we should..."

I look down at my hands. I want to tell Amin about the sparks, but I can't find the words and so we sink into companionable silence.

When we've finished our stew, Amin says, "You heard anything more? About your father?"

The hairs on my arms bristle. "I don't suppose we will."

Amin shakes his head. "He loved you very much, Émi."

Tears are prickling at the back of my eyes, so I'm relieved when we hear someone knocking on the front door of the cafe.

"Mrs Carban left her shawl," I say, hurrying to my feet, glad of an excuse to leave the conversation. "I'll see to it." I let myself in through the kitchen, unlock the front door, and hold out the shawl. "Here you go..."

"Thanks," a voice cuts in. "Not really my colour."

I look up and immediately drop the shawl. "Tsam? We thought you'd..."

"Oh, come on. I wouldn't miss your birthday," he quips, the corner of his mouth crinkling into a smile.

I almost hug him but hesitate, and then open the door wider, ushering him inside. "My birthday's not until next month."

"Close enough," he says, retrieving the shawl and locking the door behind us.

We stand for a moment, awkwardly observing one another. I am keenly aware of the dirt that's ingrained under my fingernails and on my skin. I remember, back when we were Greens, my mother saying awful things about Reds: "They might be poor, but at least they could wash." I pray Tsam isn't thinking the same about me.

Tsam's initial bravado has evaporated. The look on his face

31

asks, *What has happened to you?* But while I have become increasingly grubbier and malnourished since his last visit, Tsam exudes the glow of someone healthy and happy. Above his elbow a gold band sparkles. When he notices me staring, he nudges it with his forefinger.

"The knot is the wrong way up," I say, shocked that he would be allowed to make such a mistake. Tsam glances at his arm and begins to fumble with it. Perhaps they have people to tie their bands for them up in Gold. I help him adjust it. Tsam smiles at me and I look down at my sandals before I start blushing. He is more handsome than I remember. He used to be tall and lanky, his hair cut close to his scalp. Now, he has filled out, become more athletic, his hair flopping over his eyes. I'm about to say that we should go and find Amin when the kitchen door clatters on its hinges. Tsam's face breaks into a grin that stretches from ear to ear. He throws himself at his father. They embrace and pat one another on the back, then Amin holds his son's face in his hands. "It's been too long, son. Far too long."

Watching the two of them I remember that my mother's at home on her own, wondering where I am, and Junas is waiting for his rent. I rest a hand on Tsam's arm. "I'm sorry, you just got here, but I have to go. I'll see you tomorrow?"

Amin looks disappointed. "Émi," he says, "stay for a coffee. You have time, then Tsam will walk you back to the ferry." Amin is trying to be nice, so I resist the urge to tell him I don't need anyone to escort me. I sit down at the nearest table. "Okay, just one coffee."

Amin fetches us each a mug and fills them from the urn on the countertop. Tsam is sitting on the edge of his chair, shifting uncomfortably and looking behind him as if he's searching for a cushion. Eventually, he slides back and rests his hands in his lap. I wonder whether he is wishing he hadn't come. He turns to me and his right eyebrow tweaks upwards. "How are you, Émi? Are you alright?"

"Fine." I pause. "We're managing just fine."

Tsam's gaze flickers towards his father and back to me. "You seem... I mean, you look..." He tries to lighten his tone. "Pa's not working you too hard, is he?"

Now it's my turn to shuffle on my chair. "Of course not. I'm just a little tired."

Tsam raises that eyebrow again and I continue, "Last night was... rough. But, mostly, I'm fine."

Amin leans in, his fingers entwined around his mug. "What happened?"

I shake my head. "Just an inspection. Not us, the flats opposite. They arrested someone, and then..." I trail off. If it was only Amin I might tell him what happened, but Tsam is a Gold now. And when you live in the Red Quarter, Golds can't be trusted.

My crumpled expression betrays me and Amin pats my hand. "Émi? What happened?"

I glance at Tsam. Amin follows my gaze and says, "You can tell us."

Tsam is watching me. His eyes brim with concern and he is back on the edge of his chair. He glances at his gold sash and rests his hand over the top of it, as if covering it up will remove its implications. "You can trust me, Ém."

I tap my nails against the rim of my mug. My heart is beating faster than usual and my skin starts to prickle. *Not now, not here...* The familiar warmth starts to rise up and up in my belly. Before I can stop it, a lightning spark jolts from my fingers and sends the mug flying off the table. Coffee sloshes across the floor and I scoot my chair back.

Amin and Tsam are staring at me. I shake my hand as if something is stuck to it and pinch my wrist. "I..."

Amin leaps up from the table and closes the shutters while

Tsam watches me, unblinking. "Has this happened before?" he asks.

"Last night," I whisper. "I don't know how..."

Amin sits back down and pats my shoulder.

"How did I...?" I look up at him as though I'm expecting him to know the answer.

His usually genial expression has sharpened. He bobs down in front of my chair. "Listen to me, Émi. You did this last night?"

I nod.

"And the Cadets saw?"

I nod again. "They saw the flash of light. They came to the flat, looked around my room. I told them it was an accident with the lamp." I picture the blanket on the bed, covered in splinters of broken glass... "They believed me. I think."

Amin exhales slowly and looks at his pocket watch. "Émi, do you have anything in your flat that would get you in trouble, if they found it?"

I shake my head.

"Anything at all?"

I think of my charcoals falling to the floor. The spot where they landed, right next to the loose floorboard... They wouldn't find it, surely?

Tsam is watching me too. "Émi?"

"I... there are some drawings, but they're hidden."

"What drawings?" Tsam asks.

I blush, because it sounds childish. "Sometimes I sketch what I see in my dreams. Abilene... the Watchers."

Amin jumps to his feet. "Émi, you must go home, now. You must burn those drawings. They'll inspect you tonight, mark my words. And they won't leave until they find something."

My tongue thickens in my mouth. "What if they... With the woman they arrested... They planted something in her flat. It wasn't hers."

Amin turns to Tsam. "Go with her," he says. "They won't try anything with a Gold present."

"Are you sure, Pa?"

Amin nods and herds us towards the door. "Émi, we'll talk more tomorrow. For now, be safe."

I can't bring myself to look at Tsam as we're walking. I feel incredibly foolish. Why did I keep those drawings? Why did I create them in the first place? Thinking back, I can't believe the Cadets never found them before. If they'd moved the desk, just a little, they could have noticed the hollow creak of the floorboard, prodded it, found it was looser than the rest, lifted it up... My thoughts spiral. The Cadets could be in the flat this very moment, hauling my mother out onto the street, shoving my blasphemous pictures into her fragile hands and saying, "You must have known! Your whole family is trouble."

Tsam is talking to me and when I don't respond, he takes hold of my elbow. "Émi," he says, forcing me to meet his eyes. "It'll be alright." I want to believe him. I want him to be the boy who stopped me from falling out of the treehouse, who ran to fetch ointment for my scraped knee. But he's not that boy; he's a Gold. One day, he'll probably be a Council Official. He knows nothing of the Cadets and their cruelty.

I tug myself away from him. "We need to hurry."

When we reach the ferry, I'm relieved to see that Nor isn't in the queue. She must have caught an earlier boat. The huddle of Reds clutch their permits and jostle closer together when they notice Tsam. Again, he fiddles uncomfortably with his sash. When we board, we sit close to the front. The Cadet on deck this evening is a girl, not much older than me, who I don't recognise. She flutters her eyelashes at Tsam and wiggles her hip when she walks up and down.

He turns and whispers, "What do I tell people? If they ask why I'm with you?"

"They won't ask."

"They won't?"

Is he really so naive? I raise my eyebrows at him. "They'll think I'm..." When he still doesn't catch on I force myself to say it. "They'll think you're paying me to... spend the night."

I expect him to be embarrassed but instead he shakes his head and says, "Oh. That happens a lot?"

"In the Red Quarter? Yes. Work isn't easy to find."

For the rest of the journey, I try to see the changing scenery on the bank of the canal through Tsam's eyes – trees becoming shrubs, grass becoming grit, houses becoming shacks. In the mellow glow of the moon it doesn't look as raw as it does during the day, but I can't imagine what he will think when he sees where we live. When I first came to the Red Quarter I compared everything to our life in Green, but Tsam lives in the Gold Quarter. To him, the surroundings in Green probably seem distasteful now.

When we disembark, the Cadet snatches my permit and looks at me like I am the personification of everything she cannot stand. She doesn't speak, just flicks her eyes towards the gate and lets me past. When Tsam presents his permit, she smiles at him with her plump lips and says, "Good evening, sir. I haven't seen you around these parts before." All Golds are called 'sir', no matter their occupation. Tsam replies with a cursory, "Goodnight, Cadet," and follows me out onto the street.

Darkness has closed in upon the Red Quarter, which means the taverns are in full swing as I lead Tsam up Rygour Street towards the flat. When we reach the gate that leads to Junas's front door, and the stairs to the flat, my heart hammers faster and faster. Junas doesn't allow visitors, so I whisper for Tsam to remove his boots and carry them in his arms.

We walk up the stairs and I knock three times on our peeling front door. As always, my mother opens it just a crack and says, "Who is it?"

"It's Émi, I've brought someone to see you."

She holds the door open wider, her worried eyes nothing but pinpricks in the dark. "Who is it?"

"It's Tsam, Ma. You remember Tsam?" I push gently on the door and force her to open it; I am losing patience. My mother studies Tsam's face. "Amin's boy! Why, yes, I remember!"

I shove past her into the flat. Tsam reaches out his hand and says, "It's lovely to see you again, Mrs Fae."

My mother smiles and pats her mousy hair. "Tea," she says, "we should have tea... please forgive me... So long since we had a visitor." Tsam tells her tea would be lovely, but I'm already heading for the bedroom.

"Tsam," I call, "you wanted to see some the artwork I do for the Council?" I look back to see Tsam furrow his brow at me. He doesn't know about my posters. I'm almost ashamed of myself, but there's no time for that now. "My drawings... you wanted to see?" I nod my head at him, urging him to say yes.

Inside the bedroom, Tsam helps me move the desk and I throw myself to my knees to loosen the floorboard that's usually positioned under its back legs. I lift up the board and stick my hand into the hole, withdrawing a wad of papers and a small black sketchbook.

I replace the floorboard and hold my forbidden wares in front of me. Tsam opens his hand and I pass him the loose papers. He leafs through them, gently, carefully, as if they are precious and he is afraid of damaging them. "You drew these, Émi?"

I blush. "Yes."

"How do you... I mean, where do these images come from?"

I shrug. "I dream sometimes."

Tsam looks a little closer at the drawing in his left hand, then flicks through the others. "Who's this?"

He is pointing to the silhouette of a girl. She has dark hair and sad eyes, but the rest of her face is covered by a scarf that's wrapped tight around her mouth and nose. Sometimes I think she's me, but I know she's not. "She's in the dreams," I say. "All of them."

"Does she have a name?"

I shake my head, walk over to my bedside table and retrieve the box of matches. "No, she's just a girl. We should...?"

I drag our (thankfully) empty urine bucket out from the corner of the room and toss in the papers. When I strike the match, Tsam looks away but I force myself to watch until my imaginings have turned to ash.

I am fanning the smoke out of the window when Ma knocks and enters with two cups of tepid yellowish tea. She hands the least yellow cup to Tsam and says, "Won't you come through to the sitting room?" as if we're back home in Green with our delicate saucers. We are moving towards the door when we hear Junas shouting.

"Hey! You can't just charge in here! You could at least knock!"

My mother releases an *ohh* sound and Tsam turns to the desk. The black sketchbook sits where anyone could see it. Without blinking, he shoves it into his pocket and then puts his hand on my mother's arm.

"It's alright, Patti," he tells her. "Don't worry."

While she is distracted I grab the pee bucket and tip my tea on top of the flecks of ash, then I kick it back into its corner.

"Ma, stay here. We'll handle this." I guide her to the bed and encourage her to sit down.

This time, the Cadets really do knock the door off its hinges. As they enter, led by Falk, I jump away from Tsam and clutch at the buttons on the front of my tunic, so it looks like we've been caught doing something we shouldn't. Tsam does his best to look flustered. Falk stops in the doorway as five more Cadets plough into our miniature living space and start tearing it apart. Downstairs, crashing and shouting indicates that Junas's apartment is suffering the same fate.

Falk assesses Tsam and immediately notices the gold sash. His eyes flicker to his own, only silver, and he fixes a polite smile on his face. "My apologies for the interruption, sir." He has to shout to make himself heard as the Cadets drag our sideboard away from the window and pull its drawers out onto the floor. Our makeshift tea kettle spills its contents onto the tattered rug. My mother's last remaining china teacup smashes as it is thrown to the ground.

Tsam pulls back his shoulders. "What is the meaning of this?"

Falk chuckles. "Nothing for you to concern yourself with, sir. Just a routine inspection."

"I was under the impression we had dispatched with this kind of barbaric behaviour?" Tsam barks, as a Silver Cadet takes a knife to one of our cushions and starts to unravel its innards.

Falk clears his throat. "Unfortunately, sir, these are grave circumstances. We have been informed that this girl," he points at me with a tapered fingernail, "may be hiding forbidden goods. Perhaps even... magickal goods."

Tsam pretends to look alarmed. "I see."

"Don't worry. If there's anything here, my men will find it. And if not... We'll leave you to finish your... business." Falk turns his eyes on me as he says the word 'business' and my throat constricts. He steps closer and reaches his hand to my face. His fingertips linger by my cheekbone. "I had no idea, Miss Fae, that you were an... entertainer."

"This room's clear, sir." The Cadet who's been mauling our sofa interrupts.

Falk snaps his eyes upwards and says, "Fine, check the bedroom."

I hear my mother whimper as they shove her from the bed back into the living room. Tsam's hand twitches as she crumples onto the floor and starts to stroke her broken belongings.

"Falk, wait!" I say, surprising myself by uttering his name. "I want to watch them."

Falk opens his mouth at me, momentarily stunned, then clenches his fist as if he wants to punch me in the stomach. "What did you say?"

"I want to watch them, so I know they're not planting anything." Tsam's presence has given me a dangerous sense of bravado but, as Falk glowers at me, my faith pays off and Tsam steps in.

"That seems fair, Cadet."

Falk is bewildered, but his eyes return to Tsam's gold sash and, eventually, he tells me to go ahead. Tsam follows me, Falk too, and we watch as the Cadets tear the sheets from the bed, toss them out of the window, and overturn my bedside table. Violently, they rip the desk away from the wall and empty every one of its drawers. Then, the moment I envisioned, one of them treads on the loose board and shouts, "Stop!" He wiggles his foot up and down and when Falk hears the creaking sound he charges in and rips the board up into the air. Triumphantly, he thrusts his hand into the hole and interrogates every crevice.

"Anything, sir?" asks one of the Cadets.

Falk rises slowly. "Nothing."

"Well, then. All a big misunderstanding," Tsam says, forcing a lightness into his voice. "Perhaps Miss Fae and I can now continue where we left off?"

Falk gestures for the Cadets to leave, then takes one last look around my room. His eyes rest for a brief moment on the charred windowsill and he is about to leave when he spies the bucket.

My chest tightens, my abdomen feels hot and spiky. I clench my fingers behind my back, because maybe if I grasp them hard enough the sparks won't be able to fly.

Falk meets my eyes and refuses to break his stare as he takes hold of the bucket and pours what he thinks is urine onto my mattress. Then he peers inside the bucket.

"Just checking," he says with a thin smile. "You never can be too careful."

FIVE

My mother trembles for at least an hour after Falk and the Cadets leave. Tsam and I use my meagre selection of tools to fix the battered door back on its hinges and then he offers to stay with her while I go to check on Junas.

In the three years we've lived above him, I've never entered Junas's apartment, but as I tap on the door it swings open.

I tiptoe inside.

Junas is sitting in the dark in a corner of his sitting room. When he sees me, he croaks, "Émi, are you alright?" I tell him I'm fine, fumble for some matches and light the lamp by the window.

This room is in just as much disarray as ours – belongings smashed and strewn across the floor, pictures ripped from the walls, curtains pulled down from their poles.

Junas shakes his head. "They're getting worse. Used to always knock, at least. Now they just barge in. Sneaky, good-for-nothing, sons of Mahg is what they are..."

A pang of guilt tugs at my chest. I feel like I should apologise but if Junas knew I'd brought this trouble to his door he'd have us out on the street by morning. I start righting some of his knick-knacks but he tells me not to bother.

"I'm sure you've got your own mess to sort out, Émi."

I reach into my pocket. "The rent we owe," I say, passing him some of the crowns Garvey gave me in exchange for my necklace. Junas takes the money and counts it into a pot on his mantlepiece. "Very good," he says, then half-heartedly, "try not to be late with it next week."

When I return to the flat, my mother is lying on our tortured sofa with a cloth over her eyes. Tsam is gathering broken pieces of crockery and ornaments and dropping them carefully into the drawers in the sideboard. "I'm sure we can fix these," he says as I enter. "We just need some glue."

"Thanks," I say, "but you should probably go now. I need to get Ma to bed."

Tsam blinks at me and looks at his watch. "Émi, it's past midnight. The ferry's stopped running."

"Ah." I glance towards the bedroom. "Okay, I'll put Ma in there and you can sleep on the sofa."

Tsam agrees and when I struggle to heave my mother to her feet, he slips an arm around her waist and helps me coax her across the room. "That's it, Patti. Well done. A nice rest and you'll feel much better."

All of our bedding is now on the pavement outside, either sodden with dirt or snatched by passers by, so I tell Ma she'll have to make the best of it.

"Oh Émi," she moans as we lay her down, "the mattress is wet."

I tell her it's only tea and not to worry. Besides, the wetness will help cool her down. She grumbles, but lays down anyway and strokes my cheek.

"You're such a good girl, you don't deserve this. I'm sorry,

Émi. Your father, he'd be sorry too. It's not fair, it's just not fair..."

I pat her hand and whisper, "Night, Ma."

At least tonight she will sleep.

In the living room, Tsam perches on the sofa and I join him. I tuck my knees up under my chin.

"I can't offer you tea, we're out of water," I say, gesturing to the empty flask by the window. Tsam looks at me as though he can't believe there's such a thing as running out of water. "Usually, I fetch some from the well on my way home," I explain.

"I see," Tsam says, and I think he really is beginning to see.

Now that the flat is quiet and my mother is sleeping, the sparsity of our living quarters is thrown into stark relief.

"Well," I say, opening my arms like I'm giving him a grand tour, trying to smile. "This is home." When Tsam doesn't reply, I add, "It's not much, but Junas has a kind heart and there are far worse places."

"There are?"

"Of course. The tenements are overrun with cockroaches, and the shacks by the canal..." I stop because Tsam has reached into his tunic and is handing me back my black sketchbook.

"What do you want to do with this?" he asks. "Burn it?"

I take it from him and stroke its cover. "It's not mine," I whisper, so quietly Tsam has to ask me to repeat myself. "It's... it was my father's."

"I'll keep it safe."

"Tsam, you can't. If they find it..."

"No one will find it. Trust me, Émi."

I hug my knees a little tighter.

"You do, don't you? You do trust me?"

I tuck a stray curl of hair behind my ear and watch him for a moment. "Yes. I do."

It's getting late, so I suggest that we try and get some sleep.

44

Tsam lets me have the sofa and we use the back cushions to create him a makeshift bed on the floor. For a while we both lay perfectly still, but as the hours creep by and the stifling heat of the Red Quarter festers and intensifies, we both start shuffling about, unable to find a comfortable position. Eventually, I light the lamp and dim it to a flickering orange glow.

Tsam looks up at me, "Is it always this hot?"

"Always," I reply.

He sits up and stretches out his legs, scratching between his shoulder blades. "Ém." He called me that when we were youngsters. "I'm sorry."

"What for?"

"After your father... I wrote you a letter..."

I wheel my mind back – I don't remember a letter.

"But I never sent it. Nothing I wrote seemed... appropriate."

"It's alright," I tell him. "I probably wouldn't have read it even if you had. Things were too..."

Tsam shuffles closer to me. "Did he do what they said he did?"

Indignation flickers in my gut. Usually, when people ask about my father it is through morbid, salivating curiosity. But Tsam's face shows nothing but gentle concern so I quell my anger. "Yes, he did it. Ma said he was ill – not in his right mind."

"Was he?"

I pick at the tear on the cushion made by the Cadet's knife. "No, he wasn't mad. He knew exactly what he was doing." I gesture to Tsam's pocket, where the sketchbook lies dormant. "He always told me stories about Abilene, the Watchers, the Fire Stone. That's probably why I have the dreams... he filled my head with it. After dark, he'd bring a lantern to my room and we'd huddle together. He'd describe it all, and draw the most beautiful pictures. Of forests, lakes, the elephant riders in Tarynne, the sorcerers in Esyllt, all of it. He made it sound so

45

exciting... so different from Nhatu... places with no rules, or Quarters, or horrid old walls."

"So he went looking for them? The other Cities?"

I blink at the ceiling, trying not to let me eyes tear up. "A few months before, he told me the Council had been lying to us..." I look at Tsam to see if he is finding this absurd, or treacherous, but he is listening intently. His sleeves are rolled up, his tunic open casually at the neck, and his gold sash is crumpled on the floor. He is not like the other Golds. I should never have assumed he would be.

"Did you ask him what he meant?"

"At first, he wouldn't tell me. Then as the weeks went on, he became more and more distant. The day before he left, he told me what he was planning."

"You knew?"

"I should have tried to stop him, but he was adamant." I dip my voice into a whisper. "He said the Council lied about what happened beyond the wall. That they made it all up. He said the other three Cities were still out there, that Mahg never destroyed them. And he said he had to find out the truth."

"So he tried to scale the wall?"

I rub my forefingers against my temples. "Maybe Ma's right. Maybe he was crazy."

"You really believe that?"

I think for a moment, trying to mould my words into something intelligible. I laugh a little, even though it's not funny. "Tsam, he tried to climb over the city wall in broad daylight. If it were true... If Abilene still exists... If the Watchers weren't all killed by Mahg..."

Tsam is so close that I can almost sense his heart beating. "Émi?"

"If all that were true, how could they abandon us here?"

Tsam sits back and cocks his head at me.

I tug at the red sash that constricts my arm. "Surely, if they were still out there, they'd rescue us from all this?"

Tsam reaches out and puts his hand on mine. His eyes are brimming with sincerity. "Maybe one day they will."

We don't talk any more about my father, and Tsam doesn't ask me about those perilous sparks of light that jumped from my fingers in the cafe. Even here, just the two of us, or perhaps especially here, they are too dangerous to talk about. I want to ask him about his life in the Gold Quarter but I don't want to betray my ignorance. So we lay parallel to one another, me on the sofa and him on his cushions. Eventually, in the few fragile moments before the sun comes up, I drift into a restless sleep where the girl in the scarf dances a slow, sad dance on the surface of a sparkling blue lake.

When Rygour Street strums into life, I knock on the bedroom door and slink in to gather some things from my desk. I owe the council two drawings. Most of them are tattered and creased from Falk's angry fist, so I pick the two most presentable and slip them into the brown leather folder that Nor presented me with when I got the job.

My mother stirs and releases a groan as she remembers the events of the night before. "Émi? You're leaving already?"

"I have to, Ma." I wave the folder at her. "But, good news, Amin gave me a little bonus yesterday, so I didn't have to pawn your rings."

Ma sits up on her elbows and studies my face. If she knows I'm lying, she doesn't show it. "A bonus? Well, that's wonderful."

"And with the drawings I'm taking in today we'll have enough to last us a while." I reach into my pocket, past the spare coins from Garvey's, feeling for the rings. "Here, your hand doesn't look right without them."

Ma takes the rings and holds them to her cheek. "Bless you, Émi. Bless you."

"I have to go now. You'll need to fetch some water. I didn't have time last night..."

At this, she sits bolt upright. She hates leaving the flat because it forces her to acknowledge that we actually live here. Before she can argue with me, I kiss her swiftly on the cheek. "Bye, Ma." Then I close the bedroom door and usher Tsam out into the stairwell.

We manage to slip past Junas's door without him noticing us, and out into the early morning maelstrom of Rygour. Tsam asks me what's in the folder and I explain about the posters, indicating one of mine on the side of the ironmonger's near to the ferry station. I expect him to look disappointed, that I have lowered myself to this form of work, but he just smiles and nods.

"I need to drop these off. I'll catch the first ferry but you should wait for the next one. I'll meet you at The Emerald."

Tsam opens his mouth to disagree.

"Golds and Reds don't socialise, Tsam. If Falk were to see us together..."

He tells me he understands, but he still looks a little wounded when I turn away from him and join the queue, deliberately not looking back.

The Council's Office for Citizen Relations is a grey building that balances neatly on the border between Green and Silver Quarters. There are two entrances, one on the Green side and one on the Silver side. I knock on the Green door and present my work permit. "Émi Fae, I'm here to hand in some artwork to Mr Gauve."

The Council Official who inspects my permit is the same woman who is here every week and yet it still takes her twenty minutes to scrutinise the paperwork, take it to the office upstairs, check my credentials and return to escort me down the hall.

Gauve's office looks out on the neat green lawn at the front of the building. His desk is empty apart from an unlit lamp, an inkwell and a quill. He doesn't even have any writing paper. When I enter, he is staring out of the window and I find myself wondering, not for the first time, what he does here all day.

"Mr Gauve, I have some artwork for you." I slide the folder onto the desk and watch as he removes the drawings.

Gauve looks at me. "These are a little dishevelled, Miss Fae?"

"I'm sorry, sir, there was an... incident. They're still suitable for tracing though." To enlarge the drawings they are traced, then carved into wooden blocks that can be printed in different coloured inks. It's a painstaking process so I won't see these images up in the Red Quarter for at least two weeks.

Gauve spreads the pictures out on his desk and leans forward to inspect them. He taps them, mutters *mmm* and *very good* then shoves them in his top drawer, slams my folder shut and motions for me to leave. The permit inspector has been standing in the doorway watching us. Guave gives her a nod and she takes my arm, marching me back outside where she squints into the sunlight and watches until I'm back on the pavement.

I follow the river from the Council offices to The Emerald. The sun is already tearing through the clouds but patches of leafy shade make it bearable. The journey is so pleasant, I almost forget that I'm still wearing yesterday's tunic and that my face and hair are unwashed. I don't, however, forget that when I arrive Amin will ask me about the sparks. I don't know how to explain them and, even if I do, I don't know whether he will be able to help me.

I arrive on time, but Amin has opened early. The shutters are tied back and the unmistakable scent of his coffee is wafting out of the windows. As I draw nearer, a sense of foreboding grabs hold of my ankles and I stop just outside the door. I shake my head and tell myself not to be ridiculous, then force my feet to carry me inside. Amin is behind the counter, pouring coffee into six large mugs. He meets my eyes and I'm sure I see him flicker his gaze towards the cushions by the door. I turn and have to steady myself as I come face to face with Falk and the same band of Cadets who raided the flat. My treacherous mind reels back to the sketchbook Tsam offered to watch for me. I see him slipping it into his pocket. I see his gold sash winking at me. But then I hear him say, "Trust me, Émi," and I shake the visions loose. He wouldn't hand it over, he just wouldn't.

Falk is leaning back against the wall with a lazy grin on his face. "Morning, Émi. I'm glad you made it to work on time after your after-dark pursuits. Does the old man know this isn't your only line of work?" Falk tips his head at Amin as he says 'old man'.

I smile politely and say, "Good morning, sir. Can I get you anything?"

Falk chuckles and, on cue, so do his cronies. "Your boss is already preparing our coffee, but keep the mugs topped up. We're going to be here a while."

In the kitchen, I desperately want to ask Amin how long they have been here but I'm afraid even to whisper to him. Thankfully, I can't see any signs of Tsam. If they found him here they'd know for certain that his visit to the flat wasn't what we pretended it to be. When Amin has finished the coffees, I take them over to Falk's table. As I lean down with the tray, he catches my arm and says, "I told you I'd be watching you."

Falk and the Cadets stay until late afternoon, quaffing coffee as if it's about to be outlawed. At six thirty, they suddenly stand and, without paying Amin a cent, Falk shouts, "Sorry to leave you so soon, Émi, but we have a Punishment to prepare for." From my spot behind the counter I narrow my eyes at him. "You remember Miss Kray? Tonight is her special night and it should be spectacular! Make sure I see you there." Then he spins on his heels and leaves.

Before he dares to speak, Amin goes to the door and peers outside. "They're gone," he says, returning to the counter. "Are you alright?"

I tell him I'm fine but my face feels prickly and my head is swimming. "Where's Tsam?"

"The cellar, I thought it was best. Émi, we need to talk about your..."

Amin stops because I am untying my apron and folding it back under the countertop. "I'm so sorry, Amin. I have to go."

"Émi, you can't, we have to—"

"The Punishment starts at eight. I have to be there."

Amin sighs and tugs on his beard. "Yes. Alright. Well just... stay out of trouble."

"We'll talk tomorrow," I assure him and, before he can agree, I race out of the door.

Nor is waiting in line for the seven o'clock ferry and pulls me into a tight embrace when she sees me.

"There you are," she says, studying my face. "Junas told me about last night – the inspection. Are you alright? When you weren't on the ferry this morning..."

"I caught an earlier one... I'm fine, we're fine, really."

On board, no one is talking about the Punishment. Everyone has left work early, losing at least two hours' pay, and everyone is dreading it. But we have no choice; everyone in the Red Quarter has to attend. I wonder whether Junas has knocked for my mother. I don't have time to collect her and if she's late...

"Émi?" Nor is nudging me. "We're here."

Punishment Square is a dusty space at the top of Rygour Street, surrounded mostly by abandoned warehouses and merchant stores. Before entering, we are corralled through a narrow gateway where our permits are examined and our names crossed off the list. Avery is examining the permits and, as usual, he leers at me as I walk past. The glint in his eye is sleazier than normal and I wonder whether Falk has already started spreading word that I'm now offering 'night time' services.

The sky behind the square is mottled with grey bruise-like clouds; a rain storm is approaching. Not tonight, but perhaps tomorrow. Reds are gathering in clutches, looking at their hands or their feet, trying not to see the raised deck with its sinister stocks. The length of a person's Punishment depends on the severity of their crimes, so Nor says Jennyfer will be up there at least three days before they haul her off to jail. My father was in the stocks for two whole weeks, although he wasn't lucky enough to go to jail – he went straight to the camps.

At the front of the crowd, baying like jackals, the Green and Silver Cadets are eager to get started. Above them, high up on a balcony that juts out from one of the disused buildings, is a small enclave of Gold Council Officers. It is their job to initiate the proceedings. Gradually, we are hustled towards the front of the square. I bob up and down, trying to spot my mother's face among the sea of red sashes, but it is a thankless task. Nor squeezes my elbow and says, "Don't worry, Émi, she'll be here somewhere. Junas will have fetched her down." I wonder whether Nor is worried about her husband – usually Hedge meets us at the gate and files in beside us – but if she's concerned, she doesn't show it.

As the sun begins to set and the last few Reds scurry into the square, one of the Gold Officers on the balcony rings a large copper bell. The bell tolls three times, then the Officer calls out, "Red Quarter citizens. Thank you for joining us on this grave occasion. As always, it is imperative we are reminded of the fate that awaits those who betray their city. So, it is with great regret that I read the following Punishment." She unfurls a large scroll of paper and clears her throat. "Jennyfer Kray of the Red Quarter has been found guilty of a total of four crimes. One, that she did knowingly withhold information from a Cadet when directly questioned. Two, that she did strive to conceal forbidden goods. Three, that said forbidden goods were of an obvious magickal nature. And four, that she has used these magickal goods to perform spells that pose a severe threat to the safety of Nhatu and its citizens." The Officer pauses for effect and looks out at the crowd. "Jennyfer Kray shall spend four days in the stocks. After that time, she will be transferred to the labour camp at the Western Wall, where she will spend ten years atoning for her crimes."

Across the whole square, Reds stifle the urge to gasp. It is rare for a woman to be sent to the camp, especially for ten years. Beside me, a young woman whispers to her husband, "They're getting worse, the Punishments are getting worse." The husband tells her to shush but slides his hand into hers. Nor is shaking her head. The Officers on the balcony turn their backs and disappear into the building, which is the cue for the Cadets down at the front to start stomping their feet and banging on the platform.

It is Falk who leads Jennyfer up to the stocks. She looks dozy, like she has been sedated. When she sees the crowd her knees buckle and she falls to the ground. Falk jerks her back to her feet and pushes her to the centre of the platform. When he fastens her into the stocks her hair falls across her face, her head and arms shoved roughly into place. I want to stick my fingers in my ears and hum and look away so I don't have to witness this. Even from here, I can see her trembling as Falk announces that she must admit her guilt before the Punishment starts. I can't hear what she says, I doubt anyone can, but it will be a variation of the phrase, "I admit that I conspired to perform dangerous acts of magick and I must now be punished for my crimes."

The Cadets delve their gloved hands into their buckets of mulch, eager to be the first to throw. Images of my father flash through my mind. I see his kind eyes and the soft brown moustache I used to tease him for when I was young. I see a scene just like this one, except in it my mother is screaming and a Cadet is holding her to the spot so she is forced to watch every second of the ceremony. I feel nauseous. My head is spinning. Falk gives the signal and the Cadets at the front jeer and holler as they throw a mixture of rotten food and excrement at Jennyfer. Beside me, Nor remains completely placid. She knows that the more upset you look, the more likely it is you will be forced to take part. My jaw is tight and my fists are clenched. I am just about managing to control myself, until Falk pulls a girl of ten or eleven up onto the stage and slops a handful of putrid brown sludge into her palm.

"Go ahead," he bellows, nudging the girl toward Jennyfer. The girl hesitates so Falk grabs her arm and directs her to force the odious mixture into Jennyfer's mouth. Jennyfer coughs, choking on the putrid mess. The girl begins to cry. Nor looks at me because I'm starting to shake and whispers, "Émi, keep still. It'll be over soon." But I can't. A flash of pure, burning hatred has taken hold of me. I push forwards, driving through the swathe of Reds, my eyes fixed on Falk's face.

The square is now descending into darkness. On each corner of the platform, lamps have been lit, but even in the lamplight, Falk doesn't notice my approach until I am a few metres away. At first, he smiles. Perhaps he thinks I am trying to curry favour by showing my enthusiasm. But when I shout, "STOP!" his grin slides right off his face. At first, only a few people hear, so I raise my voice louder and shout again.

"STOP THIS MADNESS! STOP!"

This time, my cry echoes throughout the square and Falk's expression turns to stone. Beside me, Reds move aside, jostling backwards so they can't be associated with my outburst.

Falk's voice rings out. "Seize her!"

Cadets scramble to drag me up onto the stage. The square falls silent. No one makes a sound. Apart from Jennyfer, who is sobbing quietly.

A pair of Silver Cadets grab me with grubby mulch-stained hands and pull me up beside Jennyfer. I ignore the crowd and look straight into Falk's eyes, refusing to lower my gaze to the ground. I expect him to unleash a tirade of anger, to beat me to the ground, but instead he fixes a smile on his face and turns to his audience.

"Our friend Émi seems a little overexcited by all the action. She wants to take part. Shall we let her?"

The onlookers hesitate, but when the Cadets at the front start shouting yes, everyone follows suit. Falk reaches for his belt and withdraws a large knife with a curved metal blade.

"Ladies and gentleman," he hollers, "our plans this evening have changed... it has come to my attention that Ms Kray's wrongdoings are far more severe than we first thought. So our guest, Miss Fae, is going to help us rectify the situation." Falk binds his greasy fingers around my arm. "She's going to perform our execution."

SIX

At the word 'execution', a mixture of shouting and baying breaks out from the spectators at the front. Jennyfer releases a gut-wrenching howl and starts to buck against the stocks.

"Do you realise what you've done?" Falk spits viciously into my ear. "Your childish actions have caused this woman's death." He trails off and slides the knife into my hand, gripping my fingers tightly with his own so that I can't turn the blade against him.

He pushes me closer to the stocks. I can feel his sickly breath on my neck. Jennyfer is now completely still, muttering under her breath. The raw flickering heat in my gut has spread to my throat and my skin feels like it's on fire. A searing pain starts to spread through my arms and into my fingertips. I turn and grab Falk's free wrist with my loose hand. As my fingers dig into his skin I hear a sizzling sound and he cries out. He lets go of me and the knife clatters to the floor. I kick it away but tighten my grip.

"Witch! Sorcerer!" I step back as Falk shouts. He glares at

me, rubbing at the angry welts on his wrist. "Magick! The girl knows magick!"

Without thinking, I lunge forwards. I plant my palms flat on his cheeks and press down. I can feel the sparks inside me; they are bursting to be set free. The smell of charred flesh fills the air. A deep throaty roar escapes from Falk's lips as he mauls desperately at my hands, trying to pry them away. As he shouts, I release a high-pitched scream. I raise my arms, palms out, and an avalanche of bright white light bursts from my hands. The light pummels into his chest and hurls him to the edge of the platform.

My heart is thundering in my chest. I fix my gaze on the keys that are tied to Falk's belt and reach out as though I'm trying to take hold of them. The keys wrench themselves free and fly straight into my hand. Something has taken over my body, every fibre is vibrating with a fierce simmering energy that demands to be heard.

"Do something! Summon the Council!" Falk glances around wildly.

I ignore his commands and the commotion breaking out in the crowd, running to release Jennyfer from the stocks. She looks at me, at my hands. She hesitates, then she clambers to her feet and races down the steps, disappearing into the darkness at the back of the square.

When I turn around, the entire population of the Red Quarter is staring at me in wide-eyed terror. Falk is still struggling to his feet. His cheeks have been branded with my palm prints. The once-cocky Silver and Green Cadets at the front of the crowd reach for their knives but they seem rooted to the spot, afraid to get any closer.

Behind me someone shouts, "Émi, here!" Nor. I turn and bolt from the stage in the same direction as Jennyfer. In the shadow of a run-down grain store at the back of the square, Nor is waiting for me. She seizes my arm and whips me around the corner, down a side-street, then another, then another, until I have no idea where we are. I expect to hear footsteps pounding the pavement behind us but no one follows.

Eventually, we arrive at Nor's flat. She hurries me around the back and through the kitchen door, which she fastens closed behind us. I'm panting. My skin feels clammy.

"Mother of Mahg, Émi. You look like you're going to faint. Quick, sit down." Nor ushers me into a chair and forces a glass of water into my hand. Then, she throws her arms into the air. "What was that?"

I try to speak but my words have dried up. Nor tells me to breathe, take a moment. I listen to her gruff but soothing voice and drink my water and, slowly, the heat subsides. My body is returning to normal; my skin has cooled and my hands have stopped shaking. I look up. Nor is leaning on the worktop next to a small rusty sink that is stacked high with unwashed dishes. "Something you need to tell me?" she asks.

"You're not afraid of me?"

"Should I be?"

I shake my head at her although, truthfully, I'm a little afraid myself.

"Well, then..."

I barely know how to explain. "It started the night they arrested Jennyfer. Just a few sparks. I was angry and they just... happened. Then yesterday at the cafe... but nothing like this. This was..."

"Magick," Nor finishes for me, folding her arms in front of her stomach. "Magick is what it was."

"How can it be? I didn't do anything to summon it. It just..."

"Some people are gifted. The Council would have you believe it all comes from textbooks and studying and, sure, that's true for spells and potions. But what you just did, that's raw magick. Powerful magick."

"How do you know?"

Nor sighs and wrings her hands together. "I'm older than that wall, Émi. I've seen things. The Council might think we've forgotten but there's those of us who still remember what it was like."

She has never spoken like this before, never uttered a single word that could be considered treacherous. Her eyes flicker. "It was different before the wall. I've never said this to you because it's foolhardy. If we were overheard I'd be hauled up to those stocks quicker than a Cadet into a tavern, but I wouldn't be surprised if your dear father was right. No, it wouldn't surprise me in the least to discover the Council had lied to us all this time. If the other Cities were still..." She waves her hand in the direction of the Eastern Wall. "Out there."

"Why would they? Why would they want to trap us here?"

"Because they're afraid, Émi. Afraid of Mahg, and afraid of magick. They didn't care that it was only the few who misused it. They didn't care that there was a whole world out there where magick did good, where people were kind to each other... happy. All they cared about was their wretched wall. Banishing magick made sure no one could destroy it." As Nor finishes speaking she inhales as if she's been running uphill. She plonks herself into a chair beside me.

"You sound like my father."

"Well, as I said. Maybe he was right. Maybe we should all try and scale the wall."

I look down at my fingers. "I might have to," I say, "if they find me."

Nor is watching me intently. "Émi, what you did back there – do you think you could do it again?"

I shake my head and tell her I wouldn't know how. "I have no control over it. It just happens."

Nor grabs my forearm and leans in close. "But if you could... if you could use this power of yours... you could get us out."

I'm struggling to keep up with what she's saying.

"Émi, you could get us all out of here. The force of that – you could break down the wall. We could be free..."

I have never seen Nor so animated; her eyes are bright, dancing with possibility. But before I can tell her it's impossible and that we don't know what lies beyond the wall, the door begins to rattle. Nor jumps out of her chair and stands in front of me. Surely the Cadets can't have found us so quickly?

"Who's there?" she shouts.

From the other side of the door, I hear Tsam's voice. "Émi, it's me, let me in."

Nor turns to me. "Who is it? You know them?"

When I tell her it's a friend she unbolts the door but the second she notices Tsam's gold sash, Nor grapples for a kitchen knife and points the blade at him.

Tsam raises his arms in surrender. "I've come to help Émi..."

"Nor, it's alright, Tsam is Amin's son."

Slowly, she places the knife back on the counter. Then Tsam steps into the room and pulls me to him. His warmth sends a wave of calm from my head all the way to my toes and I sigh as he releases me. Now he's here, I feel certain everything will be alright.

Nor is watching us. "How'd you find us?" she asks.

"I was worried so I followed Émi home from The Emerald," Tsam says. "I saw what happened in the square. When Émi... I saw you run to the back of the platform and I followed you."

Nor frowns and sucks in her cheeks, but doesn't challenge him any further. "Anyone else follow us?"

Tsam shakes his head. "No, I was careful. Just me."

"Well then," she says. "What do we do now?"

───────

Nor paces up and down her tiny kitchen. "When Hedge gets home, we'll tell him about the magick, but I'm sure he saw it – everyone saw it! He'll help us rally the Reds... the ones who still remember the old ways. There's plenty of us, don't you worry."

She is rambling and Tsam is watching her carefully. The front door clicks and Nor stops pacing.

"Noreen? That you? You see it? Call me an old fool but it looked like Émi up there! The Cadets are..." The door between the kitchen and living room swings open to reveal Nor's wiry husband, Hedge. When he sees us, the cigarette falls from his mouth. Nor scoops up the butt and stubs it into a sooty ashtray next to the sink.

Hedge points at me. "It was you, wasn't it?" He turns to Nor. "What were you thinking? Bringing her here!"

Nor grabs her husband's hand. "Hedge, listen. Émi's going to help us."

Hedge is fumbling in his pocket for another cigarette, glowering at Tsam's gold sash. "What are you talking about? She has to go, Nor. She can't be here." When he finishes he turns to me and adds, "Sorry, Émi."

"No, no, you don't understand." Nor speaks quickly. "Think about it. Émi has magick. Real magick." Nor nods, waiting for Hedge to catch up with her.

Hedge stops looking for his cigarette and nods back at his wife. Understanding lights up his eyes. "If she..."

"Exactly! Émi's the chance we've been waiting for. She can help us. She can help us destroy the wall, break free of the Council."

Hedge slaps his thigh. "By The Four Cities, you're right." He turns to me. "Émi, you'll do it? You'll help us?"

They are both staring at me. I am utterly speechless. The powerful burning energy I felt in the square has subsided and I feel nothing other than normal.

"I want to, of course," I begin to say.

Tsam interrupts me. "Sorry, Émi, but you can't."

Nor and Hedge start bombarding him with *what do you mean* and *of course she can* and *it's our only chance, we've waited years for this*... But Tsam shakes his head. "You don't understand."

"And you do?" Nor asks, squaring up to him in the centre of the room.

"I do, yes."

"Tsam?" I ask him. "What are you talking about?"

Tsam steps around Nor's bulky frame and bobs down so he's kneeling in front of me. "Émi, I need to tell you something about your powers, and about your past."

I shake my head and almost laugh, because how could Tsam – the scholar from the Gold Quarter – possibly know anything about this? But the sober look on his face squashes the laugh before it's even halfway up my throat.

"Perhaps we could all..." Tsam gestures towards the living room. He doesn't wait for Nor and Hedge to agree before he leads me through. He tells us to stand by the window. The shutters are closed and the lamps above the fireplace paint flickering shadows on the walls. Now Tsam is the one pacing. He mutters something under his breath. Then he stops and begins to remove his shirt.

"Woah there, boy. What are you doing?" says Hedge, waving his hands in protest.

Tsam does't respond, simply unties his gold sash and shrugs off his shirt to reveal a grey vest and a silvery tattoo on his left forearm. He drapes the sash and the shirt over the arm of Nor's threadbare sofa and, as he does, I notice two large holes in the back of his vest. Tsam takes a small glass vial from his pocket, unscrews its cap and drinks down the contents in one big gulp. He smacks his lips, as if the taste is rancid, and scrapes his fingers through his hair.

"Émi," he says, "my father was supposed to be here to help me explain this to you. I'm sorry if I'm doing it wrong."

"Doing what? Tsam, what are you talking about?"

"The best way I can think of is to show you." Before anyone can say another word, he lurches toward me as if someone has kicked the back of his knees. I move to help him but Nor holds on to me. Slowly, Tsam swivels on the spot, presenting his back to us.

That's when I see it.

Beneath the holes in his vest, his skin writhes, undulating. As though there's a hoard of wriggling insects beneath the surface of his skin.

Tsam turns back around to face us. The colour has drained from his face. He bends over to grip his knees, biting his lip so hard that it draws blood. A ripping, stretching, tearing sound echoes through the room and a wave of nausea washes over me – the sound is coming from the skin on Tsam's back.

Nor's hand flies up to her mouth and Hedge juts his arm protectively in front of her. Tsam looks up. His eyes flash a brilliant shade of silver. He releases a stifled groan, then stretches out his arms.

Nor whispers, "He can't be..." Hedge's arm falls away.

A pair of enormous shimmering wings are unfolding from Tsam's back, growing larger and larger until they fill the entire room. Tsam shrugs his shoulders and the feathers flatten neatly into place. He looks taller, brighter, completely out of place.

Nor and Hedge drop to their knees but I am unable to move. I am studying Tsam's eyes, his arms. Those wings.

"You're..."

Tsam gives a gentle ruffle of his feathers. His eyes are still silver.

"Émi," he says at last."Your father... He was right."

SEVEN

"You're a Watcher..." I breathe. Tsam dips his head in acknowledgement, and tucks his wings in close to his sides. "But, how?"

He doesn't have chance to answer me because Nor and Hedge have gathered themselves and now are grasping his hands. "You've come to help us, we knew you would." Their eyes are alight with hope.

Tsam gently helps them to their feet and directs them towards the sofa.

"I'm sorry," he says, "I'm afraid it's not that easy." Tsam plants his hands on my shoulders. "Émi, we don't have much time. We have to get you out of Nhatu. It was always the plan, but what happened in the square today... Well, it's squeezed our timeline a little."

"Plan?"

Again, Tsam drags a hand through his hair. "Nor is right, Émi. You have magick. But there's a reason. This gift is no accident."

"Tsam, tell me..."

"You know the history of The Four Cities. You know that

Mahg tried to steal the Fire Stone?"

"Yes."

"Seventeen years ago, he attacked Abilene. He tried, but failed to take the Stone. After that, the Elders summoned a sorcerer to divide it, to keep it safe..."

From the sofa, Hedge interjects, "We know all this..."

Tsam ignores him. "You know that each of The Four Cities was given a piece of the Stone?"

"Yes."

"And you know that there was one more piece, a piece that was hidden..."

"Yes!" I'm beginning to get impatient now.

"Well, that piece was different from all the rest. To deceive Mahg, and make sure it was never found, the sorcerer moulded it into human form. Two humans, actually. Girls..." He pauses. "Sisters."

Tsam looks at me as if I should understand by now, but I don't. He takes my hand.

"You're one of those sisters, Émi. My father brought you here when you were a baby. He left you on your parents' doorstep and they took you in. But he stayed to watch over you. So did I."

From the sofa, Nor mutters, "Oh my..."

Hedge releases a deep whistle.

I hear myself laugh. Surely, Tsam is mistaken. "Tsam, I don't have a sister. My parents didn't find me. They told me about the night I was born. There was a storm, they couldn't get to the hospital, they..." I trail off. My thoughts are tripping over one another in the race to keep up. "They lied?" Even as the words leave my mouth, I know the answer.

Tsam is watching me. His eyes aren't silver anymore; they're blue again, but it's a sparkling blue that reminds me of skies and water and peace. He blinks. The tips of his wings twitch.

I sit down hard in an armchair next to the fireplace. My parents aren't my parents. This should feel blasphemous, foreign, nonsensical. But instead, it's as if something has fallen into place.

Tsam kneels down in front of me. "I'm sorry I left, Émi. I should have been here."

"All this time. You weren't in the Gold Quarter, were you?"

He sends a withering look in the direction of his abandoned gold sash. "No. My wings started to come through, I had to go back to Abilene."

I get to my feet. Now it's my turn to do laps of the living room. I am trying to sort through Tsam's words, line them up, see if any of them fit with my life. If I'd been told this a week ago, I'd have laughed out loud. But now? After today's magick? Because it was, undeniably, magick. "The Watchers still exist? And Abilene? Mahg didn't destroy you all?"

Tsam reaches into his pocket and withdraws my father's sketchbook. He hands it back to me. "No, he didn't destroy us. The other three cities are still there. Still thriving. Still safe – for now."

I rub my forehead with my fingers. "What you're saying, it makes sense, but a sister? I don't have a sister."

Tsam nods. "That's why I'm here. The sorcerer took your sister, Ava. He vowed to keep her safe and he didn't tell a soul where he was going. But now..." Tsam looks at Nor and Hedge and lowers his voice as if he's trying not to scare them. "Mahg's forces are growing. He's been raiding villages and towns in the outer provinces. Somehow, he knows you exist."

I think of the girl in my drawings. I see her as clearly as if she were standing in front of me. She is clutching her scarf, her eyes imploring me, and I know now she is my sister.

She is Ava.

"Mahg is looking for us?" The words drill shards of fear

deep into my bones.

Tsam's eyes fill, as though he's struggling not to cry. "Yes and, Émi, we need you to help us find Ava. Before Mahg does."

I turn to Nor and Hedge, then back to Tsam. A familiar feeling of wretched indignation tugs at my chest. "Why do you all think I can help you? What happened today – it was an accident! I can't control it!"

Tsam takes my hand again. "But you could learn, Ém. You have to learn. Ava needs you." He pauses. "We all need you."

I tug my hand away and reach up to my hair, to refasten some of the pins that have shaken themselves loose.

"Please, Émi, come with me? Back to Abilene?"

I turn away from Tsam and kneel down in front of Nor. Kind, stoic, brash Nor.

"What do I do?" I ask her.

Nor strokes my hair. The promise and excitement in her eyes has faded and she is smiling a doleful smile. "You must go."

"But if I go..." I look at Tsam. "If we go, can we take them with us?"

Tsam shakes his head and Nor clasps my hands between hers. "Listen to me, Émi. Listen close. This is bigger than me, or Hedge. It's bigger than Nhatu and that damned wall. You go with your Watcher, find your sister, and when Mahg's dead in his grave – then you can come back for us."

Hedge slides an arm around his wife's shoulders. "Noreen's right, Émi."

Again, the girl from my dreams appears in my head. Those eyes. Those pleading, desperate eyes.

"Alright," I say. "I'll come with you."

Nor springs up from the sofa.

"I assume you have a plan? A way out?" She is looking at Tsam's wings as if she's expecting him to take flight at any second.

Tsam perches on the corner of the armchair. I watch him balance his body so there is room for both him and his wings. I remember him doing the same thing back in The Emerald.

How did I not see it before? How did I not realise what he was? It is so obvious to me now; his silvery blonde hair, the ethereal glow that even Gold Quarter citizens don't have.

Tsam's feathers ripple. "The plan was to take Émi to the outer wall, late, under cover of dark. Wait until the sentries swap their watch, and fly over."

"We can't do that now?" I ask.

"I don't think so," Tsam says, rubbing his chin.

Hedge cuts in, "Impossible. It's chaos out there. The Cadets will be swarming all over the city looking for Émi."

Tsam nods. "We'd be seen. The Council can't know I'm here. If they thought the Watchers had breached the wall, brought magick here..."

Hedge looks at the clock on the mantlepiece. It is nearly half past midnight. "In three hours, I'll be starting my shift. If you two hide in the back of the cart, I can get you to the wall. Could even get you up it, if you get in with the rubbish."

Tsam is frowning so Hedge explains, "I'm a Scrappie – collect rubbish sacks from the upper Quarters and take 'em to the Tipping Point. Then throw the rubbish over the wall. If you two hide in there with the sacks..."

"We could get to the top, without being seen, and then fly," says Tsam. "Good, yes, that will work. Émi? Are you alright with that?"

"Well, yes, but Hedge, you'll be putting yourself in an awful lot of danger. If they find us with you?"

Hedge shakes his head at me. "Émi, dear, I couldn't give a jot what they do to me. Like Noreen said, this is more important than some little old Scrappie from the Red Quarter. If it helps you get out, and helps the Watchers destroy that monster, once and for all, then being caught with a couple of fugitives is a risk I'm willing to take."

"That's settled then," says Tsam.

With just a few hours until Hedge begins his shift, Nor says we should try to get some sleep. She and Hedge retire to their bedroom, leaving Tsam and I alone in the living room.

The lanterns above the fireplace are dimmed and I'm curled into an armchair with my tunic pulled tight over my knees, holding back the urge to cry. Leaving Nhatu is all I've ever wanted. I have dreamed of the Watchers, of Abilene and the other Cities, since I was a girl. But now, Tsam is telling me I'm not a girl, not really. I'm a... thing. One day, I was nothing, and then I was a person. Not even a whole person. Somewhere out there, beyond the wall, my sister – my other half – is waiting for me to find her. If he wanted to, could the sorcerer just – change us back? Could Mahg? Is that his plan?

I wish my father was here, because he would know what to say, and because he deserves to know that he wasn't crazy. But thinking of him makes me think of my mother alone in our flat, or perhaps even, by now, captured by the Cadets. Then I can't stop the tears from falling.

The vibration of Hedge's deep rhythmic snoring bleeds through the parlour wall and muffles the sounds of my sobs. Tsam is stretched out on the sofa, his fingers entwined beneath his skull so his elbows stick out and rest on the cushion of his wings. He seems to be sleeping.

As my tears dry on my cheeks, I feel the air start to change; it won't be long before it rains. Tsam shivers and curls his wings around himself, turning on his side. I take the blanket from the back of my chair and fold it over him. I am staring at the intricacy of his snowy feathers when he mumbles, "Can't sleep, huh?"

"Are you surprised?"

He sits up. His wings give a small flick.

I balance on the sofa, beside his feet. "Do you really think this will work?"

He sighs and shakes his head. "I think it's our best chance."

I know he's right. "Tsam, what about my mother? The Cadets will..."

He puts his hand on my arm. "My father will look after her. He won't let any harm come to her, I know he won't." He is sincere, but the shadow that flits across his face betrays his concern. "Hedge will be up soon."

A few minutes later, Nor knocks on the living room door and enters. Without speaking, she smothers me in a tight embrace.

"Are you alright?" I ask, struggling to breathe.

She lets me go. "Breakfast," she says, ignoring my question. "You need to eat."

As Nor busies herself at the stove, I remember the crowns Garvey gave me in exchange for my necklace. I reach for Nor's hand and drop what's left into her palm. "Will you give these to Junas?" I ask. "For the rent? I don't know how long he'll let her stay there, but—"

Nor whips around to face me. "Don't you worry about Junas," she says, sternly. "He's all talk. He'll not see her out on the street, I promise you."

My eyes start to sting. "Will you look after her?"

Nor cups my face in her hands. "You know I will."

I'm about to tell her I'll miss her when Hedge enters the room, muttering. "Nor, where in The Four Cities is my coffee? We have to leave in the next twenty minutes or the whole thing will go to pot and I can't do a darned thing without coffee in my veins!" Nor grumbles something back at her husband and shoves a steaming mug into his hands, but when he kisses her on the cheek she blushes. "Get away, you old fool."

When Hedge has left the room, Nor walks over to the pantry where she rummages around its highest shelf. She returns with a small porcelain jar that has a delicately patterned lid. She hands me the jar and tells me to open it. Inside is a pendant: a twisted leather chain with a pair of dangling silver wings. The wings are wrapped around a small white gemstone. "Put it on," Nor says, "it'll keep you safe."

I fasten the wings around my neck and they feel warm against my skin. "Are these...?"

"The wings represent the Watchers, and the stone... Well, I suppose it's you, isn't it?" She rolls up her sleeves and cracks an egg into a mixing bowl. "It's been in my family since before the wall went up. My mother wore it, for good luck."

Back in the living room, Hedge is slurping the last dregs of his coffee and lighting a cigarette. "It's almost three thirty. In a few minutes, I'll go and collect the cart from the scrap yard. I'll drive it back here and stop out front. There'll be other Scrappies and traders milling about, so Noreen will create a distraction. When no one's looking you two will jump into the back of the cart."

Nor has placed a platter of kippers and eggs on the small round table in the corner of the room and my stomach growls. We dig in, then Tsam retrieves a second blueish vial from his pocket and slurps down its contents. Slowly, his wings suck back under his skin. He grimaces and rubs at his shoulders. "That never stops feeling strange," he says.

We are almost ready to leave, when a frantic knocking starts at the front door. We freeze in the centre of the room.

"Can't be the Cadets already," Hedge whispers.

Nor holds a finger to her lips and inches forwards to peer through the shutter nearest the door. "Émi, it's your mother."

Instantly, I move towards the hallway, intending to open the door, but Tsam catches my arm and Hedge says, "We don't have time for this."

"I'll deal with it," says Nor, ushering us towards the kitchen. "Use the back door."

From outside, my mother wails, "Nor! Nor, let me in! Is Émi in there?"

"For pity's sake, woman. Let her in before the whole street hears her!" Hedge whispers, following Tsam and I to the kitchen. "I'll be back in five minutes with the cart."

Tsam is still holding my arm as I press myself against the wall next to the parlour door.

"Patti," Nor says, gently. "What in the world is the matter?"

My mother's voice is fraught and high-pitched. "Is Émi here?"

"No, Patti, she's not here. Why would she be?" I imagine Nor placing her hand on the small of my mother's back and guiding her to sit down.

"She didn't come home. I don't know what to do. Did you see what happened at the Punishment? That girl up on the platform? It looked like... people are saying it was... But it can't have been. Not my Émi."

"Patti, you need to calm yourself down. I'm sure there's a perfectly reasonable explanation. We'll figure it out."

My mother mumbles something I can't hear and I'm about to push open the door, run to her and tell her everything, when Nor suddenly raises her voice. "Oh, listen to that. It's Hedge's van. He must have forgotten his glasses again. I'll be back in a minute, Patti, dear!"

Tsam tugs at my arm and whispers, "Émi, we have to go."

I press my fingers flat on the door. "I love you, Ma. I'm sorry." Then I follow Tsam out of the back door and down the side passage that leads to the street.

Outside, the street is illuminated by the hazy half glow of

the morning street lamps. Amidst the shadows, people are already beginning to journey to their places of work. We pause at the end of the passageway. Nor is standing on her doorstep, waving her arms and hollering.

"You useless fool, what would you do without me? You'd be lost! That's what!"

Hedge hangs his head, looking dejected. He glimpses us out of the corner of his eye and twitches his index finger at the back of the cart. Red neighbours hurry past, wary of being caught in the crossfire of Nor's anger. With our heads down, we dash out of the passageway and slip through the shadows. Hedge has left the back of the cart unhooked, so we swing it open and scramble inside. Nor draws her rant to a close and Hedge catches her eye. "See you later then," he says, and the cart pulls away.

We have been crouched in the back of Hedge's scrap cart for three and a half hours when he finally announces, through the grill that separates the driver from the cargo at the back, that we will now be heading to the wall. My legs feel like they are made of lead. Tsam shifts uncomfortably beside me and stifles a cough. The odour of the rubbish is becoming unbearable.

"Tsam?"

"Mm."

"Why has this only just started happening to me? The sparks? Why now?"

Tsam thinks for a moment. "I'm not sure. The Elders will know."

I'm still sifting through the questions in my brain, trying to order them, when Tsam nudges a broken chair leg out of his field of vision and looks at me. "Maybe your age is significant. You're nearly seventeen – that's the age we turn from Fledglings to Watchers. The whole of Abilene gathers for the Ceremony. Flying displays, dancing, lanterns... it's wonderful. The next one is in a few days' time." He shuffles closer and his tone darkens. "When Mahg first attacked us it was at a Fledgling Ceremony."

"That was when he tried to take the Stone?" I still talk as though the Stone is separate from me. I feel too normal, too... human.

"Yes, seventeen years ago," Tsam says.

Before I can ask any more questions, the cart jolts violently over a pothole and Hedge swears under his breath.

"We're at the check point," he whispers. "Get your heads down."

We draw to a stop. From our hiding place, we can see the arm of a green-banded Cadet as he leans into the driver's cabin and holds out his hand. Hedge passes him a worn-looking permit.

"Fine," the Cadet says, waving us through.

When Hedge opens the back of the cart, he doesn't speak. Huddled in the corner, we watch as he starts to unload his bulging sacks of rubbish. Painstakingly, he empties each bag onto the floor and sifts through it by hand. Pieces of metal, wood, porcelain and fabric are put in a pile to return to the scrap yard, while food waste – and sometimes excrement – is stuffed back into a sack and put to one side. Through the open door, we can see a line of Scrappies with their carts, all doing the same thing. The colossal city wall rises up beside them. Its shining flint paints stripes of sunlight across the floor of the Tipping Point.

Hedge has sorted through just a quarter of the sacks in his cart when he raises his head and holds a hand across his forehead, squinting into the distance. At the far end of the line, a Cadet has stopped an elderly Scrappie and is showing him a large piece of paper. Hedge rubs the back of his neck with a handkerchief and exhales loudly, then continues to sort the scrap at his feet, glancing up every few seconds as the Cadet progresses further down the line.

"Morning, Scrappie." A silver-banded Cadet this time.

"Morning, sir," replies Hedge, offering a salute and standing up straight with his feet hip-width apart.

The Cadet steps back, wrinkling his nose at Hedge's sour overalls.

"How can I help you, sir?"

"We are in search of a dangerous fugitive. A girl. I need you to look at this and tell me if you have seen her."

Hedge rubs his chin as he studies a sketch of my face.

"Her crimes are severe," the Cadet continues. "You're aware of the incident in the square last night?"

Hedge nods and puffs out his cheeks, "Oh yes, sir. Terrible business. This is the girl?"

"Her name is Émi Fae. Redhead, medium height, slight build. Used to be a Green." The Cadet narrows his eyes and leans in closer. "I believe you're acquainted with this girl, Scrappie?"

Hedge hesitates and I pray for him to tell the truth – they will find out sooner or later.

"Well, Émi, yes. Was it really her? My word. I don't know her well myself, but my wife helped her and her mother find a place to live when they arrived from the Green Quarter. Not sure she has anything much to do with her now, mind you. My brother-in-law Junas is the girl's landlord. You could try him?"

The Cadet nods slowly. The glint in his eye says he already knew about Junas and wanted to see whether Hedge would disclose the connection. "When was the last time you saw Miss Fae?"

"Oh, not for a long time, sir. When they first moved to the Quarter, three years ago maybe, I helped them with some scrap from the yard. Between you and me, the mother is very odd. Depressive, they say. Sleeps all day, cries all night..."

"Alright, alright." The Cadet waves his hand dismissively. "We may need to talk to you again. Make sure you are available." Then he moves on, glancing into the cart as he passes.

When the Cadet reaches a Scrappie three carts along, Hedge whispers, "We need to do this now. They could start searching."

He swings a sack, which he's only half filled, onto the back of the cart and tips it over. I hesitate but Tsam nudges me. I look at him and he makes a 'hurry up' motion with his eyebrows. I crawl forwards and force myself inside, head first, then spin around so I'm facing the opening of the sack. I can see Tsam's glistening eyes peering out from the back of the cart. I smile at him, to let him know I'm okay. But my smile is still only half-formed when Hedge ties a knot in the top of the sack and seals me in. Almost instantly, it's difficult to breathe. And when Hedge heaves me onto his back, the putrid waste of the Upper Quarters smears all over my arms and face and hair.

Hedge leverages me onto a hard surface; I'm guessing the wooden deck next to the wall. I strain my ears as he does the same for Tsam, then continues to load on sacks until the deck is full. Eventually, he says, "Here we go," and the deck shudders. It is suspended beside the wall by a system of thick metal ropes and pulleys that grate viciously as our ascent begins.

The higher we rise, the more the deck sways and then, suddenly, the movement stops. From below, the burst of a Cadet's whistle cuts through the scratchy webbing that encases me. I'm certain I can hear a commotion breaking out. I start to claw at the lining of the sack, trying to find its neck and loosen Hedge's knot from the inside but my fingers are clumsy and the lack of air is making me dizzy.

I start fumbling through the rubbish, trying to find something sharp that I can use to cut through the cloth, but there is nothing other than oozing, nauseating sludge. I scratch at the fabric with my fingernails, hoping to weaken it, but my nails are blunt and useless. Panic is rising in my throat when, from nowhere, a sliver of light appears above my right shoulder. I inch sideways and the sliver widens. A knife plunges in beside me, scraping my collarbone but letting in a whoosh of fresh, breathable air.

"Émi, get out!" Tsam is shouting. I shove my arm through the hole and Tsam grabs hold of me. He pulls at me and the sack splits open. I tumble onto the floor of the deck and look down. Even though I'm on my hands and knees, I feel as if my legs might fall out from under me; we are two thirds of the way up the wall, at least one hundred metres above the ground.

"We need to get off here before Hedge is forced to bring it down," Tsam says.

I gesture to his pocket. "You'll have to bring your wings back, there's no other way…"

Tsam looks at me solemnly and shakes his head. "Afraid not," he says, opening his palm to show me the remains of a broken glass bottle – the bottle that contained his magickal wing-conjuring liquid. "We'll have to climb it."

I look up. The top of the wall seems completely unreachable but we have no choice; down below, the Cadets are multiplying. I search for a piece of flint that sticks out far enough for me to use it as leverage. I find one and take hold of it with my right hand. I tuck my left foot into a space just big enough for my toes, then raise my right foot higher. Beside me, Tsam is doing the same. We have only just begun to haul ourselves up when the pulleys start to grind and the deck clangs against the wall.

"They're winding it back down!" I call.

"Don't look!" Tsam shouts back. But, of course, I do.

The deck disappears from beneath our feet, descending at

breakneck speed. A swarm of black uniforms have engulfed the floor of the Tipping Point. Scrappies and their carts are being herded towards the far end and I can't tell whether Hedge is among them or if he has already been arrested. My hands begin to tremble.

"Émi," Tsam calls. "Look up. If we can reach the top..." A gust of wind steals the rest of his words and sends a violent shiver down my spine.

We climb, and climb, and I try to ignore what's happening on the ground – the shouting, the whistles. Time has lost its momentum and we're still at least ten metres from the top of the wall when a low, angry grumble rolls through the clouds. A drop of water lands on my forearm, then another. I try to climb quicker but the storm matches my pace and the flint becomes slick beneath my touch. I can hear the scraping of the ropes as the deck creeps its way back up the wall, and I don't need to look back over my shoulder to know the Cadets are catching up with us.

I reach above my head and find a large, protruding piece of stone. I use it to heave myself up, but I haven't made sure that it can take my weight and it comes loose from the wall, tumbling down towards the Cadets. As the stone falls, I grapple for another handhold but the surface is too slippery and I'm left hanging by one hand, the toe of a foot gripping the wall. My weight-bearing arm burns with the effort of holding on. The rain is getting faster and heavier and another crack of thunder causes the wall to shudder.

I can hear Tsam telling me to calm down but I'm struggling to catch my breath. He's trying to move sideways so he can help me but I tell him, "No, keep going!"

I close my eyes and count to ten, then snake my fingers across the surface of the wall until I find a piece that's sturdy enough to grab hold of.

I look down. Hedge's rubbish deck is halfway back up the wall, carrying a seething cluster of Silver and Green Cadets. They have stopped blowing their whistles and are staring up at us. Rain lashes across their faces but they don't flinch or try to shield themselves.

Tsam is a little way ahead of me now. When he reaches the top he lays flat on his stomach and stretches his arms out towards me. I keep climbing. As soon as I'm close enough, I take his hands and scramble up beside him.

We are here! On top of the wall – but there is nowhere to go. The side that isn't Nhatu calls to me. It is so close... closer than I ever dreamed possible. I want to pause, to see what my father gambled his life to see, but the storm has swallowed up the landscape.

Tsam takes a wooden pipe from his pocket. The pipe splits into two and he strikes the pieces against one another. On the second strike, they produce a cloud of bright blue smoke that somehow manages to twirl its way upwards, despite the rain. Tsam peers at the horizon, then turns and looks down at the Cadets, who are now struggling to keep their balance on the slippery, swaying platform.

"Come on, Lyss," he mumbles.

He's about to strike the pieces again when a fast-moving whiteish blur appears against the clouds. It's coming closer, gathering momentum. Eventually, it takes shape and I realise it's a girl. With wings just like Tsam's. She streaks towards us; then, with only seconds to spare, she slows down and stops, treading the air before gently planting her feet on top of the wall.

"Trouble?" she asks.

Tsam waves his broken vial at her. "Lucky I brought a spare," she says, reaching into a pouch that's slung across her chest. She gives Tsam a bottle, similar to the one he broke, and he hurriedly drinks down its contents.

"This isn't where we were supposed…" she says, but Tsam cuts her off.

"Long story."

The girl tips her head and pulses her wings. "Shall I wait?"

"Better had," Tsam replies, motioning to our pursuers.

The girl moves forward, just a little, not so close that she would be seen by the Cadets. She peers over the edge. "Things didn't go to plan, then?"

Tsam doesn't answer because, finally, his wings burst out of his skin and he releases a sound that's halfway between a yawn and a scream. Tsam and the girl nod at one another. She's beating her wings, ready to take flight, when a whip of lightening cracks across the sky. "Not ideal," she murmurs.

Tsam turns to me. "I'm going to have to hold on to you for this bit," he says.

Suddenly, it occurs to me that we're about to leave. I take one last look over the edge of the wall. The Cadets are no more than six metres from the top now. A little closer and they will spot Tsam and the girl and their wings. Through the rain, I see Falk standing at the front of the group, eyes like steel.

"Émi Fae," he barks, "we are giving you the opportunity to hand yourself in."

Tsam tries to tug me away from the edge but I shrug him off. Falk's eyes are fixed on mine. Even from here, I can see the scarlet burns on his cheeks where I branded him with my magick hands. He stands to one side. The Cadets behind him part and my stomach lurches up into my throat as my mother's waif-like figure is shoved to the centre of the deck. She stumbles, then looks up. For not even a second, I think she's going to be brave – tell me to go, run, save myself. But as soon as she sees me, she calls my name and her tremulous voice makes me fall to my knees.

"If you come with us peacefully, we will not harm her," Falk shouts.

Ma is shaking her head. The rain plasters her hair slick against her skull. Her sodden tunic clings to her bony hips. She is crying.

I turn to Tsam. "They have my mother! Tsam, what do we do?"

"I'm sorry, Émi, there's nothing..."

I can't speak. The Cadets are almost level with us. I look down at my fingers. I close my eyes and try to summon the powerful flames of energy that scalded Falk's face and dragged his keys from his belt. I know it's there, but it doesn't come.

"Émi." I hate that this girl knows my name but hasn't given me hers. "You're more important than your mother. She's dispensable. You're not. We have to go."

Tsam softens his voice but speaks quickly. "Émi, please. They won't let her go, not even if you stay. If you come with me, the Elders will help your mother."

Again, Falk's voice rises up above the rain. "This is your last chance, Miss Fae."

The deck's gears are grinding slowly to a halt. It's almost upon us.

"Émi..." Tsam implores me.

"Émi!" my mother screams. Her eyes are frantic and I can't do anything to help her. My powers, my great magickal powers, have deserted me. Ma stretches out her arms, straining as though she could pull me back to her.

"Ma!" I drive my voice above the wind and the rain. "I'm sorry! I'll come back for you, I promise."

If my mother replies, I don't hear her. Tsam wraps one arm around my waist and the other across my chest. Then he tears me away.

EIGHT

Plunging over the wall, Tsam launches us into a nosedive that rattles every bone in my body. We hurtle towards the ground and I wonder if he's lost control, if he's injured, if we're going to crash into the festering waste that the Scrappies toss over the Tipping Point. Then, suddenly, he slows down and turns so we're flying parallel with the ground. He is beating his wings hard and fast against the storm, hugging the Western Wall and staying low so that we remain out of sight.

Stinging columns of rain force me to screw my eyes shut. With nothing but darkness to focus on, Ma's face starts to plague my thoughts. I can't pry her loose; I see her again and again, reaching out, calling my name – her paper heart tearing into a million pieces. I squeeze tight onto Tsam's arms. *Émi, I say, using my father's voice because it is the one I always use when I am being stern with myself. You're allowed one last cry. Let it all out, here in the sky where no one can see you. Then you must be strong.* I listen, I absorb the words, and then I let the tears come. They fall and fall and bleed onto my cheeks until I can no longer tell whether they're teardrops or rain. Then, as abruptly as it began, the storm stops and the clouds dissipate.

Tsam takes us higher. Flashes of green are appearing on the horizon and I'm certain we must have passed the very last corner of the wall; I try to look back but Tsam's wings shield my view. Up ahead, a forest shimmers into focus. Destroyed, the Council told us; the land beyond the wall is nothing but wasteland – dirt and weeds and grit. But, oh, how they lied. The trees are hypnotically green, more green than anything in Nhatu; deep, sumptuous green that sings of life. So far removed from the ravaged desolation I drew in my posters that they seem as if they can't possibly be real.

Now the rain has stopped, Tsam's flying has reached a more gentle, lilting rhythm and he carries me effortlessly over the crowns of the trees. I can almost feel the leaves brushing against my legs as we fly; the sensation makes my skin hum. Soon we come to a break in the canopy, where Tsam ducks down and weaves us through a maze of branches and tree trunks. Down and down we go, descending into a pocket of muted light.

The girl from the wall is waiting for us. Tsam releases me down to the ground and hurries towards her. Instead of embracing, they push their palms together as though they're about to dance. My legs don't feel like my own. The need to vomit surges into my throat. I stagger away from Tsam and the girl, into the shrubbery, where I allow my stomach to evacuate its contents. Tsam is calling me but I can't reply.

I bend over, place my hands on my knees, and stay that way until my breath returns to normal. When I turn around, Tsam has his back to me – his wings are folded neatly, their tips resting just below his knees. The girl is beside him, gesticulating wildly. Now that the rain has subsided, I can see that her hair is the same silvery-blonde as Tsam's and delicately braided into rows that hang down between her wings.

I stare at them. They are real. Their wings, their skin, their hair, just as my father said they would be: effervescent against the dark green backdrop of the forest. I am surrounded by details that were never mentioned in the Council's textbooks, or our history lessons at school. Details that were, somehow, etched in the back of my mind and channelled into my secret sketches. Trees so tall they must have been here for a thousand years, splashes of colour, flowers peeking out from behind billowing leaves. It's as if the drawings I burned in the Red Quarter have come to life.

I touch the skin of the tree nearest to me and the life that pulses through it almost takes my breath away. There are trees in Nhatu, of course there are. But even the ones in the Green Quarter are grey, bereft and sickly in comparison to these trees. A knot catches in my throat. It's not just people that Nhatu's wall keeps hostage; it's everything.

I never saw it before. I was like everyone else. I accepted my fate. But now I see that the things they told us weren't true. I know there don't have to be Quarters, or inspections, or Cadets. And I know I am the only one who can help them. Not just Ma – everyone. I have to set them free. But first, I need to find Ava.

The heat of this knowledge sears through my veins, and I step forward clumsily. A twig cracks beneath me. The girl whips her head around, looking at me with a frown.

Tsam hurries over and brushes a stray curl from my forehead. "Are you alright?"

Before I have chance to answer him, the girl clears her throat. "I'm Alyssa." She bows at me and presses her fingertips together to make a triangle.

"Émi," I say.

"I know," she replies, smiling. Then, "We should get moving, the others are waiting at the clearing."

Alyssa strides ahead, hacking at the undergrowth and carving a ragged path between the trees and vines that surround us. She's wearing a long-sleeved wrap that criss-crosses over her stomach and up between her wings. Occasionally, she looks back at Tsam and I, or stops to check a compass that's strapped to her belt. But she doesn't speak.

Tsam is quiet too. He is trying to slow his pace to match mine but, where he and Alyssa are protected in calf-high leather boots, my sandalled feet are exposed to spiky leaves and broken twigs and he is forced to keep pulling ahead of me.

On a brief navigational stop, Alyssa notices my bleeding toes.

"The others have some boots for you," she tells me. "Clothes too," she adds, assessing my damp mud-coloured tunic.

In Nhatu, after a storm, the heat immediately rallies and sucks the moisture out of everything. Here, the sun struggles to break its way through the canopy, leaving our skin clammy. The few plumes of light that make it through bounce gleefully off the leaves, creating little wisps of steam that rise in swirls. All around us, the forest pulses with the chatter of unseen creatures.

Eventually, I ask Tsam where we are. He looks at me the way he did back in the Red Quarter, when I said we'd run out of water – as if he can't believe what he's hearing. But he quickly rearranges his expression and tells me, "The Alder Woods. They stretch from Nhatu's border out towards Abilene. I'll show you on the map when we stop."

I try to remember whether my father told me any stories about these woods. I replay visions of him sketching wildly into the night. I loop back through the tales he would share with me as he drew, but before I can find what I'm looking for Tsam interrupts my thoughts.

"Ém, your Ma will be alright," he whispers.

I don't reply. What is there to say?

It takes us almost two hours to reach the meeting point Alyssa spoke of. My limbs are covered in scratches and my hair is matted with leafy debris. The clearing is empty, just a small circle of grass mottled with light from a gap in the canopy above. Alyssa stands in the centre and makes a low clicking sound with her tongue. A higher click replies from somewhere to our right.

We wait.

Leaves rustle.

I notice Tsam and Alyssa tense and I step to one side to shelter beneath Tsam's wings. The rustling grows nearer and nearer until, suddenly, the branches part. A tall boy with scruffy hair and unkempt wings emerges from the undergrowth, grinning and waving at us.

"Émi," says the boy, "it's so good to meet you. I'm very glad you're safe." His smile is warm and welcoming. "I'm Garrett, Alyssa's big brother."

Alyssa rolls her eyes and snarks, "Only ten months bigger. Where's Kole?"

"He's setting up camp at the stream."

Alyssa's feathers bristle. "If we stop, we'll be behind schedule."

Garrett replies, in a tone that is soothing and measured. "Everyone's tired, Lyss. Especially these two." He gestures with his left wing at Tsam and I. "If we get some rest now, we might cover double the distance tomorrow."

Alyssa looks as though she is going to challenge him, but Garrett turns away before she has chance.

"You look like you've had a rough journey," he tells me.

I glance down at my bedraggled state. When I look back up Garrett is taking a flask from around his neck and offering it to me. I thank him and gulp down a few deep swigs of cool clean water, while he and Tsam exchange a brotherly embrace and a look I can't interpret.

We take it in turns to drink from the flask, then swiftly re-enter the woods and walk for another twenty minutes or so. We no longer seem to be heading in a straight line, but without sun or stars visible above us, I have no way of judging whether we have veered east or west. Up ahead, Tsam walks beside Alyssa. Garrett is by my side, struggling almost as much as Tsam did to slow his steps.

"You don't have to wait for me," I say.

Garrett laughs and pats me on the shoulder. "I'm not waiting for you, I'm *watching* you." He laughs again, amused by his own joke. "You're precious, Émi. We can't let you wander around by yourself."

The thought hadn't even occurred to me – that they're here to make sure I'm protected. I understand what they've told me. I understand who I am. But it doesn't feel real. I laugh too but it comes out wrong, like I'm trying too hard. Garrett doesn't seem to notice.

"She's not always this spiky," he says, cocking his chin in Alyssa's direction, "but bringing you home to Abilene – it's big. Incredible, really. The biggest thing since... Well, since they hid you in Nhatu in the first place. We have a lot to prove, us three."

"Why's that?" I ask.

"Until the Ceremony we're technically still Fledglings. The Elders wanted to send Watchers for you. People with more experience. But..."

"So why didn't they?" I interrupt.

"Tsam persuaded them. He didn't want you to find out from a stranger about..." Garrett blushes, clearly unsure how to phrase the next part. "About who you are."

As Garrett continues to talk, the trees part to reveal a narrow river that curves sharply out of sight. The clarity of the water startles me. Once again, I feel like I must be dreaming. We follow the river around its snake-like bend until the rocky banks peter out, replaced by tall willowy grasses. Up ahead, on an earthy patch of ground between the water and the trees, someone has lit a campfire.

Garrett squeezes my arm. "I'll get some water on. You look like you could use something to eat."

He rummages in a bulging backpack propped against a nearby tree trunk and takes out a small wooden disc. He gives it a firm shake and it concertinas out into the shape of a bucket that he takes down to the water and fills to the brim. When he returns, he places the bucket right in the heart of the fire. I wait for it to blacken or start to burn, but it doesn't.

Tsam and Alyssa have disappeared, so when Garrett flops down next to the fire and prods it with a stick, I join him.

"This must be a bit overwhelming?" he says, waving his lithe fingers at our surroundings.

"You could say that." I know I'm being curt with him but I can't help it. Under different circumstances – if Garrett had been a boy from school or a friendly customer at The Emerald – I'm sure I'd have warmed to him, appreciated his openness and easy chatter. But as he smiles at me, clearly expecting me to elaborate on how I'm feeling, I can't find the words. Not yet. Not now.

Alyssa saves me from her brother's kindness by emerging from the trees with a small leather pack. She hands it to me. "There are some clothes and boots in here. Supplies, too. It's yours now, don't lose it."

"Where's Tsam?" I ask.

"Scouting," she replies. She glances between the trees. "There's a spot over there where you can change."

I thank her and take my pack into the wood.

Back under cover, I inhale deeply and close my eyes. I try to take slow, meaningful breaths but my thoughts keep returning to the wall. My mind conjures wicked visions of what the

Cadets might be doing to my mother, to Nor and to Hedge. Even Amin.

The visions threaten to overwhelm me, to suck me down into a spiral of darkness. My temples throb. With all the strength I can muster, I snap open my eyes and shake the pictures away.

Inside the pack I find a pair of jodhpurs, a vest and a jacket. I unbutton my tunic and allow it to puddle around my feet. Then I look down at the scarlet sash that pinches the flesh of my upper arm. The sash I never take off. The sash that, even when I sleep, must stay in place. In the shade of the wood, it looks like a gaping wound against my translucent skin. I pull on the jodhpurs and the vest.

Then I start to pick at the sash.

Gently, at first, as if I should be afraid of tearing it. But, when the knot refuses to loosen, I start to tug and pull. It continues to defy me. I become breathless, frantic, desperate to be free of it. I've almost given up when a voice calls out behind me:

"Here, let me help."

Alyssa.

She takes a delicate blade from her belt. "Keep still."

I watch as she tucks the point of the knife under the sash. Then, with a single flick of the wrist it floats to the ground. I stare at it. It is nothing more than a scrap of fabric that will rot amongst the leaves and the worms.

"Alright now?" Alyssa asks.

"Thank you."

It's the only reply I can manage.

When we return to the campfire, Tsam is sitting beside Garrett with his legs stretched out in front of him and he leans the weight of his body back on his hands. Garrett sprinkles the contents of a small hessian bag into the bucket of simmering water. He turns at the sound of our approach.

"Grub's up in ten," he says.

Tsam pats the ground beside him and I sit down.

"Better?" he asks.

"Yes, thank you." My heart still hurts, but at least my clothes are a little fresher.

Alyssa doesn't mention the sash. "Anyone know where Kole is?" she asks.

Garrett and Tsam shake their heads.

"Kole?" I ask.

Alyssa's tone sharpens. "A Taman. The Elders said it was necessary for him to accompany us. Valuable skill set, apparently."

"He's not so bad," says Tsam. "A little frosty, but he's one of the best fighters in Tarynne."

Garrett nods, enthusiastically. "We saw him once at a display. Remember, Lyss? We were there for Da's birthday? He's the youngest Taman ever to reach Top Tier. He was incredible."

"You sound like a Tamanyte," says Alyssa, and I can tell from her tone that she's not paying her brother a compliment.

Tsam laughs loudly and thumps Garrett on the shoulder. "We'll see if we can get a sketch of him for your wall. Émi's great at sketching. Perhaps she can do one for you?"

Garrett scrunches his face and turns huffily back to the fire as Tsam and Alyssa chuckle at him.

"Tamanyte?" I know 'Taman' are elephant riders but I've never heard of 'Tamanyte' before.

Tsam laughs. "That's what they call the little doe-eyed Fledglings who swoon after the Taman. Kole is a real favourite of theirs."

I can't help laughing and the sound surprises me. "Well," I

say, "if Kole ever shows up I'll ask him to flex his muscles and pose for me."

Alyssa laughs when I say this, and so does Tsam. I feel pleased with myself because I'd forgotten that I can be witty. But then I realise they are looking past me at something else, or someone else. I turn and my mouth gapes.

"Kole," Alyssa says. "This is Émi..."

NINE

K ole is at least six feet tall. If I'd encountered him without first knowing he was part of our group, I would probably have assumed he was here to assassinate me. With broad shoulders and thick arms, he strides forward and bows.

At first I think he is wearing a mask, but as he draws closer I realise it's a deep purple, butterfly-shaped birthmark that covers his eyes, part of his forehead and the bridge of his nose.

"Émi," he says, nothing more. Just my name, as though it's a greeting. I shrink back. I trusted Alyssa and Garrett without question, but there's something about Kole that makes me nervous.

The Taman doesn't sit with us. He takes a cup, a smaller version of the concertina bucket, and scoops himself a portion of whatever it is Garrett's cooking, then he carries it to a boulder near the river, where he sits cross-legged facing the sun.

The sprinkles Garrett added to the water have created a thick-scented soup. I take a bowl and sip, blowing at the surface to help it cool. Its taste is utterly foreign; not a single flavour I can put a name to. I drink it down, all of it, then run my index finger around the inside of the cup. When I look up, Tsam is watching me.

I drink three cups of soup and then, my belly bloated, I lean back and sigh. Looking at my bloodied feet, Tsam tells me I should bathe them before putting my boots on, so I follow him to the river. He instructs me to sit on a flattish rock, a few metres away from Kole. I do as I'm told but, when Tsam offers to help me, I tell him I'd rather do it myself.

"Alright," he says, his cheeks flushing a little. He glances over at the campfire. "I'll wait with the others."

I wash my feet slowly. I dangle them in the water and let them be soothed, then I roll up my jodhpurs and splash my legs. The water stings, but at least it will clean the scratches. From his nearby boulder, Kole inclines his head in my direction. It's impossible to tell whether he is watching me. From this distance, his dark eyes melt into his birthmark.

Slowly, he climbs down and wades into the shallow part of the river. He makes his way towards me. I stop my splashing. That twinge of uncertainty is back, hovering around my head, whispering: *be cautious, be safe.*

Kole reaches into a leather purse on the side of his belt. My muscles tense. Now he's closer, I can see his eyes. They flicker and I wonder whether he knows that I don't trust him. He holds out his hand, offering me a clutch of purple leaves.

"Crush them," he says. "Rub them into the wounds."

I thank him and take the leaves, but when his back is turned, I slip them into my pocket.

Returning to the fire, I strap my feet into the walking boots. Garrett joins me and nods approvingly at them.

"What happens now?" I ask him.

Garrett scratches his forehead and beckons for the others to join us. We gather in a semi-circle as Tsam kneels to spread out on the ground a detailed map of The Four Cities. I eat up every detail; it's mesmerising. There is Abilene, surrounded by trees with the lake at its centre, Esyllt, on the west coast, Tarynne, with its curved rocky structure that hugs the elephants' watering hole. And Nhatu. Square. Encased in flint.

"The Council destroyed any maps like this," I say. "The new ones just show Nhatu, surrounded by wasteland." I move a little closer to the map and my skin prickles. "I never realised how close we were to the Islands. The Council talks of them, but makes them seem so distant."

"This is us." Tsam jabs a finger to a spot somewhere in the southern region of the Alder Woods. "And we're heading this way... east."

I tilt my head to take in the details.

"We need to reach the edge of the woods, then we can fly."

"We can't fly from here?" I ask.

"The Sentries on the wall watch the woods day and night. They'd spot us straight away if we took off from here."

"Is that a bad thing? If they saw you, word would spread. People would realise the Council have been lying."

Tsam rubs his temples. "The Elders said we weren't to be seen. They didn't explain why but I'd guess it's something to do with the treaty—"

Alyssa cuts him off. "It's not our place to ask why. We're given orders. We stick to them."

In the woods, when she helped free me from the Red Quarter sash, Alyssa was kind, maybe even a little soft. But now she is back to being the girl on the wall. The girl who said my mother was dispensable.

I don't dare ask about the treaty so I scrape the ground with my index finger and ask, "How long? Until we're back in Abilene?"

"A day trekking through the woods, then one more once we're out in the open," says Tsam. "We've two horses waiting by the river. One for Kole and one for you. We'll fly and you two will ride."

A little too quickly I say, "I can't fly with you?"

Tsam studies my face. "Maybe—"

"No," Alyssa interrupts, "you can't. It's too difficult. The extra weight. It's not a problem over short distances but this is too far and we need our energy in case..."

"In case, what?" I ask.

"Just in case."

As our scrutiny of the map draws to a close, so does the day. The sun disappears behind the tree line on the opposite bank and the Watchers stoke up the fire. Kole takes the first lookout, positioning himself between the trees and the river, arms folded. Garrett and Tsam grin at one another and spread out on one side of the fire. Garrett takes a small pouch out of his pack and empties the contents onto the ground – a collection of pebbles, all different shapes and sizes with swirly symbols etched into their surfaces. He and Tsam take three each and set out the rest in the shape of a multi-pronged star. I can't interpret the rules of the game; it is too fast. They exchange pebbles, balance them on top of one another, swap, take, line up – it's dizzying. Beside me, Alyssa says, "They've been playing it since they were youngsters. I've tried, but I'm hopeless."

The game lasts no more than ten minutes. Garrett suddenly whoops and beats his fist on the ground, which I assume means he's won. His outburst causes Alyssa to shush him, though the corner of her mouth curls in a reluctant smile. Garrett rolls his eyes but stashes the pebbles back in their pouch. Then he lies on the ground, arms folded across his chest, and releases an exaggerated yawn. Tsam gives the fire one last prod then follows suit, by which time Alyssa too is closing her eyes and wrapping her wings around herself.

They are so comfortable, the three of them; at ease in their own skins. They know their history, their roles, where they're from, where they're going. But me? I am disjointed. I feel like they all expect me to be something I don't know how to be. I've become hyper-aware of my thoughts, my movements, my actions. Now, as I watch them all slide into slumber, I'm left with the thoughts in my head, looping back in time to examine my life from new angles.

I scroll through the memories faster and faster, searching for clues in the way my parents looked or spoke to me, scrambling to pin down feelings that might have told me who I really was. Did I ever feel as though part of me was missing? Did I feel different? Did I always know the sparks were inside me?

The answer to every question is 'no'. I always felt normal. My life was... normal.

I release a frustrated sigh and roll over to face the fire. The weight of the last few days is beginning to drag down on my eyelids and the effort to make sense of everything is giving me a vicious headache. I shift a little closer to the fire. The flames are flickering and cracking, dancing, glowing orange, and white... and...

I wake suddenly, panting. Adrenaline makes the blood pound in my ears, my heart judders violently against my chest. Despite myself, I must have fallen asleep. I look at the spot where Kole was sitting but he has been replaced by Tsam. He waves at me through the dark when he sees me sitting up and when I join him he drapes his left wing around my shoulders. His feathers are like silk.

"Bad dream?" he asks.

"Mmm," I reply. Then, because the night makes it easier to be honest, I say, "I think I see her sometimes. Ava..."

Tsam doesn't say anything, but he must have guessed because he saw my drawings.

"I never knew it was her. She was just there," I whisper.

"What does she do? In your dreams?"

"She stares at me. Sometimes she holds my hand, asks me to go with her. Sometimes it's like we're children, laughing, playing..."

"Tonight?"

I pull my jacket closer. "Tonight wasn't like the others. There were shapes that I couldn't see properly – shadows. I was running. She was there but I couldn't see her face. It was blurry, like a painting that was never finished." I shudder. "And we were scared."

Tsam's expression is unreadable; if he's unnerved, he's not showing it.

"Do you think it means something?" I ask him.

He turns and looks at me. "I think it means that you've been through a lot. Your mind is just trying to make sense of it all." His wing curls a little tighter around my shoulder. "Don't worry, Émi. We won't let anything happen to you." He reaches out and turns my face to him. "*I* won't let anything happen to you."

TEN

The group begins to stir long before the sun comes up. Garrett makes more soup but there is an air of urgency this morning. There is no sitting by the fire or bathing feet in the river. As soon as the soup is gone, Kole extinguishes the flames and sets about destroying all traces of our presence. He carries the biggest pack, swung onto his shoulders as though it's weightless. The Watchers and I carry smaller ones, across our chests instead of our backs, and Alyssa hands me a knife similar to hers to tuck into my belt. Tsam looks at her questioningly but Alyssa simply says, "It's foolish for her not to be armed."

And then we are back in the woods.

It doesn't take much walking for us to come across vines and branches that are much thicker and more entwined than yesterday. No longer able to part them, we are forced to climb over and under them, and make lengthy detours around them. Despite this, I feel more confident in my boots and my jacket. I rub at my arm – at the place where the deep pink groove left by three years with the red sash is beginning to fade – and think of Nor's last words to me before I left.

Find your sister, and when Mahg's dead in his grave... then you can come back for us.

I raise my hand to the necklace she gave me, brush my fingers across the delicate wings.

I will, I tell her, *I'll come back for you all.*

We've been walking for an hour or so when the ground begins to squelch under our feet and it's not long before we are submerged up to our knees in brown swamp water. The tips of the Watchers' wings trail on the surface, their pristine feathers turning the colour of dishwater, and I struggle to drag my already-tired legs through the sludge. Kole, however, strides ahead, parting the water with ease.

The trees begin to thin out but long whip-like vines hang from their branches. Garrett and Alyssa are behind me with Tsam and Kole leading the way. We wade through the swamp, pause to check the compass, wade some more, until, finally, solid ground appears up ahead. We have almost reached it when Alyssa shouts: "Garrett!"

I swivel around. Garrett is beating his wings like a swan in a trap and Alyssa is grappling to catch hold of his arms. Beneath the water, something is dragging him backwards. I slosh towards them.

"Something's round my ankle, Lyss!" Garrett cries, his eyes wide. "I can't get it off!"

Alyssa's face is so white it's almost see-through. "It's a choking vine. If we don't get him free it'll drown him! Use your knife, Émi!"

I reach for my belt, for the blade Alyssa gave me. Throwing myself to my knees, I plunge my hands beneath the surface of the water and fumble for Garrett's ankle. The choking vine is solid and scaly, and my knife is useless. As I hack at it, it squeezes tighter and pulls harder.

Garrett groans. "I think it's breaking my foot…"

Alyssa bellows at me to hurry up. Tsam and Kole are at my shoulders now.

"Let us try, Émi. Out of the way!"

I shrug them off.

I abandon the knife and use my fingers. If I can loosen the vine, just a little, Garrett might be able to pull his leg free. He is still flapping his wings and the dirty swamp water floods my mouth, eyes and ears. Suddenly, my hands start to tremble. My vision shifts and blurs. The sparks are back. But this time they bypass my stomach and surge straight into my fingers.

The water begins to bubble.

Alyssa stares at me. "What's happening? The water's hot! Émi, are you…?"

I don't answer her. I can't. As I raise my hands in front of my face, beams of light pour out into the air. I grasp the vine and squeeze as hard as I can. It releases an ear-splitting squeal. Then I tighten my grip and remember the way Falk's cheeks disintegrated beneath my touch. The vine squeals again, then finally unravels to release Garrett's foot.

The sparks are gone. I'm struggling to breathe. Tsam and Kole reach for my arms and help me onto dry land, where we collapse in a heap. Garrett is rubbing at his ankle; it is already turning a mottled shade of purple.

"Émi, thank you," he says.

Alyssa looks wildly from me to Tsam. "You didn't tell us she could… did you know she could do this? Is this why the Cadets were after you?"

Tsam nods, but doesn't speak.

"You said she was in trouble. You didn't say she—"

"I can't control it," I interrupt, trying to rescue Tsam. "I can't summon it, or make it happen. It just comes." I think of the wall, and Ma. Why now, for Garret, and not for her? "And then it goes."

Alyssa looks uneasy. She is staring at my hands as though she's worried they might combust at any moment. She's angry with me, and with Tsam.

Garrett says, "She saved my life, Lyss," and, eventually, her face softens – just a little.

We rest for a moment. Then, when everyone has recovered enough to stand, we move on. This time, Alyssa and Garrett walk in the middle of the line; he is hobbling and leaning on her shoulder. I'm at the front with Kole, and Tsam is at the back of the group keeping a close eye on his legs.

"How did you do that?" Kole asks. He doesn't look at me.

"The sparks?"

"Mm."

"Like I said, it just happens."

"I see," he says, and sinks back into silence.

Once we're through the swamp, walking side by side is easier and our progress quickens. Garrett is doing his best to keep up but, before long, he asks us to stop. "Sorry," he says, "I just need a minute."

"Let me see." Alyssa points to her brother's ankle.

Garrett shakes his head. "It's fine. A quick rest and I'll be ready to carry on."

Alyssa frowns at him, then turns to Kole. "Will you look?"

Kole swings his pack down from his shoulders and crouches down, ignoring Garrett's protestations. Gently, he lifts Garrett's damaged foot onto his knee. Garrett winces as Kole removes his boot; his ankle is horribly swollen. It's almost as deep a purple as Kole's birthmark but with nasty splashes of yellow and green around the edges. With nimble fingers, Kole assesses the damage. "It isn't broken, just badly bruised."

"Do you have any lilac weed?" Garrett asks.

"Lilac weed is only for open wounds," Kole replies, glancing towards my feet. I think of the purple leaves, the ones that are still in my pocket, and feel a twinge of guilt for not trusting them.

Kole releases Garrett's foot. "You need sol flowers. Here," he says, handing Garrett a bundle of yellow petals. "Grind them into a paste, then rub on the ankle. The swelling should fade within a few hours."

As Garrett mixes up his prescription, Kole tells Alyssa, "We should camp here. Your brother's foot needs time to heal."

Alyssa is clearly torn. She looks up at the sky, which is tinged with a rapidly encroaching sunset, then down at the rolled-up map that's wedged into her pocket. Then she sighs a reluctant but loving sigh at Garrett and says, "Alright."

As soon as it's decided we are staying put, Kole, Tsam and Alyssa work seamlessly to prepare our rest stop. I offer to help find some firewood but Tsam tells me to stay with Garrett and take the opportunity to rest. His dismissiveness irritates me and I think Garrett must sense it because he smiles and pats the ground next to him. I sit down and slide off my boots. The grazes on my feet are still angry and sore so I reach into my pouch for the purple leaves Kole gave me.

"Are these safe?" I ask.

Garrett frowns at me. "They're lilac weed leaves."

"Kole gave them to me yesterday but—"

"You nut." He laughs. "If you'd used them last night those scratches would be all cleared up by now."

"I forgot," I say, because I don't want to admit that I was

suspicious of them – of Kole. The others trust him, seem in awe of him almost, so why does my stomach still tighten whenever he looks at me?

With Garrett beside me, I squeeze the leaves until they turn to mulch, then smear them onto my wounds. When I'm finished, my feet look worse than before. The leaves have created a blotchy stain, but my skin already feels less tight.

Tsam and Alyssa return from the trees with arms full of kindling. They're followed by Kole, who promptly hands me half of the branches he's gathered and tells me to sort them by size into piles of logs and kindling. When Tsam notices, he whispers something in Kole's ear. Kole's forehead creases sharply.

"Émi?" he says to me. "Are you capable of lifting firewood?"

His question is so oddly direct that I laugh a little. "Yes, of course."

Kole turns back to Tsam. "She's capable. We are here to protect her, not serve her."

A flash of anger that I haven't seen before crosses Tsam's face as he squares up to Kole. "She's not like us, Kole. She's..."

I step between the two of them, branches still in my arms. "It's alright," I tell Tsam. "I want to help. I want to be useful." Tsam looks at me and his face softens. Kole walks away.

Later, when we've finished eating, Tsam apologises to me. "I'm sorry about before – with Kole. I know you can look after yourself but it's different now, Ém. You were safe in Nhatu. Out here, you have to be more careful."

Safe? In Nhatu? It's almost laughable. Since we left, Tsam has been treating me like I'm a baby bird with a broken wing, but I'm more resilient than he thinks. I'm about to tell him exactly the kind of danger I faced every day in the Red Quarter when Alyssa suddenly raises her hand in warning, telling us all to be quiet.

I hold my breath, my eyes scouring the darkness. I see nothing but shadows. Eventually, she shakes her head and we all relax.

The interruption has muted my annoyance so I tell Tsam I'm tired. He helps me unfurl a sleeping mat from my pack and, as I lie down, he crouches beside me.

"I'll be right by the fire if you need me," he whispers.

Only a few days ago, I'd have given anything to be out of Nhatu, by a campfire, with Tsam. I'm certain I dreamed of it, more than once, on those long torturous nights in Red. Now here he is, and here I am. But it's all wrong; he feels further away from me than ever.

"Sit for a moment?" I ask.

Tsam glances back at the others, then folds his legs and crosses his hands in his lap.

I lean up on my elbows. "What's going to happen when we reach Abilene?"

Tsam absorbs the question, blinking slowly, his feathers illuminated by the glow of the fire. "We'll meet with the Elders. They'll tell us what to do."

I feel myself frown. "You don't know what they're planning?"

Tsam rubs at his forehead. "I'm just a Fledgling, Ém. Until the Ceremony, I'm not a Watcher, not really." He glances at the others. "The Elders only allowed us to come and fetch you because my father and I persuaded them it would be better for you to learn the truth from someone you know. And because we agreed to bring Kole. But whatever intelligence they have about Mahg, his plans, Ava... They have to keep it closely guarded."

"Oh," I say.

"They have a team of Watchers tracking Mahg. But the details of their work remain secret. Out of everyone in The Four Cities, our group and the team tracking Mahg are the only ones who have been allowed to know that the last piece of the stone was made into human form. We're the only ones who know you and Ava exist."

"What about Mahg?" The question is out before I can stop it. "He knows. If Ava and I have been such a closely guarded secret, how did he find out about us?" I'm sitting up now. Tsam's silver-blue eyes darken but I push on. "Could there be spies in Abilene? The Council do that sometimes, send Cadets into the Red Quarter, dressed like us."

Tsam shakes his head. "For all our sakes, I hope not." He stands up and tells me to rest. The conversation is over.

I lie back down and close my eyes, folding my knees up into my chest. Back at the campfire, I can hear Tsam whispering with the others. The rustling of paper tells me they're plotting our course on the map. Behind me, the trees are silent. I open my eyes. I'm right. The four of them are hunched in a circle.

I climb off my sleeping mat and slip into the shadows of the forest. I step between trees. The deeper I go, the darker it becomes but – somehow – the blackness is comforting. No stars, no moonlight, just endless dark. It's as though I'm invisible. No one is watching me. Not the Council or the Cadets. Not my mother or Tsam.

It's just me.

Ahead, something flickers, disturbing the curtain of darkness. There it is again; the palest of shimmers. I squint and it brightens, like a shadow in reverse. I move closer. The trees in front of me are now illuminated from behind as though someone has lit the flame of a blue-green lantern.

By the time I am close enough to see what's producing the light, it's too late. A glowing woman stares back at me. Her eyes are sunken, her cheeks hollow. Her hair flows lank and loose. But most of all...

She's translucent.

She points at me. "What are you?" Her voice is thin and breathy. She begins to float towards me, the branches of the trees passing through her as if she is made of nothing but air.

I can't speak.

A chill rocks my body.

"What are you?" she asks again and again. "What are you?" She seems to be getting bigger, taller, filling the space between us. "Not human," she says. "Not real. Not here."

I try to run, but when I turn she is already in front of me. I trip and fall to the ground. She hovers over me, stretching her skeletal fingers towards my face...

Someone calls my name.

The ghostly woman snaps her head up and stares wildly into the trees.

I scramble backwards and then, suddenly, Kole steps in front of me.

"Spectre!" he bellows. "You do not belong here!"

The woman smiles. "What *is* it?" she asks him.

"You have no jurisdiction in these woods!" Kole replies.

The Spectre – that's what he called her – tilts her head to the side and stretches her mouth wide as though she's about to yawn. But she doesn't yawn. She screams.

And it's as if my ears are bleeding. My teeth vibrate in my skull and my skin feels as though it's being stripped from my bones.

Then, as quickly as she started, she stops.

She leans closer, until Kole's features quiver in her eerie glow. "What. Is. It?" she spits, looking at him but pointing at me.

Kole keeps his eyes fixed on hers, like an animal challenging its opponent to fight. "This orphan is in my charge. I must return her to the Islands."

The Spectre laughs. Her matted hair falls across her face. "There are no Taman on the Islands." She reaches out, pressing her index finger against his temple and stops laughing. "I can see inside your mind, Taman. I can see if you are lying."

Kole doesn't blink. "I am no Taman. My loyalty is to the Overseers. This girl is a fugitive." He grabs my arm, tight. "She must be returned." His face has contorted into something harder. Beneath his birthmark, his eyes are like steel. He is so convincing, I almost believe I am his prisoner.

The Spectre doesn't. "You want the prize, don't you? You filthy, lying Taman!"

"Prize?"

"The prize! The prize!" She is shouting now. "Freedom!"

Kole keeps his eyes fixed on her, still gripping my arm, saying nothing.

"Find the girls. Take them to him and in return he will set us free! You want it first. This is one. This is she. This is it!"

"He?" asks Kole. "You speak of Mahg?"

The Spectre nods. "Mahg the Dissenter, who forced us from our homes. He sent us to be his eyes. All of us – the Spectres, the Kelpies, the Ogres. Eyes and ears, eyes and ears..."

Kole laughs then, and plants his hands on his hips. "You expect me to believe Mahg sent you here? Even he could not wield such power over a Spectre..."

She lowers her gaze. Fear flashes across her face. "Dark magick," she says, shuddering. "Controls us, binds us. We are his. He is ours." She is silent for a moment, then her head snaps back up and her gaze fixes on me. "Oh," she breathes, as though suddenly understanding. "Could it be?"

Kole tries to push me back into the trees, and raises his arms up as if he might be able to fight her off. But she surges forwards, straight through his chest, and he falls to the ground, convulsing like he's been struck by lightning.

She strokes my hair, tweaks her finger under my chin. "Are

you the one he seeks?" The finger that was under my chin moves to my temple.

From the ground, Kole shouts, "No!" But it's too late. A brutal mind-numbing pain swallows me up. Waves of it ricochet through my body. I want to burn the Spectre like I burned Falk and the vine, but I can't catch hold of my sparks, I can't focus. The fire is there and my hands are fizzing but the pain tramples it back down.

The Spectre is on me now, surrounding me, mauling my skin. I feel as if I'm being sliced open. I try to hone in on the energy in my gut. I find the sparks and I latch on to them. I coax them up into my throat, into my chest, into my arms, and they bleed into the pain, eat it up, then churn it out. This time, the energy doesn't just flow from my fingertips, it seeps from every pore.

I stagger to my feet. The light is pouring from me now, battering the ground like a forcefield. A tree catches fire. The Spectre is forced backwards. She is clamouring to reach me. I open my palms at her and the sparks burst out like an explosion. I am blinded by their brightness. Everything is white.

And then it turns dark.

When I open my eyes again I am on the back of a horse, slumped over with my cheek pressed against its mane. An arm is around my waist. It is tanned and muscular – Kole's arm. A second horse is trotting beside us. I try to sit up and Kole whispers, "Easy."

My words are thin. The effort of speaking makes my head throb. "What happened?"

Kole waves a signal up at the sky. Then he tells the horse to stop, dismounts and lifts me to the ground. My knees wobble but he helps me to a nearby tree. I sit down and lean against the trunk; the pressure of the bark against my skin makes me wince. Every part of me throbs.

I look around. We are no longer in the Alder Woods; grassy tree-scattered landscape stretches as far as I can see, undulating in peaks and troughs beneath a cloudy blue sky. The Watchers glide down and land gracefully at my side. Tsam takes hold of my arm, gently, like I'm made of glass. "Émi," he breathes, brushing his fingers across my forehead.

Alyssa is standing in front of me, blocking the light. "Are you alright?" she asks sharply.

"I think so."

"Good. Then perhaps you can tell us what in The Four Cities you were thinking? Running off on your own like that?"

I try to remember. The camp fire, slipping out into the trees. It all comes rushing back.

"I'm sorry. I just needed some space – time alone."

Alyssa snorts. "You needed space?"

I try to stand up but I wobble and sit back down again. I hate how close I am to crying. "I didn't mean to..."

"Do you think this is a holiday? Whatever difficulties you faced in your walled city are nothing compared to what will happen if Mahg finds your sister before we do. Or captures you, or—"

"Lyss," whispers Garrett, "I think that's—"

"No! If I'm the only one willing to tell her the truth, that's fine." Alyssa crouches down so her face is close to mine. "If that Spectre saw inside your mind, she knows who you are. And she's working for Mahg. He could be following us right now. He could be attacking Abilene right now. This isn't just about you. It's about keeping everyone in The Four Cities safe. You stupid, naive—"

My eyes are swollen. Tears threaten, but I promised myself when we went over the wall that I'd be strong.

"That's enough," says Tsam softly.

"No. It's not enough. From now on, one of us is with her at all times. She's not to be trusted."

"Tsam's right," Kole interjects. "Enough now."

Garrett tries to take his sister's arm but she pulls away and looks at him as though she is deeply disappointed. Then she opens her wings and swoops back up into the air.

"Don't worry, Émi. No one's following us," Garrett says. "Alyssa's just..." He shrugs.

"I'm sorry," I whisper.

Tsam tuts at me. "You have nothing to be sorry for. I should have been more clear. It really is dangerous for you here, Ém."

"I know that now," I say. I overestimated myself, and I underestimated Mahg. I must not make that mistake again.

Tsam and Kole help me back into the saddle. Kole tells me that my horse is called Pascha and his is Orie. Pascha is grey with a white splash on his nose and four white socks, while Orie is black and altogether more stoic. They are different from the horses in Nhatu – their coats are smoother and glossier, their physique more toned. These are not horses used for dragging carts, or shifting the rubble of the fallen-down Red Quarter tenements. These horses are cared for.

With the three Watchers up in the sky, Kole and I are effectively alone but he doesn't look at me. His eyes stay fixed on the horizon, and when he does turn in my direction it's only to survey our surroundings.

After an hour or so, we reach a sharp incline that winds up through a copse of trees. Surely Pascha can't carry me up there? It's too steep. I tense, and Pascha slows down. I wonder whether

I should climb down and walk but, ahead, Kole has risen up into the stirrups so he's leaning into Orie's neck. He is gripping Orie's mane, pressing his weight in just the right place to propel them up the slope.

Pascha shakes his head as though he's waiting for me to take the same stance as Kole, so I take a deep breath and heave myself up. I grasp a chunk of Pascha's mane in my right hand and hold the front of the saddle with my left, then push myself into his strong muscular neck.

Pascha makes a *snuff* sound as he marches us up the hill but it takes only minutes to reach the top. When I sink back into the saddle, I'm exhausted and panting. Kole and Orie fall in line beside me.

"How's the pain?" he asks, finally acknowledging me.

"Not terrible."

"A Spectre's touch can be deadly," Kole replies.

"She passed straight through you..." I say.

Kole barely blinks. "I'm unharmed."

"What are they?" I ask. "The Spectres?"

Kole frowns. "You don't know?"

I feel my cheeks flush. "The Council rewrote our history books. We know nothing of anything."

Kole nods. "Spectres are malicious female spirits. Hundreds of years ago, after the Dark Quarrels, the Elders gave each dangerous Magickal race its own territory. The Spectres were sent to the Whispering Forest near Esyllt and they have remained there, peacefully, ever since."

"She said Mahg made them leave?"

Kole dips his head. "For some time now, there have been rumours that Mahg is recruiting the more unscrupulous Magicks to do his bidding. Now we know this is more than rumour."

We sink into silence but my mind is still churning with questions.

"Who are the Overseers?" I ask.

"They work for Mahg. They keep the inhabitants of the Islands in line. Especially the orphanage."

"Orphanage?"

Kole straightens his shoulders. "There are no families on the Islands. At birth, infants are sent away from their mothers. The weak are destroyed, or kept as slaves. The strong are trained to fight for Mahg." He pauses. "The Islands have always been different from The Four Cities but Mahg has harnessed their darkness and turned it into something bigger. If he succeeds in seizing the Fire Stone..."

An icy shudder ripples through my body. "Is Alyssa right? Do you think the Spectre saw inside my mind? What if she tells Mahg we're going to Abilene?"

Kole's jaw twitches. "I do not believe she saw inside your mind. You repelled her before she could connect with you. But your magick proved she was right... proved you're one of the girls Mahg's looking for."

"So I've put everyone in danger?" Prickles of dread are creeping under my skin.

Kole turns so he's facing me. "No. She knew I was hiding something, but she thought I simply wanted the glory of returning you to Mahg myself. She didn't see the Watchers, only me, so there's no reason for her to connect you with Abilene."

I don't know how to respond. Once again I feel like I'm going to cry. *Please, please let Kole be right.*

We keep going, even when the sun disappears and the sky is dotted with stars. We don't stop. Exposed, and without any trees to trap the day's residual warmth, the air turns bitterly cold. Kole is wearing only a vest and a waistcoat, his arms exposed, yet he seems not to feel the cold. I can't wrap my arms around myself because I need to hold Pascha's reins, and soon my teeth begin to chatter. Kole glances at me, then takes a blanket from one of Orie's saddle bags and passes it over.

Perhaps I was wrong not to trust him? I try to meet his eyes, but he stares straight ahead so all I can see is the way he looked when he told the Spectre he was working for Mahg, the metal in his voice, the way he gripped my arm. No, I must not drop my guard. I must remember this feeling.

For another hour, at least, we trek on. Then, suddenly, the horses stop, and I look up from my half slumber. We are at the edge of another forest. This one, however, is different; it isn't trees in front of us, but bamboo. Huge thick canes, silver in the moonlight, stretch up and sway in greeting. I stroke Pascha's neck, then climb down from his back. A warm breeze ripples through the air, dancing across my face. It weaves through the bamboo so that the canes chime softly against one another, sending out a hollow, whispered greeting. *Welcome, come inside.*

"This," says Kole, "is Abilene."

ELEVEN

The Watchers land in front of us. Garrett leans onto his knees and exhales deeply. Alyssa wipes her forehead, her wings sagging. Tsam, however, doesn't stop for breath.

He asks Kole to take the horses to the Academy and inform the Elders of our return. Then he tells Alyssa and Garrett that he's going to take me home with him to rest for a few hours – we will reconvene in the morning.

It is a short journey. We fly over the tops of the bamboo until it becomes trees and, within minutes, Garrett and Alyssa break away and dip down beneath the canopy. Seconds later, Tsam does the same.

We land on a suspended wooden walkway where flickering lanterns light the way to a house that is nestled between thick entwined branches. Its walls curve and twist, making it impossible to discern where dwelling ends and tree begins. It has glowing windows and a pointed chimney, which is puffing out light grey smoke.

Tsam releases his hold on me and I wobble after him, finding my legs again after the journey. When we reach the front door, he doesn't knock – just opens it, ushers me in beside him and says, "This is home." Inside, intricately carved pieces of furniture sit snug against the undulating walls. There is a kitchen area, a round table with chairs that have bright blue legs and a crackling fire.

I sit down next to Tsam, wondering whether he lives here alone but feeling too exhausted to ask. A glass teapot rests in the middle of the table, on top of a small copper frame with a candle in its centre. Inside the pot, heavily perfumed tea simmers patiently. I sit back in my chair. It is quiet here; Abilene doesn't chatter like the Alder Woods or hum like Nhatu. It is still, as though frozen in time, with Tsam and I the only creatures still moving.

Tsam pours us each a cup of tea, as if it is the most normal thing in the world to be sitting here together. The liquid is a deep ruby; sweet and hot. I wrap my fingers around the mug's warmth. As Tsam sips, his muscles visibly relax. He is different here; he fits.

"It's been a long couple of days," he says, lifting a foot to balance on the rim of his chair. "Tonight, we'll rest. Tomorrow, I'll take you to the Elders."

"And they'll help Ma? Get her out of Nhatu?"

Tsam picks at his thumbnail then looks up. "I'm sure of it."

"We can't see them tonight?" I ask. Every part of me vibrates with fatigue, but I can't help feeling we're wasting time.

Tsam looks at the window; its shutters are open, framing a square of heavy darkness. "There's nothing they can do tonight, Ém. They can't just charge over the wall and snatch Patti back."

I know he's right and, really, I wasn't expecting him to say yes. He is watching me as if he can hear my mind whirring. He motions to the tea. "Drink up. It will help you sleep. Stop your brain feeling fuzzy."

We drain our cups in silence then he guides me into a dimly lit corridor lined with doors. He points to one of the doors on the right. "That's the bathroom." Then, next to it, as if I was always destined to come here: "This is yours. Night, Ém."

I step into the room. When Tsam closes the door behind me, I take off my boots and fold myself into the softness of the bed. I can't remember the last time I slept in sheets this soft. Ma would like these sheets.

———

I wake to the smell of freshly brewed coffee. It reminds me of weekends in the Green Quarter, when my father was still with us. Every Saturday he would make a large pot of coffee and scramble some eggs, then the three of us would eat together while he read out articles from the newspaper. For one cloudy moment, I hear his voice calling, "Émi, breakfast!"

I shake off the memory and stretch my arms up above my head, feeling my shoulders click and groan. At the foot of the bed, Tsam has left me a towel and some fresh clothes, with a note: *Morning. Breakfast's ready when you are.*

I pad barefoot to the bathroom, and pause in the doorway. This isn't really a room; it's more like a balcony. Circular, like the living quarters we were in last night, but with a shoulder-height woven screen in place of a wall. There's no ceiling – just a patch of clear blue sky and a few sinewy branches where the roof should be. Strung from one of those branches is what looks like an upside down bucket with holes in it.

I lock the door and hang my clothes and towel over a branch that seems to have grown precisely for this purpose. Then I step under the bucket. I prod it, thinking that perhaps it will tip up and pour water over me, but it doesn't move. I tug at its handle, wondering if I'm supposed to lift it down and fill it from some-where, but it is fixed in place. And anyway, it couldn't possibly be filled with water because of all those holes.

Then I notice a small wooden lever protruding from the trunk of the tree. I pull it. I hear the sound of something sliding away and, instantly, blissfully warm water bathes my skin. Clouds of steam billow into the sky. I step closer and the contrast between the cool air and the warm water makes me sigh into myself.

My muscles relax. I close my eyes. And, for just a moment, I allow myself to forget why I'm here, what's to come and what has been. Too soon, a knock on the door drags me back into the present. Tsam's muffled voice asks, "Émi, you okay in there?" I shout that I'll be out in a moment, scrub the dirt from my skin and hair, then climb into a clean set of clothes. Damp from the steam, my curls will dry thick and wavy so I pin them up out of the way and steel myself to leave the solitude of the bathroom.

When I enter the round room, Tsam greets me with a broad grin and presses a mug into my hand.

"You look rested," he says, pleased.

"And a lot cleaner," I reply, presenting my hands for inspection. Tsam gives a soft laugh that reminds me of Amin and ushers me into a seat at the table.

While he opens the oven to check on a loaf of bread, I lean back in my chair and look out of one of the windows. In the morning light, I notice a flurry of greenery. Above our heads, a hatch in the ceiling welcomes in a column of sunshine. I'm desperate to poke my head out and see where we are but, at the same time, my body twitches with the need to get going. It's as if I have two separate Émis in my head – one who can't believe she is in Abilene and who's longing to explore, take it all in, marvel at it. And one who knows she is here for much more severe purposes – to rescue a sister and save a mother.

Tsam joins me at the table. He is relaxed, content, at home. I'm about to ask him what will happen today when the front door swings open. A middle-aged Watcher with silver-tipped wings and hair down to her waist enters, carrying a sack of groceries. When she spots Tsam, she abandons the sack on the counter and they press their palms together before embracing.

"They said you were back." She smiles, tousling his hair.

Tsam turns to me. "Émi, this is Rumah. My aunt."

"You're Amin's sister?" I ask, immediately seeing the resemblance to Tsam's father.

Rumah nods and her eyes twinkle as she hugs me. She smells of rosemary. "It's lovely to meet you, Émi. Tsam has told me so much."

I glance at Tsam and I'm sure I see him blushing. He turns quickly to the counter and starts unpacking the food.

"How is Amin?" Rumah asks, her expression creasing with concern.

I'm not sure what to say. I think he's alright, but so much could have happened.

Luckily, Tsam jumps in. "When we left, he was safe. But I'll dispatch a messenger to him this morning. Our departure wasn't quite as smooth as we'd hoped."

Rumah frowns and folds her arms so Tsam tells her about my sparks and Jennyfer's Punishment. When he reaches the part where we escape over the wall, leaving my mother in the hands of the Cadets, Rumah gasps and her feathers ripple.

"Don't worry, Émi, the Elders will know what to do," she says sincerely.

The breakfast Rumah brought home is a large green fish, which she fries and divides into three portions. While we eat, I make myself smile and chatter as if we have all the time in the world. But a voice in my head chants, *Hurry up, hurry up, hurry up!*

Eventually, Tsam asks if I'm ready and, although I'm not sure what I'm supposed to be ready for, I say yes. We leave Rumah at the house and step out onto the boardwalk. Now it's daylight I can see that the Watchers' round houses are scattered at varying heights throughout the trees, all connected by suspended wooden walkways. The trees themselves aren't like the ones in the Alder Woods. There are no creeping vines or twisted trunks; they stand tall and straight and proud, and their leaves shimmer in the sunlight.

We follow the boardwalk down to ground level. When we arrive at the forest floor, we are greeted by a host of bright purple flowers, spread out before us like a carpet. I'm afraid to step on them but Tsam doesn't hesitate; the flowers simply spring back up as soon as he lifts his foot. I wish I wasn't wearing boots so I could feel them between my toes.

"We're not flying?" I ask, hurrying to keep up.

Tsam laughs, flitting his wings outwards a little. "Not this morning. I need to keep my legs in shape somehow, Ém."

I glance at his legs and blush, looking away quickly before he notices. I forgot he could be like this. *Charming*, that's what Ma used to call him. "Tsam is so charming, Émi," she'd say. "He's going to be a real dish when you're older, you'll see. You really would make a delightful couple..."

As we walk, the trees are slowly replaced by bamboo. It creates a silvery fence around the Watchers' homes, towering up so the houses are obscured from view. I am walking backwards, staring up at the delicate bamboo leaves, when Tsam grabs my elbow and says, "Best watch where you're going..."

I turn around and my breath catches in my throat. We are standing on the edge of a cliff face that drops down so sharply it's as though we're looking at the end of the world. I want to tiptoe closer and peek over but Tsam motions for us to keep walking.

Moving away from the forest, the bamboo is on our right and the cliff on our left. After a few minutes, the ground begins to dip; it slopes down and down until finally, hundreds of metres below us, vast and glimmering and so blue it's as if someone painted it there, I see the lake. The one from the stories I wasn't supposed to know, from my father's drawings, and my own vivid dreams. I feel like I might cave inwards because I can't absorb enough of it.

I take a deep breath and let the cool air wash over me. Tsam points to the other end of the lake where a white stone building stands tall and proud.

"That's the Academy," he says. "It's where we train, and where the Elders meet." He steers my gaze to the rocks below the building where a waterfall spills out. On either side of it, Watchers stand in hollowed-out enclaves guarding the water – guarding the Fire Stone. At the thought of the stone, I look down at my hands. Do they feel different? Or is it my imagination? I haven't felt my sparks since the encounter with the Spectre. They've become a fizzing memory that I can't quite conjure. But now, looking down at the lake, my pulse quickens and something stirs in my belly. Does the Fire Stone know I'm here?

From our vantage point I can see that the Academy stretches back in a U-shape, with two large turrets at either end. We continue down the sloping cliff path until we reach the eastern side of the U, where an archway opens onto a large square courtyard. It is empty except for a tree in its centre, a circular wooden bench built around the trunk.

We cross the courtyard, then climb some steps that have been carved into the side of the Academy building itself. They lead to a small stone landing with a big wooden door. Tsam pushes it open and we enter a high-ceilinged room with rows of small windows. Above us, hundreds of birds, all of different colours and sizes, flit back and forth between criss-crossed beams.

Tsam looks up and whistles an intricate, high-pitched melody. A bird with bright red feathers and black circles around its eyes flies down to him. It lands on the crest of Tsam's wing and chirps something into his ear. Tsam takes a piece of paper from his pocket. It is curled into a tiny scroll and tied with a piece of twine. Gently, Tsam parts the ruffled feathers below the bird's neck to reveal a tiny tube-shaped pendant. He unscrews the lid of the pendant and slips the scroll inside. Then the bird shimmies and its feathers fall back into place, obscuring the message that's now strung around its throat. Tsam says, "Thank you, Fin. It's for my father." Fin blinks, chirps and leaves us.

"This is how you've kept in touch with Amin, since you left Nhatu?" I ask.

Tsam nods and points up at the birds. "See how they're all different colours? No two look the same, so they're not easily distinguishable as messengers."

I'm about to ask if we could send a message directly to Ma, or Nor, when Garrett's booming voice drifts in from the steps. "Tsam-uel! You in there?"

When Garrett enters, Tsam scowls and says, "You know I hate that."

Garrett winks at me and, out of the corner of his mouth, he whispers, "Well, it wouldn't be any fun if he liked it!" Then he wraps his arm around Tsam's shoulder and ruffles his hair.

"Oh come on, then," Tsam mutters, struggling to hide a smile.

Garrett is wearing the same dark blue outfit as Tsam and, when we reach the bottom of the steps, Alyssa and Kole are waiting for us. Alyssa is dressed similarly to her brother – the only difference being that she is in leggings and has a belt strung around the waist of her tunic. Kole, however, is in the same clothing as yesterday, standing with his feet apart and his arms behind his back. He greets me with a nod but Alyssa doesn't acknowledge me.

"Are you ready?" She speaks directly to Tsam, her voice high and quick as she hurries us towards the Academy's entrance.

Garrett puts a hand on his sister's arm and slows her down. "Lyss, stop worrying. We did our job. We got Émi back safely."

Alyssa ignores him. "Tsam, do you know what you're going to tell them?"

Softly, Tsam echoes Garrett. "Alyssa, it'll be fine. Things didn't go to plan, but we dealt with it."

"Tsam, you have to explain why you left Nhatu so suddenly." As Alyssa speaks, she angles herself away from me and shields Tsam from my view. "You have to tell them about Émi's powers."

"I'll handle it, Alyssa," Tsam says. "Just leave it to me."

She shakes her head. "Why am I the only one taking this seriously?"

Inside, the Academy is cool and grey. But it isn't the oppressive grey of our flat in Nhatu – it's a shiny, bright type of stone and when you look closely you can see veins of silver and white trickling delicately through it.

Our footsteps echo as we cross the entrance hall. Older Watchers nod hello as we pass through, then do a double take when they notice that I don't have wings. Kole walks at the back of the group and he too stands out amongst the others. He is taller than the Watchers, broader, and his hair is pure ebony. I try to hold myself the way he does – straight and unashamed.

The Elders' chambers are high up in the western turret of the Academy, behind a pair of huge double doors that reach all the way to the ceiling. The doors are wooden but painted in a coppery varnish and decorated with intricate carvings in the shape of feathers. We pause in front of them. Alyssa brushes down her tunic and picks a stray hair from Garrett's shoulder. Tsam inhales deeply and steps forward but, before his hand can come to rest on the door handle, Kole clears his throat.

"The Elders informed me that they wish to see Émi alone," he tells us.

Alyssa whirls around. "Alone? Why?"

"I didn't ask why."

Alyssa looks at me, then Tsam. "But..."

"They'll see us when they've spoken to Émi," Kole replies, unblinking.

"Come on, Lyss," says Garrett, swiping a hand through his messy hair. "You can use the time to quiz me, ready for tomorrow. You like quizzes." He winks at her, but Alyssa scowls.

A coldness sits inside my belly. Tsam takes hold of my forearm and dips to meet my eyes. "Émi, you'll be fine. They just want to meet you. Get to know you."

"Should I tell them about..." I lower my voice, "... the sparks? The Spectre?"

Tsam opens his mouth to answer me but stops because the huge double doors are creaking inwards.

A voice calls. "Émi, please enter."

Without a backwards glance, I step inside.

The doors close behind me and it takes a moment for my eyes to adjust. The chambers are round, like the treehouses, with windows that frame snippets of the lake, the sky, the cliffs. Sunlight streams in, bouncing off the walls.

In front of me, four Watchers are seated in large stone chairs – two women and two men, each with silver-tipped feathers, like Rumah's. The woman on the left stands.

"Welcome," she says, waving a hand to take in her companions. "We are very glad to meet you, Émi."

I don't know what to say so I dip my head. She smiles at me. Her skin is smooth and dark, her eyes fiercely blue. Her hair is the same ashen shade I've noticed on almost every Watcher I've seen, twisted at the nape of her neck in a series of elaborate braids.

"I'm Hitra," she says, a melodic lilt in her voice. Then, looking at the Watchers either side of her, she continues, "We are the Elders of Abilene."

I can't bow again so, this time, I press my hands together the way I've seen the others do it.

Hitra smiles and returns the gesture. "Please, come closer."

I step forwards. I was expecting the Elders to be... old. But they all have the same flawless glow.

"Émi," says Hitra, "you must have had an exhausting journey?"

"Yes." I shuffle my feet. I feel awkward, on display. Which, of course, I am.

The Elders appraise me with solemn eyes. I wonder how they see me? A girl? Or a thing? To be feared? Or revered?

As if reading my mind, Hitra says, "The four of us have waited a long time to meet you, Émi. But I'm sure what you've learned about your past has been difficult to absorb?"

I almost laugh. I know I should be editing my speech but I've done that for too long now and, despite the sensation of unbridled awe that is clenching my stomach, I intend to be myself here. I pull some air past my teeth and down into my lungs, then look at each of the Elders in turn.

"You created me," I say. A statement, not a question. "And then you sealed me up in Nhatu. Behind the wall. You left me in a city where using magick is a crime. Where Watchers and sorcerers were fairy tales we weren't allowed to repeat.

"My whole life, I thought Mahg had destroyed The Four Cities, that Nhatu was the only thing left, that their wall was protecting us!"

Hitra blinks at me, opening her mouth as if she's going to interrupt, but I rush on.

"My father was tortured because he was certain this story was a lie. Everyone thought he was mad. My mother and I have been humiliated, starved... And, all that time, you knew. You knew who I was and where I was and you left me there." I feel my cheeks flush and my speech get faster. "How could you let the Council do that? How could you leave us there? All of us? Why haven't you helped us?"

Hitra's eyes narrow.

My limbs are flooded with heat. It pulses through my veins, threatening to ignite the sparks that simmer beneath my skin.

The Elders are still. I can't read their expressions.

Smoothly, Hitra starts to talk. "We are truly sorry for your troubles, Émi. We believed we had chosen parents who would protect you until you needed to know the truth. What happened with your father was unforeseeable."

The man sitting to Hitra's right clears his throat. "In times like these, difficult decisions have to be made. The situation with the Council of Nhatu is far from ideal. We're aware their methods have become extreme. But behind their wall, you were protected from Mahg."

I breathe out quickly, almost snorting my reply. "So if it wasn't for me you'd have stepped in? Prevented them from outlawing magick?"

The man makes a ticking sound with his tongue. "My dear, it's not quite that simple..."

Hitra waves her hand, stopping him mid-sentence. "What Brock is trying to say, Émi, is that if we could have intervened, we would have. Believe me. But it just wasn't possible."

She wants to move on, start discussing the real reason I'm here. Perhaps I should remain quiet. Perhaps it's not the right time, but I've been ignoring the ache in my chest ever since we left Nhatu and I can't hold it back any longer. "Now that I'm out," I say, "you can, though? You can intervene?"

Hitra tilts her head at me. "It's certainly something we can discuss, but it's not the most pressing—"

"It is. It is pressing," I say, my hands starting to tremble. "They have my mother and my friends." A spark leaps out of my palm and dissolves in the air.

Hitra doesn't flinch. In fact, she almost looks pleased. "I think it's time for the Fledglings to join us. Don't you?"

When Tsam and the others enter, I grip my hands together in front of my body and try to stay calm. They file in. Tsam, Alyssa and Garrett on one side of me, Kole on the other.

"Welcome, Fledglings, Taman. Thank you for bringing Émi back to us safely. We owe you a great debt."

Alyssa's cheeks turn pink with pride. Garrett gives a dimpled smile and exchanges a look with Tsam that says, *We did good.* Kole stands with his hands behind his back and nods.

"Tsam," Hitra says, "Émi tells me her mother is in danger. Does this relate to your unexpectedly quick departure?" Her voice is sing-song, but I can see Tsam swallowing hard as he prepares his response. I want to tell him that I haven't explained about the Punishment, or the sparks. I meet his eyes but I can't impart what I want to say in just a glance.

Tsam straightens. "Yes, Ma'am. Events took place that altered our planned course of action considerably."

Hitra smiles with the corner of her mouth. "A succinct answer, Fledgling, but not very detailed. Could you explain?"

Tsam takes a deep breath and launches into a speech that is so smooth, he must have rehearsed it. "Ma'am, Émi's magick began to show itself about the same time I arrived in Nhatu. She seems to have the ability to conjure sparks – tiny balls of light.

They appeared for the first time when she witnessed an unjust arrest outside her home. The Cadets saw the sparks and became suspicious.

"The day after I arrived, the woman they arrested was due to be punished in the Red Quarter. Émi stopped it – she used her powers to free the woman from the stocks. But this put her in great danger. The whole of the Red Quarter, and at least twenty Cadets, saw what she did. We had to escape, quickly. We couldn't wait for my father so I revealed my wings and told Émi the truth about Mahg and the Fire Stone. Then we fled over the wall.

"We were helped by a Scrappie and his wife from the Red Quarter. We believe the Scrappie was arrested when we were scaling the wall, although we're unsure about his wife." Tsam pauses. I know what he's about to say and I brace myself for it. "The Cadets also arrested Émi's mother. They pursued us and tried to force Émi to hand herself in but she, bravely, refused."

I can't stay quiet any longer. "Tsam said if I came here you would help get my mother back."

The way Hitra looks at Tsam tells me she wishes he had not made this promise.

"We understand," she says, after a pause. "Of course you want to help them. But a long time ago, to ensure peace between Nhatu and the other three cities, we promised the Council we would not interfere. We promised that no Watcher, or Taman, or sorcerer would set foot inside the city wall."

"That's why they couldn't know Tsam was there," I breathe, almost to myself.

Hitra dips her head solemnly. "If we break the treaty, the Council will take action against us."

I look around the room, exasperated. "But what could they possibly do to you? You're Watchers."

Brock looks like he wants to rise out of his chair and shake his fist at me. "You have told us yourself how ruthless the Cadets are. We do not want a war."

Hitra nods in agreement. "And, Émi, Nhatu has its own piece of the Fire Stone. If the Council was to join forces with Mahg, we would lose any advantage we currently have."

My bottom lip is beginning to tremble. Tsam reaches for my hand but I snatch it away. I close my eyes and try to focus on breathing. All four Elders are speaking at once, over and under and through one another. Alyssa and Garrett are bickering. I can hear Garrett saying that surely there must be a way, and Alyssa telling him not to get involved. Tsam tries to quiet them, with little success.

Only Kole is silent, his energy smooth and unmoving. I latch on to it and calm my thoughts to a reasonable pace. Then I open my eyes and step into the middle of the room. No one notices me. Without thinking, I clap my hands together. On releasing them, a flurry of sparks shoot into the air, slicing through the disarray. Now they are all looking at me.

I turn to the Elders. "I understand your position. I don't want to make you enemies of the Council, and I don't want Nhatu to fight for Mahg."

Brock inclines his chin and Hitra smiles gently.

"But I do need to help my mother." I know what I'm about to say and I'm certain it's a bad idea but I can't help myself. "And if you won't rescue her, I'll return to Nhatu and fetch her myself. I'm sorry. You'll have to find Ava without me."

When I finish, I take a few steps towards the double doors, as if I'm going to leave. Alyssa's mouth has fallen so far open I can almost see her tonsils. Tsam takes hold of my elbow. "Émi, you can't—"

Hitra allows me to reach the door before she says, "How will you find your way back to Nhatu?"

I freeze to the spot, my cheeks starting to flush. I try to

sound confident as I turn back around. "I'm quite skilled at navigation," I say quietly.

Hitra has pressed the tips of her long slender fingers together. "And after your long, treacherous walk, you will climb back over the wall? Defeat the Cadets? And rescue your mother? You'll do all this alone?"

I lower my eyes to the ground. I have been outplayed.

Hitra's voice is like poisoned honey as she continues to speak. "I don't blame you for trying, Émi. Your passion is admirable. But you don't need to leave. Of course we will help your mother."

I look up sharply. Brock and the other two Elders are wrinkling their foreheads as if to say, *We will?*

"*After* you bring Ava back to us," Hitra finishes.

She has me trapped. There is no way I can help Ma, Nor and Hedge on my own. And it's not just them I want to free. I want everyone in the Red Quarter to know the Watchers still exist. I want to give them hope, bring magick back. Perhaps if I have Ava on my side, if there are two of us, and the Watchers too... "I have your word that as soon as we return with Ava you will help free my family? Despite the deal you made with the Council?"

Hitra nods. The others follow suit.

I take a deep breath. "Alright. Then what do we do now?"

TWELVE

After my failed attempt at bargaining, the meeting gathers pace. Alyssa starts to tell the Elders about the Spectre, but it seems Kole has already informed them because Hitra smiles and says, "Thank you for your concern, Alyssa. But we have the situation under control. We have doubled the number of Watchers on duty in Abilene, although I have to say I agree with Kole – the encounter could work to our advantage if Mahg is now scouring the Islands looking for a pair of orphan girls with powers, rather than watching Abilene."

Alyssa clears her throat. "Of course, Ma'am. And, what about us? Where do we go now? When do we leave?"

This time, Hitra's smile doesn't reach her eyes. Looking at Tsam, Alyssa and Garrett in turn, she says, "Thank you, Fledglings, for your bravery and service. But you will not be accompanying Émi any further on her journey."

Alyssa doesn't move. "Then who...?"

Hitra looks at the two Elders who have not yet spoken, "Sayah and Roan will be joining Kole and Émi."

Unexpectedly, Garrett interrupts. "I'm sorry Ma'am, but we thought... Have we not proved ourselves?"

The female, who must be Sayah, answers him. "Of course you have, Garrett. But we can't send three Fledglings on a quest of such magnitude. Roan and I have fought in more battles than you have seen full moons. And Kole is the most experienced Taman in Tarynne. We are best placed to protect Émi."

Tsam looks deflated. Alyssa is biting her lip, and Garrett's complexion has turned sallow. I can't let this happen.

"I need them with me," I say, as forcefully as I can manage.

Hitra shakes her head at me. For the first time, her feathers visibly prickle. "I know you think you're helping your friends, Émi. But you're not. Encouraging them to go on this journey with you will only put them in harm's way."

"You don't understand. I can't do this without them." My stomach is whirling. "Everything inside me is saying that *they* are the ones who are supposed to help me."

I'm telling the truth. When I think of doing this without Tsam – or even without Garrett and Alyssa – a cloud of darkness presses down on my shoulders.

Sayah whispers something in Hitra's ear. Hitra blinks slowly. Then turns to me. "Why are you certain the Fledglings must go with you?"

I consider her question. "It's like the feeling I get when I know a storm's coming. Something under the surface of myself, warning me. When I think of being without them, I feel as if something terrible will happen."

Sayah rises from her chair and walks over to the window overlooking the lake. "Hitra, you know I would give my life to protect our people, to protect the Fire Stone..." She turns back. "But we cannot forget that Émi was created from the stone – the very thing that keeps The Four Cities alive. I believe we should listen to her intuition."

Hitra turns to the only Watcher still seated. "Roan?"

Roan speaks without hesitation. "I agree with Sayah."

"Kole?" Hitra asks.

Kole doesn't speak, simply dips his head in agreement.

Hitra breathes in through her nostrils. I open my mouth to speak but she raises her hand. "We will consider this, Émi. But we will not be rushed. You'll hear our decision tomorrow, after the Fledgling Ceremony." Then she turns away and the three of them gather to talk in hushed, urgent tones. It is time for us to leave.

No one says a word until we are outside, sitting under the tree in the courtyard.

"You didn't have to do that," Alyssa whispers, which I think is her way of saying thank you.

"Yes, I did," I reply, pleased that her anger towards me has softened.

Tsam sighs and shrugs his wings. "I don't know. Maybe they're right. Maybe we're not ready for this?"

Alyssa throws her hands up in the air. "How can you say that? We've trained for this. We know what we're doing."

Garrett puts his arm around his sister and squeezes her. "Lyss, it's not an insult. Tsam's right. We don't know what we're up against. Mahg's army is growing and, even if that Spectre has diverted him, it's still not going to be easy."

Alyssa wriggles out of Garrett's hug and scowls at him. "I know that. But I think we can handle it."

"So do I," I say. "I can't explain it. I just know you have to come with me."

"What do we do now?" Garrett asks, drumming his fingers on his thighs. "Just sit and wait for them to make their decision?"

Alyssa stands and rests her hands firmly on her hips. "Well, I don't know about you two but I'm going to practise for tomorrow. If we want them to believe we can do this, we have to put on a good show."

Garrett stands too. "Not a bad idea. Tsam?"

Tsam looks at me, unsure whether to stay or go, but Kole interjects. "I have to take Émi with me for a few hours. You should go and practise. We will find you later."

Tsam rests a hand on my shoulder. "You'll be okay?"

I glance at Kole, then back at Tsam. "Of course," I say, although I'm not sure I mean it.

When the others have taken flight, I ask Kole where we're going. "To prepare you for the journey," he says, leading me to the back of the courtyard and through an archway that opens onto an expanse of meadow. It should remind me of the field behind The Emerald, but it doesn't. The grass is taller and greener, and it's speckled with yellow flowers. It reaches all the way up to my forehead, so I have to concentrate on Kole's back to avoid being swallowed up by it as we make our way across. I let the fronds run through my fingers, tickling my skin.

The long grass stops about three metres away from the trunk of an oak tree, and so do we. Kole looks up, searching for something. He moves slowly around the trunk, stepping over its protruding roots, then bends down. One root in particular sticks out further than the others. Kole tugs it and my eyes widen as a square of earth folds inwards like a trapdoor. He steps down into the opening and motions for me to follow him. When the trapdoor closes, we are encased in a thick, earthy darkness that makes my heart beat faster and my breath catch in my chest. Kole draws a match from his pocket and strikes it against his belt, chasing away the closeness.

We are inside a tunnel that winds down through the soil. Kole has to lean sideways so that his head doesn't bash the ceiling. We walk, one behind the other, for what feels like an eternity. Then, a pinprick of light appears in the distance. As we draw nearer, I can see that it is a torch, fixed in the centre of a large wooden door. Kole taps the door four times. The tap tries to echo but it's contained by the tightness of the tunnel. Claustrophobia scratches at my skin. My heart jumps and the torch flickers from the draught as the door opens.

We are greeted by a tall, lithe Watcher whose wings are puffed out to the sides. She flicks her feathers in greeting and lowers her head at us. Kole presses his hands together and says something I don't understand. She ushers us inside. The room we step into is cavernously tall and illuminated with hundreds more torches.

The Watcher flashes her teeth at Kole. "It's lovely to see you again, Taman. Is this…?" She trails off and looks at me with her diamond-grey eyes.

Kole nods. "This is Émi." Although he speaks quietly, at the sound of my name the others in the room look over.

"Émi, it's an honour. I'm Rhea."

I smile, allowing Rhea to take my hand and press her lips on top of it. When she releases me, she says, "Only a few of us know about this place, and about you."

In the centre of the room, there is a large table strewn with small wooden structures – miniature mountains, trees and people. Rhea notices me staring.

"It's a replica of The Four Cities," she explains. "We use it to track Mahg's movements, his army…"

I walk over to it and brush my fingers over the little wooden elephants beside Tarynne's lake. I try not to look at Nhatu, which is depicted as merely an empty square box. No Quarters, no camps. But I can't help it. Ma is there. So far away…

Perhaps misinterpreting my gaze, Rhea points to the cluster of islands beside Nhatu. "We believe Mahg is still on the Island of Bones. We have scouts keeping watch throughout the Cities, but so does he."

She catches me nodding. "Kole informed us of your encounter with the Spectre. It was unfortunate, but at least we have proof that Mahg is employing creatures like her to do his bidding." She turns to Kole. "You say he promised them freedom?"

"It seems he is using dark magick to control them. He has told them that if they bring him the girls, he will set them free."

Rhea strokes her chin. After a moment, she says, "We need to find out which other creatures are working for him."

"She mentioned Kelpies and Ogres," I say, remembering my father's, almost comical, drawings of the Ogres near Esyllt.

"That's a start," says Rhea. "Thank you, Émi."

Kole nods, almost impatiently, then changes the subject. "Rhea, I believe you're to inform us of our plan for departure?"

Rhea blinks at him, then taps the wide open space on the table that indicates the desert between Abilene and Tarynne. Speaking more to me than Kole she says, "We need you to travel to Tarynne. It's a short journey, only a day's walk. We suggest you go by foot. It takes a lot of energy for Watchers to carry passengers, especially in the heat, so it's best preserved for when it's most needed."

"Why Tarynne?" I ask. "You think Ava is there?"

"No, not Ava. But someone who can help you find her. A woman called Silvana." She pauses. "Mahg's mother."

I frown. The words don't make sense. "He has a mother?"

Rhea laughs. "Well, yes. Everyone has a mother, Émi." Then, immediately, she flushes. "Oh I'm sorry. I know you don't... that was thoughtless of me."

At first I don't understand why she's embarrassed. Then the realisation hits me. I have no mother. I wasn't born. I was conjured.

Rhea clears her throat. "Silvana abhors her son's actions. She is a kind and gentle woman. We trust her."

Kole *mm*'s in agreement.

"She was very close to the sorcerer who created you. His name is Søyen. He entrusted her with a message that will tell you where to find Ava."

"Mahg's mother knows where Ava is?" I ask, wondering whether they can hear how that sounds.

"Not exactly – Søyen's message can only be opened by you, Émi. That's why we need you. Silvana is simply guarding it."

"But surely Mahg could—"

"He could try," says Rhea, "but think about it – who's the one person, in all The Four Cities, Mahg wouldn't be willing to kill?"

"Oh." I see now.

"Even Mahg wouldn't kill his own mother," she says, although I'm not sure she believes it.

"What about Søyen?" asks Kole. "When we locate him and Ava, are we to bring him back to Abilene also?"

Rhea hums and strokes her fingers across the little wooden hills that represent Esyllt – the Third City – the true home of magick. "Esyllt are our friends, but they prefer to remain distanced. Søyen is different. We hope he will return with you. He would be a great asset in our fight."

Kole nods slowly, then says, "Émi is still learning to control her powers. They are unpredictable. Can you provide her with a weapon?"

Rhea smiles. "Certainly. Émi, follow me."

We leave Kole studying the map and walk towards a door that looks identical to the one we arrived through. Just above the handle, there is a dial which Rhea turns until it makes a *clunk* sound. She pushes the door open and allows me to enter first. The room is full, from floor to ceiling, with weapons: crossbows, swords, arrows and daggers. They all glint wickedly in the half-light.

Rhea assesses me. "I see you already have a blade," she says, motioning to the one Alyssa gave me. "So..." She walks about halfway down the wall on our right until she arrives at an empty shelf. She presses the wall behind the shelf and a drawer slides out. From it, Rhea takes a glass vial that reminds me of the one Tsam used to bring his wings back. Except this one is full of dark green liquid.

Rhea hands it to me. I hold it up towards the torchlight and notice there are tiny gold specks floating inside. "When Kole said a weapon, I thought he meant a sword or something?"

Rhea flicks her hair and chuckles. It's the same sound Amin's coffee pots make when they're warming up in the mornings. "Émi, you'll be leaving Abilene straight after the Fledgling Ceremony tomorrow. I don't have time to teach you to sword fight."

My cheeks redden.

"This is a very powerful potion," she continues. "Use it only in an emergency. One drop of this will dissolve whatever it comes into contact with. It acts like acid, but twice as fast."

I think of Falk's face. Melted. The way I dragged the keys from his belt. If all they're going to give me is a dagger and a potion, I need to learn to control my powers.

When we return to the three-dimensional map, Kole is talking to a Watcher with cropped hair and chunky features. They are clearly disagreeing about something.

"It is not appropriate," Kole says. "Not now."

"I'm sorry. Hitra insists..."

When they see me, they immediately stop talking.

"Gentlemen," says Rhea, raising an eyebrow, "is everything alright?"

Kole says nothing, just makes a tutting sound and walks away, shaking his head.

"Émi," says the Watcher with short hair, "I'm Cai. Hitra asked me to come and meet you." He pauses and glances at Kole, who is standing by the entrance with a stony expression on his face. "She thinks it's important for you to understand a little of where you came from."

"Alright," I say tentatively.

"If you'd come with me?"

I look back at Kole. He doesn't move. Doesn't smile or say, "Go ahead..." Just stares straight ahead.

Cai rests his hand on my elbow and guides me forward. "It won't take long," he says, crossing to the far side of the room and opening another identical-looking door. "Just through here..."

The space behind the door is empty, other than one solitary torch on the back wall. Cai tells me to stand in the centre of the room.

"That's perfect," he says. "Now, what you're about to experience will feel very real, Émi, but it's not. It's a projection of what has been, not what is. Do you understand?"

I don't.

"It will begin when I close the door."

"What wi—"

He is gone.

The torch flickers, then dies.

The room is black.

The floor beneath my feet quivers and the sensation makes me want to hold on to something but there is nothing there. The blackness vibrates. I feel like I'm spinning, the room disintegrating. Nausea springs into my throat and I close my eyes. Then, it stops.

I open my eyes.

I am by the shore of the sparkling lake. There are pebbles

beneath my feet. The sun is slipping lazily beneath the horizon, giving way to twilight, and the cliff where Tsam and I stood earlier looms up behind me. To my right, the Academy glistens. To my left, a bridge arcs from one side of the lake to the other. The underneath of the bridge is in shadow, but someone is there. I move closer. The someone doesn't look up. It's a boy – perhaps sixteen or seventeen – scrawny and pale. He can't be a Fledgling because he has no wings. He is hunched over a large tattered manuscript, muttering strings of words I don't understand, running his fingers over the lines of the page.

A sharp gust of wind whips across the lake. The boy's mutterings grow louder. He looks out across the water, holding his palms out and staring up at the sky. Time accelerates. The sun is gone but there is no moon. I want to leave – find my way back to the torchlight and the warmth but I can't move. The surface of the lake is becoming unsettled, as though a storm is on its way.

A dark mist seeps in from the water's edge. The boy's breath puffs in icy clouds as I feel the temperature drop. He begins to shiver and I notice that I am too. The mist clings to his feet. He looks down and his eyes widen as it coils itself around his legs, up towards his waist, over his chest and around his arms. When it reaches his throat, he begins to panic. Like an animal caught in a trap, he tries to break free. But it's too late. It smothers him, whole. He cries out and I try to run to him, to help him, but I can't.

"Someone help!" I shout, searching for the Watchers, or for Kole. "Help him!" I am shaking uncontrollably. When I look back, the mist is retreating and the boy is lying unconscious on the pebbles.

The scene before me starts to bleed into itself, like one of my posters, drowned in a rainstorm. I turn around and I'm no longer on the beach – I'm on the bridge. It is heaving with people: men, women and children, all with majestic white wings folded neatly against their backs, smiling and patting each other's shoulders and pressing their palms together in greeting. Flickering lanterns adorn the edges of the lake below us and, on the shore near the bottom of the cliffs, a towering bonfire blows blue-grey smoke into the air. Somewhere, music is playing.

Behind me, a voice shouts, "Inta!"

It's the boy from under the bridge. He breaks through the crowd, scanning faces, searching for someone.

"Inta!" he calls, looking straight at me. Except he's not looking at me; he's looking *through* me. I turn to see a girl, about my age, with elfin ears and long wavy hair. The feathers on her wings rustle as she sweeps past me to embrace the boy.

"I was looking for you," he says. "You'll never believe what's happened!"

"What is it?" the girl asks.

"It's incredible!" he replies. "I knew it would work, I just knew it!"

"What, Mahg? Tell me!" Inta replies, grinning.

Mahg. The young boy I'm watching is the one who wants to destroy me. The thought tears through my bones. The Council told us he was born with black wings. But this boy has none.

Suddenly, I know what is going to happen next.

Inta is still smiling when Mahg's face contorts and he falls to his knees. The shirt on his back splits open. He reaches around, desperately trying to understand what is happening. I have seen this before. When Tsam drank his potion – but it wasn't like this.

"What have you done?" shouts Inta. "Mahg, what have you done?"

The boy starts to scream. Mothers grab their children and husbands shield their wives. The girl called Inta is trying her best to calm Mahg down, but it's no use. And then, Amin – or a young version of Amin – is there too.

"Did you know he was going to do this, Inta?" he asks. "Did you?"

"No, Amin, I swear," she gasps. "I had no idea..."

Between them, they struggle to restrain a petrified Mahg as he thrashes and shouts. But his wings don't stop growing; they get larger and larger, and they're different to any others I've seen. His feathers are jagged, sharp, solid – like jet-black scales bursting from his skin. They grow and grow until they are all I can see.

Then I run.

I run from them as fast as I can. I push through the crowds and don't stop running until I reach the top of the cliffs. When I finally look back, the scenery shifts and the bridge is calm again. The light is different. Mahg is gone. The Watchers on the bridge gaze quietly across the lake. This is a different night. A different Ceremony.

From the Academy, a voice booms. "Welcome, all of Abilene! Tonight, another class of Fledglings will become Watchers of the Fire Stone. Tonight, we celebrate!"

Cheers and whoops ripple through the air.

"Let the festivities commence!" cries the voice.

The hammering in my chest should be slowing but it's not. Something is wrong. Something is going to—

Before the thought even has time to form, the ground shifts. A deep rumbling thunderclap rips through the air. Except it's not thunder; it's an explosion.

I fall to my knees. The bridge has collapsed. Huge chunks of it splinter into the lake below. A handful of Watchers manage to fly, but the rest are taken by surprise and they plunge towards the water before they have time to spread their wings.

After the combustion, there is silence. And then there is

screaming. So much screaming. And more thunder. The Academy is on fire.

I don't want to see it, I don't want to see any of it. I close my eyes but when I open them I'm on the beach again and there are bodies all around me. I see my posters, the ones with the blood and the dead, and their messages: *What Mahg's evil magick did to The Four Cities*. Then I see Amin, older than before but not as old as he is now. He's running towards me, shouting, "Tsam! Inta!"

From the commotion beneath the rubble of the collapsed bridge, Rumah appears. She is holding her arm and her wings are bent at a sickening angle.

"I can't find them, Amin," she sobs, her cheeks grey from the smoke. "I can't find them." Blood trickles down her face. "They were here, and now I can't find them…"

Her voice fades and so does the landscape. I shove my hands over my eyes and hear myself whispering, "Please, make it stop. Make it stop."

I am still hunched in a ball, shaking, when Cai returns for me. He doesn't say much, just helps me to my feet and takes me back to Kole and Rhea. Rhea offers me a flask of water but my hands are too unsteady to hold on to it, so she apologises and opens the door for us to leave.

Back in the open, Kole tells me to sit down. I fold myself into a nook beneath the oak tree and take some deep breaths. He sits beside me. "I didn't know they were going to do that," he says.

"I can't stop seeing it. It was…"

Kole nods, solemnly. "I imagine so."

"The Council told us he was born that way. Mahg – his wings."

"I see."

"He was just a boy."

"A boy who turned to darkness because he wanted to be like his peers," replies Kole.

"But how did he go from that, to—"

Kole rises up and helps me to my feet. He starts walking back towards the Academy. "After the spell, he fled to the Islands. He stayed there for seventeen years, building an army. Then returned to capture the stone."

I am still shaky, struggling to keep up as Kole strides back through the long grass. "When he blew up the bridge?"

"Indeed."

We break free of the grass and I step in line. I take hold of Kole's arm and he stops. "I saw Tsam's father and – I think it was his mother?"

Kole's forehead wrinkles. "You should talk to Tsam. I'll take you to him now."

THIRTEEN

We walk back along the cliff edge. As we draw closer, I find myself taking long, deep breaths and trying very hard to see what's there now instead of the terror they showed me in that room. Just before we reach the bridge, Kole stops and turns to me.

"The Elders wanted you to understand what Mahg is capable of. Do you see now?" His dark eyes search my face.

"Yes. I see." And I really do.

In the sky above the lake, Tsam, Alyssa and Garrett are performing dips and whirls in the air. When Tsam spots me, he waves and the three of them glide gracefully down beside us. Before I even have time to speak, Tsam can see from my face that something has happened.

"Émi? Are you alright?" He looks at Kole, then back at me. "Where have you been?"

I shake my head. My curls have untucked themselves and are frizzing around my face. "I'll tell you later."

I know Tsam wants to push for an answer, but he doesn't, just narrows his eyes at Kole. After a long pause, he tells me that Rumah wants to see us all for dinner. Kole turns back towards the Academy, but Tsam adds, "All of us, Kole. You're invited, too."

Kole hesitates, then replies. "Thank you."

Rumah is delighted that Tsam has brought us home. She hugs Alyssa and tells her she's looking tired and mustn't forget to eat, even if she is sick with nerves about the Ceremony. Garrett receives a hug too, and he blushes when Rumah tousles his hair. Kole, however, stands stiffly by the door, until Rumah notices his awkwardness and beckons him inside. "You must be Kole," she says, pressing her hands together and bowing. "You're famous, I believe."

I watch all of this from the doorway, trying to erase the image of Rumah with a broken arm and two broken wings, screaming for Tsam. The chaos, the dying. The calamity in my brain causes my knees to give way and I have to steady myself against the door frame. Kole moves to help me but, in a flash, Tsam is there and he's lowering me into a chair.

Rumah fetches some water and bobs down in front of me. "Émi?"

I don't know what to tell her.

Tsam glares at Kole. "What happened back there? What did you do to her?"

Everyone is staring at Kole now, waiting for an explanation. He tells them about Cai, and the room. And Tsam explodes. His face turns puce and he bangs his fist on the table so hard it causes my water to jump out of its glass.

"They did what? You let them—"

Kole allows him to shout, while Rumah strokes my arm and Alyssa and Garrett huddle together, clearly wondering whether they should leave. Finally, when Tsam is calm enough to sit down beside me, Kole starts to explain.

"I had no choice."

Rumah hangs her head. "Tsam, I don't agree with it either, but the Elders clearly felt Émi needed to know..." Her voice fades into a whisper. "What he did to us. What he could do again."

No longer trembling, I reach for Tsam's hand. "It was awful," I say, close to tears, "but I needed to see it." I look around at the others. "I didn't understand before. Not really. I thought I did. But being there, in the heart of it... I get it now." Something deep in the basement of my stomach sets into a steely determination. "We have to find Ava. We have to stop Mahg." I turn back to Tsam. "When I came with you, all I was thinking about was saving my friends, breaking down the wall and setting them free. But Nor was right, this is so much bigger. *I'm* so much bigger."

Alyssa is nodding. Garrett looks down at his feet. Kole unfolds his arms and tucks his hands behind his back. I think I see him blink at me, but I'm not sure. Rumah nods and thumps the table, but merrily, not the way Tsam did.

"Right," she declares. "If you're going into battle, you need to eat!"

The room softens. Garrett offers to help prepare the food, and Alyssa sets about lighting the fire while Rumah instructs Kole to open the roof. When he pulls on a lever by the fireplace, the chimney drops down and the ceiling splits open, revealing a blue-pink evening sky, peppered with leaves and branches.

Rumah sings to herself, the way Amin does, as she busies around the kitchen. But Tsam doesn't move from my side. Soon, though, with food in front of us, everyone relaxes – even Tsam, who rocks with laughter as Garrett acts out exaggerated impersonations of their professors at the Academy.

We have almost finished eating and are beginning to sag backwards into our chairs with full stomachs and heavy eyelids, when Alyssa asks me about Nhatu. They have heard stories, she says, but no one except Tsam has ventured beyond the wall since it went up.

I fold my arms across my chest. "Earlier," I say, "after I saw Mahg's attack on the bridge, I thought that perhaps the Council weren't so bad after all. Maybe they were right that we were safer behind the walls. But then I remembered the endless Punishments, and the labour camps and the inspection. And it's not safer. Not even a little bit. The danger is real. It's just less violent, less explosive than Mahg's. It's slow, pervasive. It drips into every corner of the City and poisons it from the inside out."

The others are all staring at me, listening, so I explain about the Quarter system, how we are required to carry permits everywhere we go, the coloured sashes that tell everyone who you are and where you're from. I tell them about the Cadets ripping through our houses, destroying our possessions, and the Punishments where young girls are forced to throw excrement at vulnerable women.

When I finish speaking, the room is sombre and quiet, and I feel sorry for dragging the atmosphere back down. "I know Mahg's threat is more immediate," I say, "but I still intend to rescue my mother and my friends. After this is over, I will get them out of there."

No one speaks. Garrett and Alyssa rise from the table and say that they had better be getting home. Kole offers to walk with them and, almost instantly, it becomes just Tsam, Rumah and I.

Rumah closes up the roof. "I'm going to bed. You two stay up as long as you like, but remember you have a big day tomorrow, Tsam." She squeezes his arm as she speaks.

Tsam nods. "We won't be long."

And then it is just the two of us.

We haven't been significantly alone since the ferry ride to

the Red Quarter three nights ago and I find myself unsure what to say. Luckily, Tsam starts.

"Are you sure you're alright, Ém?"

I nod and pick at a splinter that has loosened itself from the smooth wood of the tabletop. There are a million questions I could ask, but I don't think it's the right time to mention Inta, the woman I'm certain was Tsam's mother. Instead, I settle on the most immediate question.

"What do you think the Elders will decide?"

Tsam breathes out a long sigh and folds his wings inwards so they're hugging his arms. "I hope they will let us go with you. I can't imagine staying behind and just letting you leave." His voice is melancholy and I can't decide whether it's because he would be sad to miss the adventure or me.

"I meant what I said, Tsam. I won't go without you."

Tsam's mouth crinkles into a smile but he doesn't say anything. He glances up at the clock. It's late and if we don't go to bed now there's a danger we'll end up talking all night, so we extinguish the fire and head to our separate rooms. When we pause in the hallway, opposite my bedroom door, I think he's going to hug me but, instead, he waves and mumbles an awkward, "Night, then," and shuts himself away.

With my bedroom door closed, I am cocooned in the silence of the treehouse. I strain my ears but all I can hear is the rustle of the leaves next to my window. Last night, I was so exhausted that, despite everything, I slept without any trouble. Tonight, the thunderous quiet allows thought after thought to flash across my mind and I can't shake them loose.

I see my mother in the Council's putrid jail, petrified and alone. I used to wonder whether she had ever been strong, whether it was losing my father that broke her. But I think she has always been this way. He was her strength. He was her sun, her moon, her reason for breathing. When she lost him, she lost herself too.

My treacherous mind tortures me, on and on. Swerving between my mother and Mahg, Nhatu and the bridge, the arrest and the explosion, until, eventually, when it feels like I have been lying here for an eternity, I decide to get up.

In Nhatu, I could wander around in the middle of the night and still find my skin stinging with sweat. But, here in Abilene, a sultry coolness drifts in as soon as the sun goes down. I shrug my jacket on top of the nightdress that Rumah has lent me. Then I tiptoe out onto the boardwalk. Most of the treehouses are in darkness but small orange lanterns illuminate the walkway so I can follow it down to the ground. When I reach the purple flowers, the lanterns disappear. I'm not sure how I will find my way to the edge of the forest but I take off my boots, leave them where the carpet of flowers begins, and step forward, wiggling my bare toes into the silky petals. As I lift my foot, a host of fireflies wisps upwards, bobbing between the branches of the trees above. I follow their glow, and the distant chime of the bamboo at the forest's edge, until I break out onto the cliff top.

I walk to the edge, closer than Tsam would allow, and stretch out my arms. It is hard to imagine that something so terrible happened here. All around me, blinking constellations of stars decorate the night sky. I imagine I am flying again – for pleasure this time, not because I am fleeing or escaping. I move my arms up and down, beating them softly, letting the air cushion them. In the distance, the Academy glows white in the moonlight. Its reflection on the water is still as glass. But, in the center of the lake, something is glowing, like flames beneath the water. As I stare, my skin prickles.

What is that?

I lower my arms and climb down the steps to the beach

where Mahg cast his spell. At the water's edge, a breeze that wasn't there before whispers. *Émi... Émi.*

I know I shouldn't go in. I know it will be cold and that I'll ruin Rumah's nightdress but I can't stop. I shrug off my jacket and dip in my toes, paddling at first. Then I wade towards the glow. When the water is far enough past my ankles that it meets my pale legs, it begins to shimmer. Despite its icy temperature, my skin is alive with heat.

I keep walking. The water is up to my knees now and the hem of my nightdress floats on the surface. When the water reaches my thighs, I stop. I lower my hands until my palms meet the ripples and, instantly, the glow becomes brighter – so bright that the cliffs around me are drenched in a blinding light.

Clouds of smoke – no, not smoke – steam start to rise from the surface. My fingers are fizzing. I look down. Sparks are shooting like lightning rods from my fingertips, through the water, towards the centre of the lake. My vision begins to blur and I shake my head to clear it. Pushing through the clouds of steam, a figure appears. It's the girl from my dreams, Ava. She is standing on the surface of the water. A black scarf is wound tightly around her face and neck and all I can see are her eyes, wild and pleading. The steam swirls up around her. It's black now, like the mist that swallowed Mahg, like her scarf, wrapping itself tighter, squeezing the breath from her belly. She reaches out to me and I reach for her but the second my hands break contact with the water everything plunges into darkness. I whirl around, searching for her. I call her name, "Ava?" and the sound of my voice bounces off the cliffs. I begin to swim, out to where the water was glowing. But the glow is gone, Ava is gone.

Something grips my elbow. I thrash out. It's a person, pulling me towards them. They're saying my name, holding my arms. "Émi, you're alright."

I look up, panting, struggling to tread water.

"Kole?"

He holds on to me until I am calm enough to swim. He doesn't offer to carry me, just waits until I am strong enough to carry myself, then leads the way back to the beach.

At the shore, three angry-looking Watchers are waiting for us. One of them barks, "Kole, what happened here?"

"My apologies. Émi is a visitor, she wasn't aware of the rules."

"Swimming is only permitted on the night of the Ceremony."

Kole dips his head, "I should have informed her."

The Watchers observe me for a moment, then swoop silently into the sky and leave us.

I am shivering and my teeth chatter. Kole retrieves my jacket and wraps it around my shoulders.

"That's it?" I ask.

Kole frowns at me.

"They didn't ask about the light..." I stop speaking because I can tell he has no idea what I'm referring to. I cross my arms over my body, aware that I'm soaked to the skin and desperate to warm up. "What did you see?" I ask.

"I saw you in trouble."

"That's all?"

Kole nods.

I want to tell him. I want someone to know what happened. What I saw. But the way he is looking at me tells me it can't be him.

Kole walks with me all the way to the purple flowers and waits until I've stepped onto the boardwalk before turning back to the Academy. He doesn't say that we'll talk about it tomorrow, or tell me why he was there too, wandering around in the middle or the night. Just blinks his deep cavernous eyes at me and walks away.

I'm aware that I'm paddling a trail of water behind me as I tiptoe back to my room. But I don't have the energy to mop it up. I hang my nightdress on a branch outside my window, hoping it will dry a little by morning, and pull on my vest and jodhpurs.

Back between the sheets, fingers of ice itch through my bones. Have I caught a chill? Or is it the memory of Ava, throttled by poisonous steam, that freezes my core?

I still don't sleep.

I turn over and over. I pace up and down. I rub at the pimples on my arms. I shove my feet into three pairs of socks. I close the window. I open it again. Eventually, the leaves beyond the window begin to brighten. With the sun taking over from the moon, I gather my things.

In the bathroom, I stand under the water, watching my skin blemish beneath its heat and, when I emerge, I am no longer chilled. Daylight is softening the memory of last night. The idea I might have dreamed it all comforts me, until I find Rumah scrubbing the kitchen floor.

She looks up when she hears me and smiles. Sitting back on her heels, she gestures to her hard work. "Tsam says he knows nothing about it, but I'll bet you all the fish in Abilene that he and Garrett were off making mischief last night." She doesn't sound angry, more amused, but I think of the damp nightdress that's now hidden under my bed and a pang of guilt makes my cheeks flush.

"Pfft, don't mind me," Rumah tuts, springing up and deftly setting a pot of water to boil. "Coffee?"

I nod and take a seat at the table.

"You look tired. Couldn't you sleep?"

I watch her, trying to figure out if she suspects it was me who left the wet footprints in her kitchen. But she is open and genuine. "Just restless," I reply.

Rumah hands me a mug. The coffee is just like Amin's. I wonder whether he's readying the cafe for the morning rush, or if it is closed and shuttered up. Deserted. Abandoned.

"It must be difficult," Rumah says, leaning her wings against the kitchen counter, "not knowing what happens next, worrying for your mother and your friends."

I consider telling her about last night. The way I told Amin about my sparks. But I can't.

"The Elders will make the right decision today. You must trust them, Émi. They know what's best."

I feel like asking, "Best for who?" But I don't.

It's not long before Tsam joins us. His hair is damp. He nudges me and says good morning as if we've been waking up in the same house for as long as there have been mornings to wake up to. He's smiling, but his face sharpens when he notices me yawning.

"You didn't sleep?"

I look at Rumah and she replies for me. "Émi's just worrying, that's all. About what the Elders will decide. I told her it will be fine."

Tsam rests his coffee on the worktop and takes hold of my elbows. He's taller than me, by at least a foot. His feathers puff as he speaks. "Ém, stop fretting. There's no way they'll make us stay. Not after what you told them. If you say we have to go with you, then we have to. They know that." Tsam turns to his aunt. "I don't suppose... Have you heard anything?"

Rumah gives him a withering smile. "You know I can't tell you, even if I have."

"Sorry, it was unfair of me to ask."

"You never need to apologise to me. But promise me something, Tsam?"

"Of course."

"Today is the day you graduate from being a Fledgling, to

154

being a Watcher. It's the most important day of your life. So promise me you'll enjoy it? Forget all of this, forget why Émi's here. Just enjoy the fact that she *is* here. Worry about the rest tomorrow."

Tsam nods then bites his lip. "What about Mahg?"

Rumah's eyes soften. I shuffle my feet. I feel like I'm intruding on a private moment, something that should be just between the two of them, but Rumah slips one arm around me and one around Tsam, tucking us into the curve of her wings. "Mahg would be a fool to attack us today," she says. "We'd be expecting him and that's not what he wants. So you two just go out for a few hours. Explore." She turns to Tsam. "Introduce Émi to her home."

Hearing Rumah call Abilene my 'home' feels strange. I don't live here. Though I suppose, now, I don't really live anywhere. Unless I'm turned back into a piece of rock. Then I might live at the bottom of the lake.

We leave Rumah stringing a garland of small white flowers above the door in preparation for tonight, and make our way down to the ground. At the purple flowers, instead of heading to the Academy, we veer east, away from the lake and the bridge.

The trees around us are buzzing with activity. Above, walkways and front doors are being adorned with lanterns, flags and flowers. Watchers call good morning to one another, saying *see you later* and *we wouldn't miss it*. Friends and neighbours wave down at Tsam, then look a little closer when they see my flame-red hair and my lack of feathers. Tsam notices me fidgeting.

"They'll think you're a visitor from Esyllt," he reassures me. "Don't worry."

It occurs to me then that I have always looked different

from everyone else. Growing up, I was the only person I knew with red hair, freckles and papery skin. So different from my parents that, once again, I can't believe I never realised they weren't mine. And, if I look like I come from Esyllt – the City of Sorcerers – is it any wonder the Cadets were suspicious of me?

"Where are we going?" I ask Tsam, pulling back from my remembering.

"You'll see when we get there." He winks. Charming.

We've been walking for a little over two hours when we leave the treehouses behind and the forest envelops us in a cocoon of peacefulness. It is quieter here, but not dark and clammy like the Alder Woods. There is room to move freely between the trees, with dappled sunlight and luscious leafy shrubs.

Eventually, we stop in front of a tree that is almost double the size of the others. Its bark is closer in colour to the silvery sheen of the bamboo at the forest's edges. "This is my favourite spot," says Tsam, standing behind me and wrapping his arms around my waist. "Ready?"

"Yes," I reply, letting myself lean back against his chest as he beats his wings and propels us up into the air.

Tsam weaves us through the tree's thick upper branches. Up and up, until we emerge above the canopy. We land on a branch that is large enough and flat enough to hold us. Then we sit, side by side. Before us, the First City, Abilene, which for so long I believed was gone, stretches as far as I can see. Behind, mere whispers in the distance, the Tsamur Mountains quiver in the sun.

For a while, neither of us speaks. Then Tsam points north, towards Nhatu. "When I first came back – when you thought I was in the Gold Quarter – I used to come up here all the time and wonder what you were doing, how you were." He looks at me, then back into the distance. "I'm sorry I wasn't there for you when your father was sent away."

"You couldn't have done anything even if you were."

"I should have written. Especially when—"

I shake my head. "You know, they never told us what happened to him. They just sent a letter. Three lines: *To whom it may concern. Theiss Fae: deceased. Cause of death: unknown.*"

"That was all?"

"That was all."

"Do you know what they did with his body?"

I shudder, and swallow hard. "People who die in the labour camps are flushed away," I say. "Under the wall, out into the ocean."

Tsam's wings droop. He rakes his fingers through his hair. "I'm sorry, Ém. At least with my mother, we were able to say goodbye."

His mother. I brace myself to ask. "Tsam, your mother. She died in the attack on the bridge?"

Tsam nods, solemnly. "She was badly injured, and died a few days later."

"What was her name?"

Tsam frowns a little, then he smiles. "Inta, she was called Inta."

I don't know how to say what I need to say.

"What is it?" Tsam asks. "What's wrong?"

"I think I saw her. In the vision they showed me."

Tsam shimmies around so he's facing me. "How?"

"She was on the bridge when Mahg's wings started to grow." I hesitate, then push on. "I think she was his friend."

Tsam shakes his head, gazing out over the lake. Finally, he looks back at me. "Are you sure?"

I nod.

"And did you see her when the explosion happened?"

"No," I assure him. I did not see that.

Tsam exhales deeply, then forces a smile. "Who'd have thought it, hey? When we were playing make-believe behind the cafe. Climbing trees in the field. That this is where we'd end up."

I shift a little closer to him. Tsam moves his wing so it is almost touching my shoulder. I look up at him. "Did you always know who you were? Who I was?"

I think he's going to look away, but he doesn't. His eyes continue to meet mine, pure and blue and silver. "Yes."

"Always?"

He nods. He's closer now. Or, at least, he feels closer. His feathers flutter in the breeze. He tucks a stray curl behind my ear and his hand lingers by my cheek.

Then something that sounds like a foghorn blasts through the forest. It trumpets a brief, jolting melody and Tsam quickly looks up at the sky. "We should go. The Fledgling Ceremony begins at sunset."

I want to tell him to wait, make him slow down, but he has hold of me and we're in the air before I know it. The moment is gone.

FOURTEEN

Tsam offers to fly me back, but I tell him to conserve his energy for the Ceremony, so when we return we are very close to being late. I expect Rumah to be pacing back and forth, wringing her hands the way my mother might have, but she greets us with a smile full of warmth and places her hands on my cheeks.

"There you are," she says, giving me a peck on the forehead. "Tsam, go and change. Émi, I've left a tunic on your bed for you."

I go to my room, and struggle with the tunic for at least ten minutes before Rumah comes to help me. It is shaped like a normal piece of clothing all the way up to my waist, but then it becomes nothing but two wide strips of fabric. I assume I'm supposed to wind them around myself. But I have no idea how. Rumah laughs gently at the confusion on my face and shows me how to wrap them – around my abdomen, criss-crossed over my chest, small gap at the shoulder, then down and around my arms. When she has finished, she says, "There..." and stands aside so I can see myself.

I don't look like me. My skin has lost its sickly grey pallor and the freckles on the bridge of my nose seem more prominent than before. The dark blue of the tunic makes my hair seem redder, too. Hair which is still piled in a nest-like tangle at the back of my neck.

When Rumah leaves to finish getting ready, I reach back and pull the pins loose, allowing the curls to tumble down over my shoulders. I give them a little shake and they settle into place. The necklace Nor gave me sits around my neck, the charm resting against my collarbone. I touch the wings, and the stone in between, and whisper, "I haven't forgotten." Then, I inhale deeply and give my shoulders a wiggle to release the tension. I'm ready. Even though I don't quite know what I'm ready for.

Tsam and Rumah are waiting for me on the boardwalk, just outside the front door. They turn when they hear me walking towards them. Tsam smiles, steps forwards and knocks his head on one of the lanterns Rumah has strung above the door. His ears redden first, and then his cheeks. "You look..." He pauses and loses his chance to finish because Rumah interrupts.

"You look beautiful, Émi."

I tuck a lock of hair behind my ear. "Thank you."

The three of us head to the edge of the forest, where Garrett is waiting for us. "Tsam!" he calls. "Ready?"

Tsam tells me he'll see me later, then jumps into the air, spreads his wings and swoops out of sight.

When Rumah and I exit the trees, my breath catches in my chest and my feet take a few seconds to catch up with the rest of my body. As far as I can see, swathes of Watchers are making their way towards the bridge. The Academy is resplendent in the glow of the fading sun and a rhythmic drumming drifts up from somewhere near the lake.

On the bridge, with our bodies crammed together, the drumming and the memory of Mahg's attack makes my heart jitter uneasily in my ribcage. Rumah and I take a spot near the steps that lead down to the beach. Below, the bonfire I saw in my vision is being lit. Rumah points in the direction of the Academy. "When the sun reaches the spot just above the western tower, the Ceremony will start. All the Fledglings have to perform. It's a group display but they're judged individually too."

"Like in an exam?" I ask.

Rumah hums. "In a way. Their rankings are unlikely to change at this stage, but it's possible. If they really impress the Elders, they can move up. Or, if they make a horrible mistake they might find they graduate lower in the class than expected. But Tsam will be just fine." Rumah smiles, proudly. "That boy hasn't made a mistake since the second he first took to the skies." Then, the smile dips a little and she adds, "I only wish his parents were here to see it."

When the drumming stops, everyone becomes still. Even the trees seem to be waiting. The sun is almost in line with the western tower. Rumah points at the cliffs on the opposite side of the lake, where the Elders of Abilene stand in flowing white robes, with Hitra at their centre. Hitra waves towards the bridge. In one seamless motion, every single Watcher lowers their gaze to the ground. I hastily follow suit, out of sync and hoping no one notices. When I look back up, the sun is in position. Rumah reaches for my hand and squeezes, her eyes darting backwards and forwards.

"There, look..." she whispers.

Winged figures have appeared at each of the windows on the Academy's top floor. Then there are more, on the roof and on the rounded spires of the two sparkling towers. They are utterly motionless, their wings stretched out, their feathers glistening brilliant and white against the pink sunset. The drummer restarts his drumming. The sound is low and rumbling, barely audible but enough to make my skin vibrate.

Suddenly, the Fledgling on top of the eastern tower falls, toppling like a domino over the edge, straight as a board, plummeting parallel with the waterfall. The figure falls faster and faster and the people on the bridge gasp. Then another Fledgling tips over and begins to fall, and soon they are all falling. Straight down, as if they are made of stone.

The audience holds its breath but when it looks as though the first Fledgling is about to plunge into the water, he suddenly rights himself, just a hand's breadth above its surface, wings beating as he flies straight towards us. Then I realise. That first Fledgling? It's Tsam. He is flying the same way he did when we jumped over the wall. Rumah knows it too and she stands beside me, fizzing with pride.

Tsam keeps flying towards us, so close to the surface of the lake that the power of his wings causes the water to spray out. As each Fledgling reaches the bottom of the waterfall, they turn and fly in the same direction. Some are closer to the water than others, some faster, some slower. Alyssa, who left her perch after Tsam, has managed to level herself with him and Garrett isn't far behind them.

The crowd turns, expecting the frontrunners to emerge the other side of the bridge.

But they don't.

A few moments pass and then, as the last Fledgling flies beneath us, the entire group bursts out, as one, and sweeps upwards in an arc that bends over the bridge and up into the sky. Above our heads, they gather and position themselves into the formation of a giant bird.

The crowd on the bridge gasps and some of the younger ones give jubilant cries. Somehow, the Fledglings coordinate their bird to flap its wings and open its beak. The drummer is keeping time with their movements, quickening and slowing his pace.

Alyssa is the first to break away from the group. When she does, the others move to fill her spot and quicken, as though they are chasing her. They climb up and up into the pink, cloudless sky. Alyssa and the giant bird begin a delicate dance in which she somersaults, weaves and dips as it pursues her. Seamlessly, she swaps places with Tsam and he performs his own version of the flying dance. Then, the Fledglings become two birds instead of one, and Garrett takes his turn.

Two birds become three, then one again, and then they are a tree, swaying in the wind while a Fledgling with long white hair flies as though she is a child swinging from its branches. And all the time, the drum beats on.

When each Fledgling has had their turn, the sun is a mere whisper and the sky has darkened. The girl with the long white hair breaks away from the group and swoops along the edge of the lake. As she does, multi-coloured lanterns spring into life. She rejoins the others, who are hovering in a line. They beat their wings slowly and delicately as though they are treading water. When the line is complete, they bow. The crowd on the bridge erupts into the loudest cheers I have ever heard.

Rumah is clapping, bouncing up and down and calling Tsam's name. Beside us, a man wipes a tear from his cheek. From their vantage point on top of the cliffs, the Elders are applauding too. Then, Sayah steps forwards and flies down to hover in front of the line of Fledglings.

"I'm going to call you each by name," she sings out, "with the highest ranking students first. Before I do, I will say that you are an outstanding bunch of students and it has been my pleasure to see you grow and to announce that today – you become Watchers of the Fire Stone!"

The crowd cheers and the drummer plays a drum roll.

"The first name I am calling is... Tsam Djaran!"

Tsam moves forward, bows and then flies down to the beach where he stands with his hands behind his back, clearly struggling not smile or to jig up and down. Rumah looks like she's going to jump out of her own skin, or perhaps hurtle over the bridge so that she can smother her nephew with kisses.

Alyssa takes second place, then Garrett and then the girl with white hair. I can't see Tsam's face properly, he's too far away, but I know he is happy. I can feel it. And I am too. When the last name is called, the applause slows, and everyone looks back towards the cliffs. Sayah rejoins the Elders and Hitra moves to the front of the group.

"Thank you," she says, "for, I think you'll all agree, one of the most creative and adventurous displays we have seen at a Fledgling Ceremony!"

Everyone cheers.

Hitra waits for us to quiet before she continues. "Tonight is a night for laughter and celebration, a night for family and friends. A truly wonderful night. But it has not always been so." Her tone becomes more solemn. Rumah sighs. The man who wiped away the tear stands straighter and his feathers twitch.

"I shan't remind you of the detail of that Ceremony, nearly seventeen years ago. I know it is etched in your minds, as it is in mine."

Rumah squeezes my hand.

"But I do have to remind you that, while we celebrate, Mahg's evil forces are getting stronger." Hitra's voice grows louder. "Mahg is still determined to take control of the Fire Stone. More now than ever before. And he will do anything to have it all in his possession. But," her voice lifts, "do not fear! There are plans in motion to protect you all and to save The Four Cities from his wicked ways."

Hitra is staring at me. I can feel it. I shuffle sideways, so that I'm hidden behind Rumah. "Watchers of Abilene, trust us. Stay vigilant. Do as we say, and we will ensure you are safe. When the time is right, we will share our plans with you all. But for now – enjoy the festivities!"

As Hitra finishes her speech, the drumming becomes more melodic and is joined by a cohort of flutes and pipes. The crowd of Watchers from the bridge begins to flow down to the beach and Rumah and I follow them. By the water's edge, the newly anointed Watchers have moved from a line into a huddle, where they are congratulating each other and chattering excitedly. I catch a couple of them glancing over at me. I'm desperate to talk to Tsam, but I can't see him.

Rumah tells me she's going to speak with a friend, and I'm not sure what to do. I feel like everyone is looking in my direction. Noticing that I don't fit. My skin tingles and I tell it not to. Not now. No sparks tonight. Finally, I see Tsam. He emerges from the crowd with a grin that stretches from ear to ear. He's wearing the same shade of blue as me, but his robes have delicate embroidery on their cuffs and collar. He jogs towards me, doing a half-jump half-flutter to speed himself up.

"Did you see?" he asks, sounding just like he did when we were young and he'd done a handstand he was proud of.

"Of course," I reply, hugging him awkwardly. "You were incredible."

Alyssa and Garrett arrive by our side, buoyed up with pride, cheeks flushed with adrenaline. Behind us, along the underside of the cliffs, a collection of market stalls have sprung up. Garrett drags us to one that serves tiny chunks of fish, fried and tossed in something that looks like salt but tastes a thousand times better.

After we've eaten, we dance. At first, I sway from foot to foot, happy to watch them, absorbing their elated smiles, forgetting why I'm really here. Then Garrett drags me to my feet and starts to twirl me around beside the bonfire. Tsam is dancing with Alyssa, the drummers are drumming, we swap and I dance with Tsam. I spot Kole, by the bridge, watching us. I beckon him over, giddy with the joy that hums through the air. Kole shakes his head, but walks slowly towards us. He might even be smiling. Alyssa and I grab a hand each and start to drag him into the circle. Tsam makes a joke about Garrett getting jealous, and all four of us laugh.

Then something cracks. Like a firework. But small. Distant.

I tell the others to stop. They ignore me. There it is again.

"Stop!" I shout. "What is that?"

The drummer stops, his hands frozen in the air. The revellers stumble to a halt. Then...

BOOM.

Just like the vision they showed me. A thunderous explosion, but not from the bridge – from the Academy. A voice cries, "There! The western tower!" and we look up to see dense grey smoke tumbling out of its windows.

BOOM.

Another, somewhere in the forest.

From the clifftop someone shouts. "The houses! They're on fire!"

Tsam, Alyssa and Garrett encircle me. Watchers begin springing into the air, some towards the Academy, some to the forest but Kole ushers us to the far end of the beach, into an alcove just beneath the waterfall.

"What's happening?" asks Garrett.

"It's him, isn't it?" says Alyssa. "It's Mahg. He's come for Émi. I knew that Spectre..."

"Not now, Alyssa!" shouts Tsam, in a tone I haven't heard him use before.

Kole steps between them. "I don't know what's happening but we have to get Émi out of Abilene."

"Shouldn't we find Hitra?" I ask. "Rumah?"

"There's no time," says Kole, glancing back into the alcove. "This way..."

We follow him to a spot where the rock is slimy and damp. He wraps his fingers around a gap in the stone and starts to pull. Garrett helps him and the gap gets bigger. When it is big enough for us to fit through, we run. Into a cold, narrow passageway that winds down and down until it's far beneath the City. We keep going. When we emerge, hours later, we are at the edge of the forest, just before the bamboo, and it is sunrise.

Behind us, Abilene is still, except for columns of dark grey smoke, trickling up from the trees and into the sky. Alyssa is breathing heavily.

"What do we do now?" she asks. "Where do we go?"

"We follow the Elders' plan," says Kole. "We take Émi to Tarynne."

"Tarynne?"

"Silvana has a message for her, it will tell her where Ava is. We need to hurry."

Alyssa peers out past the bamboo. "We don't have any water. If we leave now we'll be crossing the desert at midday, we'll fry out there."

Tsam and Garrett exchange a worried look. Kole is the only one to speak.

"We have no choice."

And he marches on.

FIFTEEN

A t school, we were warned about the wasteland between
Tarynne and Abilene. The Council told us that when
Mahg destroyed the other cities, the desert spread until it
engulfed every living thing. Everything, except for Nhatu.

They lied about that, but it wasn't a lie when they said no
one could survive out here. Nothing could have prepared me for
the ferocious, unrelenting heat, which dries up all the air in my
lungs and burns my arms even through the sleeves of my tunic.

There is nowhere to hide, no place to shelter. Every now
and then, the Watchers stretch out their wings to provide shade,
or to shield us from a flurry of sand that is being whipped up by
the wind, but they can only do so for a couple of minutes before
the fragile skin beneath their feathers begins to burn. So we
soldier on. I don't even look up as we walk. I just bow my head
and stare at my feet. No one speaks.

We walk through the midday sun and into the afternoon. It
is only when I finally step into the cool of a shadow that I allow
myself to look up. Ahead, the smouldering pinnacle of Tarynne
reaches up towards the clouds. Its height casts the boulders
below into a greyish half-light, offering salvation from the blaze

of the desert sun. Kole leads us closer, and it seems as if he is going to try and walk straight through the rock itself. He beckons for us to follow him, then steps sideways around a section that sticks out further than the rest, and disappears.

We copy him and pass through a narrow gap that widens out into a winding corridor. Pinholes of sunlight stipple our path and the walls radiate an earthy coolness that I simply have to touch. If I was alone, and if I wasn't so thirsty that I couldn't see straight, I would press my cheek against the rock and stay here, absorbing the drop in temperature. But the others charge ahead until, suddenly, we burst out on a busy street.

Above us – way, way, above us – a slash of bright blue sky divides the pinnacle into two halves. On one side, market stalls have been chiselled out of the rock. On the other, an elaborate mural of elephants and Taman stretches for as far as I can follow it down the street.

At the nearest stall, Kole asks for some water. The vendor, who has a birthmark like Kole's on his left ear and part of his chin, hurriedly offers a flask. Taking in our sun-scorched cheeks and dusty appearance, he asks what's happened. Kole tells him about what happened at the Ceremony, tells him to find Tarynne's Elders and send help to Abilene. Wide-eyed, the man leaves his stall and runs down the street.

We share the contents of the flask between us. All around, stall holders chatter amicably with their customers and a temperate air of calmness makes me feel as if someone is holding their hands over my ears. The quiet, coupled with the air-born scent of sage and lavender, has an almost soporific effect. My eyelids grow heavy and, after the effort of the journey here, I find it hard to start walking again when the group sets off once more.

Everyone we pass has a purple birthmark somewhere on their face or arms, although I don't notice any that are as prominent as Kole's. We continue down the main street and, eventually, the stalls peter out. For a while, there is nothing ahead of us other than the street and the dancing sunlight. There are no doors here, just a series of unrecognisable symbols carved into the limestone wall at regular intervals. When we come to a symbol that looks like a spiral with a cross through its centre, Kole presses his palm onto it. The stone depresses slightly and the imprint of a door appears. It sucks inwards and sideways, revealing a cavernous living space with high ceilings and bright white walls. Kole ushers us in, then disappears into a side room, returning with a carafe full of water and five large tumblers. Again, we drink without stopping for breath. Then Kole tells us to wait while he goes after the stall holder.

It's impossible for Tsam, Alyssa or Garrett to keep still. They try to recline on the floor cushions in the centre of the room, but they end up back on their feet and pacing. Like the market stalls, Kole's dwelling has been carved into the limestone but, with no windows, it is completely sealed off from the street. From the back of the room, an archway ushers in the hint of sunlight. Above our heads, a circle of fist-sized holes in the ceiling illuminate the room. It is cool here, and quiet, and it's hard to believe that the chaos we left behind in Abilene really happened.

While we wait, we do not speak. Then, after what feels like hours, when the sunlight from the ceiling is fading, Kole returns to us. Alyssa pounces on him immediately, asking what's happening, what he's heard, what we should do. Kole reaches into his pocket and hands her a tiny scroll of paper, like the one Tsam gave Fin. Alyssa unfurls it and reads quickly.

"They're alright?" she asks, looking back up at Kole.

"No one was hurt," he replies, "but many houses were damaged."

"I don't get it," says Garrett. "Did Mahg attack us?"

Alyssa waves the scroll at him. "Hitra thinks it was just meant to scare us, prove he could hurt us if he really wanted to."

"What about Émi?" asks Tsam. "Do they want us to wait for Sayah and Roan? Take her back to Abilene?"

Alyssa looks at the scroll again, then shakes her head. Her voice is slow and small, as if she can't quite believe what she's reading. "No. They want us to go with her."

As the Watchers gather around the scroll and read through it again and again, Kole slopes off into the kitchen. I follow him, and find him leaning against the sink, breathing deeply. When he sees me he straightens up, but I fill a tumbler and pass it to him.

"You should rest," I say.

He takes the tumbler from me. "There's no time. It's almost sunset. Maya is waiting for me."

Immediately, and I don't know why, my cheeks flush. Of course he has someone. Someone waiting for him.

His eyes twinkle as he asks, "Would you like to meet her?"

"Now?" I reply.

"She's at her best at the end of the day," he says.

Unsure, but feeling unable to say no, I follow him past the others – who are scratching out a reply to Hitra on the back of the scroll she sent them – and through the archway at the rear of the living quarters.

We emerge on a veranda that protrudes about an eighth of the way up the northern side of Tarynne's limestone pinnacle. Below us, there is a reed-lined pool, not quite big enough to be a lake, and beyond, grassy plains melt into the horizon. Kole waits for me to absorb the view. A breeze drifts over us, carrying a delicate chiming melody. From archways all along the rock face, Taman like Kole are humming as they make their way to the pool.

Kole and I make our way down a series of stone steps. When

we reach the bottom, doleful calls trumpet out from somewhere behind us. Holding my elbow, Kole turns me around.

"There she is..." His eyes are sparkling, his features lighter.

I laugh, because I can't believe I didn't realise sooner that Maya is an elephant. One of at least fifty, who are emerging from a group of caves below the verandas. Kole raises his arm, waving. An elephant at the front of the herd lifts her trunk into the air as though she is waving back. When she reaches Kole's side, he places his hands on her trunk and she sighs into him, closing her eyes.

Kole tells me to wait here, and the pair of them walk side by side to the water's edge. I sit and tuck my knees up under my chin, watching them gently pace their way through the reeds and out into the water. A few metres in, Maya stops and huffs at Kole as if she is scrutinising his travel-worn clothing.

Kole shrugs apologetically and she twitches her ears at him.

The other Taman are dressed in white billowing trousers and matching shirts, but as they wade further into the pool they remove their shirts, scrunch them into balls and dip them in the water. Beneath their shirts, they wear dark purple vests, the colour of their birthmarks. When Kole removes his tunic, however, he is naked from the waist up and I have to lower my eyes before my cheeks have the chance to blush. A little further out, when Kole is knee deep in the water, Maya lowers herself and rolls onto her side. Chanting under his breath, Kole gently and painstakingly washes her, using his bunched-up tunic to caress her thick, crumpled skin.

The Taman finish bathing their elephants, then kneel so that the surface of the water rises most of the way up their chests. They continue to chant. From the shore line beside me, a young boy – only five or six – rings a large copper bell four times. The elephants rise and turn to face the Taman. Kole reaches to the back of his neck and untwists his hair from its braid. He presses his palms together and closes his eyes. Maya takes a step towards him and, more gently than I imagined was possible, releases a stream of cool, clear water from her trunk onto the top of Kole's head. Then she strokes his face, and bows.

When each pair has finished, the elephants trumpet in unison, the small boy rings the bell and the Taman lead the way back to shore.

Kole joins me and sits down. Maya rests her trunk on his shoulder.

"So this is Maya?" I ask.

"Yes," he says. "This is Maya."

I turn to her. "It's lovely to meet you."

She puffs her cheeks at me.

"She likes you," Kole says. "We do this each night – a bonding ritual. The young ones bathe in the mornings. First light." He pauses, looking at me from the corner of his eyes as if he's not sure whether to go ahead with what he's about to say. "We can come back and watch the morning ceremony, if you like?"

"Yes. I would like," I say.

"Good. After that, we'll go to Silvana."

"You don't think we should see her tonight?"

Kole shakes his head, and glances up towards his home. "We are all exhausted. We know Abilene is safe, so we should rest tonight."

"Alright," I say.

Kole gazes out at the water for a moment, then says, "Émi, do you mind giving me some time with Maya?"

"Of course. It was lovely to meet you, Maya. I'll see you tomorrow."

As I leave, she blinks at me and her eyes are just like Kole's – deep and full. I feel my distrust starting to waver. How can I be afraid of him when a creature like Maya has given him her soul?

When I reach the veranda, Tsam is waiting for me, stretching his wings.

"Quite a spectacle," he says.

I stand beside him, looking down at the pool. "They're so in tune with one another," I murmur. "It's like they know what the elephants are thinking, and the elephants know them too."

"I think they do," Tsam says. "If a child's sick, the Healers ask the elephants for advice about which herbs to use. If the Elders are struggling with a decision, they ask the elephants. The Taman trust them completely. They're almost symbiotic. One being, instead of two."

"If I'm honest, I'm a little jealous," I say.

Tsam's eyes flicker down to Kole.

"Oh, no! Not jealous of Kole and Maya. Just jealous of their bond. I don't think I'll ever know what that's like."

"You might," says Tsam quietly. "When we find Ava."

When Kole returns, we have supper and take ourselves to bed before the moon has chance to fix itself firmly in the sky. We sleep in Kole's bedroom, stretched out beside one another on the cool smooth floor. I think perhaps we won't sleep, that we'll all lay here restlessly, thinking of Abilene and how much worse things could have been. But the tumultuous emotions of the Ceremony and our departure lie heavy on our eyelids. Within minutes, we're all sinking into a deep sleep.

SIXTEEN

K ole wakes me at sunrise and takes me back down to the bathing pool to see the young elephants. At the water's edge, the boy who rang last night's bell bounds up behind us.

"Morning, Kole!"

"Good morning, Bael," Kole replies.

"Who's that?" Bael asks, looking at me.

"This is Émi. She's a good friend of mine."

Bael bows at me. "Pleased to meet you, Miss."

I smile and say, "Likewise."

The sun is a little way above the horizon now so Bael eagerly rings the bell again, four times, as before. Then I hear the sound of trumpets and stamping feet coming from inside the caves.

The elephant caves stretch all the way along the underside of the verandas. On the third chime of the bell, shapes start to emerge. This time, calves as well as adult elephants amble down to the water's edge. From above, a mixture of Taman and Tarynese children start to descend the limestone steps.

When Kole spots Maya, he waves and she makes her way

towards us. Behind her, bothering her tail with his trunk, follows a calf. Maya pushes it towards me.

"This is Niri," Kole says. "Maya's son."

Niri waggles his ears at me and scrapes his right foot in the dirt. Then he reaches out his trunk towards me and tries to prise open my fingers!

"He thinks you have food," laughs Bael. When Niri sees him, he bolts towards the boy, and wraps his trunk around his shoulders in what looks like an embrace. Then, just as suddenly, he releases Bael and rushes towards the water.

"Bael will be Niri's Taman," explains Kole. "When they've grown, they will join the adults in the evening ceremony. Until then, they practise here in the mornings."

Maya watches carefully as Bael and Niri wade into the pool and perform a more playful version of the ritual I saw the night before. Bael washes Niri gently from head to foot, then Niri squirts water over Bael's head. But when they are splashed carelessly by a nearby calf, they retaliate and the ritual becomes a mixture of squirting, laughing, dunking and wrestling as the children and the calves tumble around one another.

As the sun begins to rise, Maya tickles Kole's ear with her trunk and he sneaks her a piece of bread that I didn't know he had brought with him. Then he pats her leg and says, "Sorry, Maya, we have to go now."

Maya tilts her head and it feels almost like an eye-roll, fed up that he's leaving her so soon. But then she wraps her trunk around his body in farewell and forgives him.

Silvana's dwelling is just five symbols away from Kole's. This time, when he rests his hand on the shallow, intertwined grooves, we have to wait before the outline of the door appears and slides inwards.

Silvana is not what I expected. Despite her living in Tarynne, I had assumed she was a Watcher, that she'd fled Abilene after her son's treachery. But her dark hair and complexion indicate immediately that she is Tarynese. Her hair is short, exposing elfin ears that are pierced from top to bottom with copper-coloured loops, and she wears a bundle of scarves tied on top of her head. She smiles broadly at Kole as she steps aside to let us in. They embrace, and the way Alyssa looks at them tells me their closeness is a surprise to her too.

In shape, Silvana's living quarters echo Kole's, but hers are decorated with an array of herbs and flowers, hung from the ceiling with thick, plaited twine. Despite the morning light that streams through the pinholes and the archway, Silvana has lit candles and arranged them in grooves either side of an empty fireplace.

A teapot rests in the centre of a low square table. Silvana sits down, cross-legged, and swills the tea around, anti-clockwise, four times, before pouring it. Kole sits beside her and I follow suit but the Watchers remain standing. Kole ignores them, touches the rim of his mug to Silvana's, then mine and sips the green tea.

"How are you, Silvana?" he asks, finally.

She smiles and sets down her mug. "I think your friends are eager to skip the small talk."

Tsam presses a hand on Alyssa's forearm to stop her from speaking, flicks his feathers and takes a cushion opposite Silvana.

"I'm sorry," he says. "But I'm afraid time isn't on our side."

A shadow crosses Silvana's face. "Because of my son," she says. She darts a look at Kole. "I heard about Abilene. Was anyone hurt?"

"No," says Kole gently.

Alyssa folds her arms. "Many homes were destroyed. It could have been much worse."

"I'm sorry," says Silvana, her eyes watery.

Kole puts his hand on her sinewy shoulder then looks at Alyssa. "Silvana is a friend. She's trying to help us."

Alyssa unfolds her arms and sits down. Garrett too.

Silvana's face clears. "Thank you," she whispers.

Kole tells her to speak only when she is ready.

She smiles sadly around the table. "You're here because the sorcerer who divided the Fire Stone is a close friend of mine. His name is Søyen. When he created the girls and took Ava away, he entrusted me with a message for Émi. He knew the day would come when she would need to find her sister."

"How did you meet Søyen?" asks Tsam, cautiously.

"My husband was a Watcher, but I'm a Healer. I grew up here, in Tarynne. Søyen came to my mother's stall when I was a girl, to buy herbs and discuss remedies. When I moved to Abilene, he visited me often. Many times I asked him for advice —" her voice falters - "about my son."

"Advice?" I prompt.

"Mahg was a troubled boy. Even before his wings failed to come through. But when he turned eleven, when all of his class-mates developed and he didn't, he withdrew even more. My husband wanted to consult the sorcerers in Esyllt, but Søyen didn't think magick was the answer and I agreed. We spent a lot of time discussing holistic remedies – things that might help Mahg's emotional state – to help him to come to terms with who he was and embrace it."

Alyssa nods curtly. "But Mahg turned to magick anyway."

Silvana sighs. "Yes. Dark magick. And I will never forgive him for what he did. I will never understand it. But Søyen believed that, despite everything, Mahg would not harm me. That I was the only one who could keep his message safe."

Alyssa blinks twice, in quick succession. "So, do you have it? The message."

Silvana rises from her place at the table and looks at me. "I do. But I would like to be alone with Émi."

Alyssa looks at the others. "I don't think—" But they walk towards the door. Reluctantly, she follows them.

Silvana and I are alone.

She unhooks a dark blue pendant from around her neck and places it on the table in front of me. "When you touch the amulet, you will see Søyen's message. Are you ready?"

I stare at the jewel and the blueness begins to swirl. It latches on to me and pulls me in. My fingers begin to prickle. Pins and needles of energy dart from my hands through my elbows to my chest. I reach out and place my hand over the amulet. What happens next is not like the vision in the room Cai put me in. This time I find myself drowning in images, battering into my mind as though they've been there all along.

I see the bridge explode. I see dirty, yellow-toothed men tearing through the Academy with swords and daggers. I see Watchers falling from the sky and then a vast, black shadow swallowing up the lake. I see Mahg diving for the stone. Hitra, Sayah, Amin and Rumah follow him, along with other Watchers. They fight him in the air; they fight him in the water. Finally, he flees, injured. His soldiers retreat through the woods. I see the Academy burning, hear the screams. Then the Elders, in their chambers, frantic.

We should divide the stone!

No, keep it whole.

Splitting it is the only way to keep it safe.

No, it must stay here with us.

We must consult the Elders of Tarynne, Esyllt.

Nhatu?

No, not them. The Council must not be told. Not yet. They will use it to their advantage.

Then there appears a figure I've never seen before, but who I recognise instantly. Søyen. The sorcerer who created me. He tells them it can be done; the stone can be broken. As long as the pieces remain connected, the power of the stone will hold true. One for each of The Four Cities – even Nhatu. That's how it must be.

But Mahg will know. He'll know where they are. He'll attack again.

Then we'll divide it six times. Four for the cities and two to be hidden. Hidden where Mahg will never find them.

A room, dark. No, not a room – it's a cave, hidden behind the waterfall.

Søyen kneels in a circle of flames. He's holding something. The Fire Stone. Smaller than I thought, and brighter. So bright. So beautiful. He is chanting, his eyes closed. The flames go out. The stone gets brighter. Brighter. Sparks, like mine, burst out of it, bounce off the walls and the floor. Darkness. Then a baby cries. Two cries. My cries. And Ava's.

Amin is crouched beside a hospital bed. Inta lies still. Her cheek is bleeding. "I love you," he says. "I will take Émi and Tsam. I will protect them both. Goodbye."

Amin is holding me. I'm not crying. Søyen kisses my forehead and whispers into my ear. He is holding Ava. He takes her away. I'm crying now. So is she.

It starts to snow. Whirling, white, cold...

My eyes snap open. "I know where she is..."

———

As I leave Silvana's, I feel strangely calm. I know everything now, and it feels as though I always have. Every fibre of my skin fizzes, but the sparks are calmer, constant, a part of me. Silvana didn't ask me what I saw, just hugged me and told me to be careful. Her smallness as I wrapped my arms around her reminded me of my mother. But she is stronger than my mother.

The others are waiting for me outside. Kole's arms are folded. Alyssa and Tsam pace the ground as Garrett leans against a wall, chewing on something that looks like a long blade of grass. When Tsam sees me, he rushes over and checks me from head to toe. "You're alright?" he asks.

I brush him away. "It wasn't as bad as before. It didn't take me to the memories, it gave them to me. As if they were always mine."

Tsam frowns, as if he doesn't quite understand. "Did it work?" he asks.

I glance up and down the street. I'm not sure I want to say the words out loud. Understanding, Alyssa takes the map from her pocket and holds it out in front of me. I point to the mountains, west of Tarynne. She exchanges a worried glance with Tsam.

"Are you certain?" she asks.

I nod.

"Do you know where?" asks Tsam.

"I'll know when we get there," I tell him.

Tsam peers closer at the outlines on the map. "The mountains aren't really... habitable. No one lives there, Ém."

"Ava lives there," I say, firmly.

Instead of returning to Kole's, we split up in order to gather supplies for the journey. Alyssa and Tsam go to dispatch a messenger to Abilene. They decide it's not wise to tell the Elders where we're going in a letter, so plan to simply inform them that we have a location and that we'll be out of contact until we return. Kole goes to ready some horses and, I suspect, say goodbye to Maya, while Garrett and I are tasked with sourcing clothes and food.

As the two of us walk through the market, I find myself fighting the two Émis in my head. Serious Émi, the one who is trying to prepare herself for what's to come, simply wants to collect the things we need and be on our way. Émi from Nhatu, who always dreamed of going over the wall, can't help feeling a prang of excitement at the journey ahead.

The market is buzzing with activity. It is calm, like Abilene, but more vibrant. Last night, I didn't notice the brightly coloured scarves or flowers, the wind chimes or the incense. But today they seem to have multiplied. Each stall is different, and each vendor is smiling. The markets in Nhatu are ruthless, full of people trying to barter, steal and fleece each other. Here, in the middle of the giant limestone rock that forms the Second City, trading is amicable. Herbs are swapped for potions, wool for cotton, scarves for incense. Not once do I see someone offering money in exchange for goods.

Garrett is still chewing his piece of grass and, after procuring some snow boots from a tubby retired Taman, he offers me a piece. It is sweet and salty at the same time and it makes my tongue tingle. I wrinkle my nose and Garrett laughs.

"It's an acquired taste," he says. "Reminds me of when we were little. Da used to bring us for the displays and he'd let us chew as much Lye as we liked."

"Displays?"

Garrett's eyes twinkle. He explains that, at the turning of the season, the Taman and the elephants put on a display of their fighting skills.

"It's more like a dance, really," he says. "Have you seen the baton Kole carries on his belt? It folds out so it's almost as tall as he is. Every Taman has one. They use them like swords – fence with them." Garrett does a little jig, spinning around and pretending to fight me with one of the boots he's just purchased. I remember Alyssa's jibe about him being a Tamanyte and I have to suppress a smile.

"Kole is the best," he says. "Really, the best. You know he's only two years older than us? It's unheard of for someone so young to be a Top Tier Taman."

"What makes him so good?"

Garrett gives an exaggerated shrug. "Probably it has to do with his parents." He lowers his voice. "From what I've heard, they were Healers. They were out looking for herbs and they were attacked by a changeling. Kole was too young to fight it off. Ever since then, he's trained harder, fought better—"

"Ahem." A voice interrupts and we turn to find Kole standing behind us. I'm not sure who blushes more – me, or Garrett – but Kole's expression doesn't falter. If he heard us, he doesn't betray any hint of anger or embarrassment. When he's like this, stony and closed off, I feel my distrust of him ebbing back in waves. I try to remember how gentle he was with Maya and Silvana. But then I search his eyes and they're so utterly still that I can't help shuddering.

"The horses are ready," he says. "We will leave when the midday sun starts to wane."

"Good idea," says Garrett, overly jovial, compensating for gossiping. "We've bought boots, wraps, food packs. Should have enough to last."

"I need some medical supplies," says Kole. "I will meet you back at the dwelling."

"Right," says Garrett. Then, as Kole walks away, he adds, "He heard us, didn't he?"

I shake my head. "It's hard to tell. He's so..."

"Aloof?"

"Exactly. I don't understand it. With Maya, he's so different. It's like she softens him at the edges. Even with Silvana, he was kind."

"Probably an orphan thing," says Garrett, immediately flushing red again. "Sorry, Émi, I didn't mean..."

I wave away his embarrassment. "I wish everyone would stop being so careful around me. I'm not that fragile. And I'm not an orphan." Not yet, anyway.

"Course. Sorry, Ém."

He looks genuinely sorry, so I nudge him playfully in the ribs. "Come on. Give me some more of that Lye."

When Kole returns to his quarters, he finds us in a state of utter disarray. Alyssa is clutching her side and trembling with laughter as Garrett hops on one leg, trying to squeeze his foot into one of the boots we bought. When he sees Kole, Garrett huffs and waves the boot at him,

"That Taman said these would fit but we need to ask for our money back. I've been trying for ages!"

I'm laughing too now, reminding Garrett that we didn't actually give the Taman any money – just a few pouches of tea – so we probably can't afford to be choosy. For a fraction of a second, Kole allows a smile to wrinkle the corner of his mouth. Then he takes the boot from Garrett, reaches inside and says, "You have to unclasp the laces first."

With the laces undone, the fabric falls open wide enough for Garrett to insert his foot. He wiggles his leg and grins.

"That's fantastic!" Then, he rounds on Alyssa. "Did you know? Were you deliberately watching me struggle?"

Alyssa shrugs and seamlessly ties up her own pair, winking at her brother. Garrett flutters his wings and charges towards her but, before they can engage in a full-scale skirmish, Tsam shouts, "Okay! That's enough!" He is smiling but they immediately straighten themselves up, muttering, "Sorry," and, "Got carried away."

It is past midday now and the map is spread out to plot our journey. With the horses, Kole says we should make it to the foothills of the mountains by nightfall. "We'll camp there tonight, then at sunrise we'll begin our ascent." He looks at the Watchers. "You won't be able to fly once we're past the foothills. The weather will be too unpredictable."

"How far are we going to have to climb?" Alyssa asks me with just a hint of nervousness in her voice.

I shake my head. "I'm sorry. I don't know. I just know she's there."

SEVENTEEN

When we are ready, Kole walks us through the market, past the elephant murals and under a narrow archway that leads to a winding staircase. The stairs circle down through the limestone and emerge at the western edge of the pinnacle. A pair of horses are waiting for us. The Watchers take flight immediately and, for a moment, I let myself marvel at them. Then I climb onto my horse and we set off.

Every hour or so, we stop for the Watchers to rest their wings. The terrain is sparse but unchallenging, similar to the landscape between Nhatu and Abilene. But when the mountains come into view, their tips obscured by low-hanging clouds, the temperature drops. Our travel tunics are similar to the one I wore for the Ceremony in Abilene, with winding straps of fabric that can form either short or long sleeves. Balancing as best I can in the saddle, I wind mine down around my elbows and forearms.

We reach the foothills just before sunset and find a spot beneath a rocky alcove that will shelter us from the increasingly determined wind. Tsam and Garrett light a fire, while Kole gathers everyone's rations, and I help Alyssa to fetch water from a nearby stream. When the water is bubbling in a pan suspended over the camp fire, Kole tips in each of our ration packs and stirs them into a thin brown broth.

After we've finished eating and the sky is a dark blueish grey, Garrett reaches into his pocket and pulls out a small red harmonica. He grins. Alyssa groans. Tsam claps his hands.

"Do you have to?" Alyssa asks, groaning again.

Garrett answers her with a wink and begins to play a soft, lilting melody that reminds me of after-school dances in the Green Quarter, before they were banned. Kole looks uncomfortable, as if he's worried someone will hear us, but the music is soothing and normal, helping us to forget about tomorrow's climb and what it might bring.

Eventually, with the sun firmly retired and the sky full of stars, Garrett draws his tune to a close. Without it, everything is quiet – too quiet. I glance over my shoulder at the mountains.

"It really is just us, isn't it?" I whisper.

Tsam edges closer to me. "Yes. But we can do this, Ém." He takes hold of my hand. "*You* can do this."

Garrett shuffles up on my other side. "Course you can."

Of course I can.

Garrett takes the first watch, and, when I know Tsam, Alyssa and Kole are safely asleep, I go to sit with him. In the beginning, I found his liveliness unnerving. But now, he is the only one I feel at ease around. Tsam's fussing irritates me, Alyssa's frostiness is unpredictable and Kole's stoic indifference makes me feel twitchy and exposed.

My father's sketchbook is still in my pocket. I carried it over the wall, through the woods, to Abilene and to Tarynne. Now, I take it out and settle it in my lap. With a nub of charcoal that I snatched from the fire, I start sketching. I draw the Watchers, flying above me. The Spectre in the woods. Mahg as a boy, under the bridge. Time slips away.

Garrett clears his throat. "Tsam was right. You're good."

Finally, I look up. "My father taught me," I tell him. "I know he'll never see them, but I feel like I need to capture..." I wave my hands, "... all this. For him. Does that make sense?"

Garrett nods and smiles, then points to the page where I've sketched him, Alyssa and Tsam. "I'm much better looking than that, you know."

I laugh lightly. "I'll have to work on the likeness."

Soon, it's time for Garrett to switch places with Alyssa. I'm not called on to keep watch, because they want to save my energies for tracking Ava. So I curl back down, hugging my sketches to my chest, and close my eyes. Garrett is asleep and snoring almost before he's lying down. For the rest of the night, I tread water below the surface of sleep. I hear Alyssa swap with Kole, Kole swap with Tsam and Tsam begin to boil water for our breakfast.

When I join him, he notices the grey circles beneath my eyes but doesn't remark on them. He hands me some drinking water and places his wing around my shoulder. I let myself sink into him for a moment, pretending perhaps that we're ten years old again and camping in the field behind The Emerald, with Amin keeping watch over us from the window.

Alyssa is warmer towards me this morning and asks if I need help fixing my cloak, ready for the trek into the cold. I am starting to learn that her spikiness is a side effect of her need to prove that she is her brother's equal. I must learn not to take it personally.

Shortly after sunrise, we are ready to begin our trek. We leave the horses by the stream and, as I pat them goodbye, it occurs to me that when we return they will have an extra passenger: Ava. Maybe even two. Surely Søyen will come back to Abilene with us. If he was powerful enough to create twin baby girls from the Fire Stone, then he must be able to help us defeat Mahg. I decide, then, that I will convince him to come. No matter what.

Despite being wrapped up, it is not long before the cold begins to nip at my skin as we wind our way higher through the rocky landscape. The further up we go, the more breathless we become but, as my chest tightens, a flicker of energy ignites in my belly and propels me forwards, closer to Ava. For the first part of the morning, we climb an obvious, well-trodden path up the mountain. Then we come to a fork in the path. There are two routes we could take. One goes east, the other west.

"Which way?" asks Alyssa, pulling her cloak tighter against the cold.

Tsam turns to me. "Émi? Do you feel anything?"

I close my eyes and try to summon the image of Ava. I think of her as the girl in my dreams, the girl from Nhatu – running, playing and laughing. Not the girl on the lake who was consumed by black mist. I picture the swirling white from Silvana's pendant, the snow and the ice. Then I hear Ava's voice, like a distant echo, bouncing between the rocks to our right.

"West," I tell them. "This way."

We climb slowly now. Our hands are wrapped in fur-lined gloves, our cloaks tied tight. The Watchers wear their cloaks over the tops of their wings to protect their feathers. They look like three haggard hunchbacks, silhouetted against the sun.

To begin with, the snow appears in tiny little drifts, surviving only in the shade of the rocks. But, just past midday, the sky thickens with whiteness and I suggest that we should take shelter.

We find a crevice that opens into a small cave, just big enough to accommodate the five of us, and shuffle inside. We have only just finished sharing a pouch of dry oats between us, when the snow storm begins. It is sudden and violent, bleaching all colour from the mountains. The others huddle far back into the cave, but I position myself at the entrance. I have never seen snow fall before and I am desperate to touch it, but when I reach out my hand, the icy strength of the flakes feels like tiny bee stings on my palm.

Tsam calls to me. Reluctantly, I slink back into the cave. We have no way of lighting a fire and, even if we did, the smoke would be too much for our tiny hiding spot. So we huddle together, staring out at the blizzard, waiting for it to stop.

It doesn't stop. It snows, and snows, and soon we are all shivering. My fingers twitch. At first I think it's from the cold, but then they start to tingle and a thought occurs to me – if I can make sparks, maybe I can turn them into something bigger, something warm?

I don't tell the others what I'm going to do. The pressure of them watching would be too much. Discreetly, I rub my palms together, as if I'm trying to warm them. I close my eyes, because concentrating is easier that way, and breathe deeply. There they are – the sparks – simmering somewhere between muscle and skin. I picture them flowing through me, from my stomach, into my lungs, down my arms.

When I open my eyes, the others are staring at me. I grin at them, holding out the white-hot ball of light that floats between my open palms. Tsam and Alyssa look concerned, as if the ball might suddenly explode, but Garrett says, "Amazing!" and folds his gangly frame down beside me, warming his face and hands.

I keep the ball alight as long as I can but, after a while, I feel overwhelmingly tired.

Tsam notices my eyelids drooping. "That's enough now, Émi."

I don't argue with him. I just let the sparks die down and then I lean back against the cave wall.

"Looks like it's going to stop soon," Alyssa says. "Tsam, come with me and see?"

Garrett insists on going too, which leaves Kole on Émi-sitting duty.

He stands beside me. "You're learning," he says.

I smile weakly. "I'm trying. I think I need to learn a bit quicker though, don't you?"

"Søyen will help you."

I look up at him. "Kole, can I ask you something?"

He inclines his head.

"I keep thinking about Silvana, all alone. What happened to her husband?"

"He was killed in Mahg's attack."

I breathe out.

"When she came back to Tarynne, my parents looked after her. When they died, she looked after me. She's a good woman."

I'm steeling myself to ask about his parents, curious to know if what Garrett told me is true, but I lose my chance because the Watchers return and tell us the storm has died down. Tsam wants us to leave straight away, but Kole isn't sure. He says it's too close to nightfall and that we should stay here in case we can't find shelter further on. They're squaring up to one another when Alyssa steps between them. "For once," she says, "I agree with Kole. If we keep going and get stuck out in another storm, we'll be dead. No matter now many balls of light Émi can conjure."

Reluctantly, Tsam concedes defeat.

We just manage to find enough dry kindling, hidden from the snow beneath rocks or under plants, to make a fire at the cave's entrance. When it's lit, we stretch ourselves out in a row. Tsam is beside me. I remember that night in the Red Quarter, after the Cadets, when we lay in the living room, restless in the oppressive heat. I was nervous then, nervous of his closeness, and it surprises me that the feeling has faded. I think of our moment, looking out across the treetops of Abilene. We were so nearly something. But perhaps it is gone. I shiver and Tsam moves closer to me. I think perhaps he will wrap his wings around me to keep me warm, but he doesn't. He is already asleep.

The next morning, the snow is almost blinding. At least three metres deep, solid but crunchy underfoot. Walking is difficult, but the sun livens our spirits and we make steady progress. I am at the front of the group and every time I pause, the others look at me eagerly, wondering if we are almost there.

We're not. We climb for an entire day, shelter again overnight, then climb some more. It is mid-afternoon of our third day on the mountain when I feel a short sharp prang in my stomach and stop walking.

"Here," I whisper, out of breath and with my hands on my hips.

Tsam looks at me, then at our surroundings. "Here? Ém, there's nothing here, it's just rocks."

Alyssa rubs at her temples, clearly wondering whether our entire climb has been a fool's errand. Garrett rotates his ankle, still sore from the choking vine and now aggravated by the arduous journey. Then Kole points at something. At first, I don't see what he's seeing. From my lower vantage point, all I can see is snow and rock and the odd tuft of frozen grass. Then I notice two pairs of eyes, silently blinking at us, camouflaged against the rocks.

The eyes disappear.

"Quick," whispers Alyssa, "after them!"

Exhausted, we chase after the figures, up a section of large sharp rocks. We are trying to hurry, but it is almost impossible to get a firm foothold so we have to tug and pull at one another.

When we finally haul our aching bodies over a jagged snow-covered ridge, we are greeted by a host of silent children, their faces wrapped tightly against the cold, their bodies padded in thick clothing. Two of them step forwards and I realise they're not children but adults who are barely as tall as my waist. They come to stand either side of me and lead me through the crowd, still not speaking.

The others follow, and we are taken to a cluster of small round huts, balanced at varying heights on the rocky cliff face, each with a thatched roof and a door, but no windows. As we near the huts, my skin begins to prickle and I'm sure I hear the wind whispering a name. "Émi," calls the voice, as it whips through the craggy mountainside.

Our escorts knock on the door of the first hut. It is answered by a man with a thick, grey beard peeking out from the bottom of the kerchief he wears over his face. He scowls, scrutinising us, one by one, and peering deep into our eyes as he shakes his head. When he reaches me, he takes a few strands of my hair between his fingers. Then he suddenly yanks and I wince as he tugs them loose from my scalp. He sniffs them, nods and shuffles back inside.

"What's he doing?" whispers Garrett, but the others shush him.

We are beginning to shiver when the old man returns from his hut. He beckons for us to follow him and climbs up to a neighbouring hut. He doesn't knock, just impatiently ushers us inside.

In the centre of the hut, a fire crackles beneath a suspended chimney and we hastily gather around it. On one side of the fire, a pile of rugs indicates a sleeping or sitting area, while the other side houses a low slatted worktop and a metal tub. The old man leaves. The moment he closes the door, every part of me, from the tip of my toes to the top of my head, begins to tingle and fizz.

Alyssa breathes out sharply. "Émi..."

They are all looking at me, their eyes wide. Tsam takes my arm and rolls up my sleeve.

"Émi," he says, "you're glowing."

He's right. My skin is sparkling. I remove my gloves and turn my hands over. They crackle like they're made of lightning. I look up. A girl steps out of the shadows. She moves towards me and as she passes the fire its flames billow and whoosh upwards. Everyone steps back, but I am rooted to the spot. She stops, an arm's length in front of me, and dips the upper half of her body into a bow.

"Ava," I breathe. Not a question, because I know it's her.

She nods.

"Do you know who I am?"

She nods again and takes my hand in hers, pressing it to her cheek. Her face and hair are wrapped in a thick grey scarf so I can't feel her skin, or tell if she is glowing too. Only her eyes are truly visible, and they are just like mine. When she loosens the scarf, however, she isn't glowing, and her hair isn't red or curly. It is darker and straighter, and her cheeks are pinched. The skin around her eyes is grey and sallow and she looks as though she has been crying.

"Ava?" I ask again.

This time, she clears her throat and croaks, "Yes."

"Are you alright?" I ask.

"We don't—" Her voice is barely audible above the snapping flames.

Garrett steps forward then and reaches out his hand. Ava extends hers too and Garrett shakes it cheerfully.

"You don't speak?" he asks.

Ava shakes her head. "The people here cannot use their voices."

"Well, that makes sense," says Alyssa. "No one would be able to tell Mahg she's here, even if they wanted to."

At the mention of Mahg's name, Ava stiffens and pats at the scarf which now rests on her shoulders.

"It's alright," I tell her. "He doesn't know where you are. We're here to protect you – to make sure he doesn't find you."

Ava nods slowly. "You must be hungry?" she asks, her speech stilted and unsteady. Without waiting for an answer, she goes to the worktop in the corner and fetches some bowls. A pot in the middle of the fire is bubbling and Ava spoons us each a portion of clear tepid broth that tastes of absolutely nothing. I force it down and smile encouragingly when I notice her watching me.

"Mmm, delicious!" Garrett announces loudly. Alyssa sharply reminds him that Ava isn't deaf and Garrett blushes, but Ava smiles and offers him some more.

When we have finished eating, Tsam gives me a meaningful look, so I nudge a little closer to Ava and rest my hand on her shoulder. I have stopped glowing now but when I touch her, the tiniest flicker of energy passes between us, like static.

"Ava, you know who I am?"

"You're my sister," she says, smiling.

"And you know who we are?"

She nods fervently. "Oh yes, Father told me. We're special, you and me. We're the most special."

I glance at the others, then back at Ava.

"Made from fire, aren't we?" She is still smiling.

"Yes, yes, we are. Your father, Søyen, he told you why he brought you here?"

"To keep me safe. But you couldn't come," she says, her expression faltering. "I was very sad about that."

"Me too," I say, because it doesn't feel like the right time to explain to her that I had no idea who she was until a few days ago. Ava is still smiling at me. We are the same, two parts of one whole, and yet she feels younger, more fragile. "Your father," I say, "Søyen? Is he here, Ava?"

"*Our* father," she corrects me. "Oh yes. He is always here."

Again, I glance at the others. "Will he be back soon?"

Ava frowns then, and wrings her hands together in her lap. She is wearing silky elbow-length gloves. "Oh, I shouldn't have thought so," she says. "But I can take you to him if you like?"

"Yes," I say firmly. "Yes, we'd like that very much."

EIGHTEEN

Ava takes a long time readying herself to go outside. She wraps and re-wraps her head scarf, changes her boots at least three times, and paces up and down at the back of the hut, muttering. When she finally opens the main door, we are met by darkness.

"Oh," she says, "I think we're too late."

Alyssa sighs and pulls off her boots.

"I'm sorry," says Ava, her eyes watery. "I didn't realise the time."

"It's alright," I tell her. "You'll take us to see Søyen in the morning?"

"Oh yes. Of course. Tomorrow morning."

We don't speak much after that. We are exhausted from our climb, and Ava seems preoccupied with her own thoughts. I feel oddly disappointed. We found Ava – I found her. And yet, something is off balance.

Later, when we're almost asleep, I whisper to Alyssa, "Do you think she's alright?"

Alyssa lies on her back, cushioned by her wings. At first, I don't think she's heard me but then she rolls over and says, "She's odd. But it's hardly surprising – growing up here."

"Mm."

"You think it's more than that?" Her eyes are sharp now, assessing my response.

"I'm sure it's nothing. Let's see what happens tomorrow."

Tomorrow, Kole is the one who wakes me. He taps me, then Alyssa, and gestures urgently to the door. "We overslept. It's mid-morning."

I sit up too quickly, my head still fuzzy with sleep. Alyssa squints around the room and says, "Where's Ava?"

Kole wakes Tsam and Garrett too and they are equally thick-headed, unaccustomed to so much rest.

"She's gone," says Kole.

"Gone?" Alyssa is jumping to her feet, pulling on her boots. "Well, we have to find her."

"I'm sure she just went to fetch water," I say, although I feel anxious too.

We are still lacing up our boots when Ava returns. She is smiling and holding out a basket of gnarly-looking vegetables. She places the basket on the worktop, then embraces me, tight.

"Good morning," she sighs, as if she's been waiting a lifetime to say that to me. I am stiff and awkward. I feel guilty for not returning her enthusiasm, but she doesn't seem to notice. "I brought breakfast," she says, gesturing to her basket. Then, to Garrett, "Would you like to help me prepare it?"

Alyssa steps in, more tactfully than I'd have anticipated. "Actually, Ava, perhaps we could meet Søyen first? Then all have breakfast together?"

Ava laughs. "He won't want any breakfast, silly."

Alyssa glances at me, losing her patience. "Well," I say, "perhaps we could meet him first anyway? I've waited so long to see him..."

That seems to do the trick. Ava wrings her gloved hands and shakes her head. "Of course. So selfish of me. Of course you must see Father. Come... come."

I expect Søyen to be nearby, but Ava hurries us past several huts, clambering higher with each one. She scrambles over the rocks with practiced ease, but we are clumsy and slow. When the huts peter out, we keep climbing, then come to a place where the rock sticks out and curves around, making a path that's only just big enough to stand on. We shimmy around it, Kole and I more cautious than the Watchers, whose wings could save them if they fell, and arrive at a stop when the path becomes wider again. We gather around Ava.

"Surely Søyen doesn't live up here?" Tsam whispers to me. I shake my head at him. It doesn't seem possible. Ava's hut is isolated enough, but living all the way up here? Why would he? Instead of being with her?

"There he is, the middle one," says Ava, pointing.

She is gesturing almost straight into the sun so it takes a moment for my eyes to adjust. When they do, I gasp. There on the mountainside, dangling like morbid wooden fruit, is a row of rectangular boxes.

I look at the others. "Are those...?"

"Coffins," replies Kole darkly.

Ava is smiling. "Father's is the one in the middle. The very best. I painted it myself. See the clouds? He liked clouds."

Any words abandon me. Søyen is dead. Sealed in a wooden box and hung from the side of a mountain.

"What happened to him?" asks Garrett, touching Ava's elbow and causing her to twitch.

"He died," she replies, as if we're all very stupid. "He was scavenging for nettles, to make tea. He fell and banged his head. But he is at peace now." She smiles. "Shall we have breakfast?"

When we return to Ava's hut, Tsam discreetly whispers to Garrett to distract her. Garrett nods and begins to ask lots of questions about the vegetables she gathered and how best to chop them. My stomach is somersaulting uneasily.

"Søyen is dead," I mutter, trying to make it sink in. "From a bang on the head?"

"Something doesn't fit," says Alyssa, glancing over at Ava.

"I agree, it's odd," says Tsam, "but the plan hasn't changed. In fact, I'd say it's even more urgent. We need to get her back to Abilene..."

"Get who back?" Ava's mousy voice drifts across from the other side of the room and the look in her eyes tells me she has heard every word we've been saying. Too late I realise that, living in a commune where speech is rare, Ava must be attuned to every sound.

Tentatively, Tsam asks her to sit down and explains that we are here to take her back to Abilene. He tells her that Mahg is getting closer to finding out where we are. He tells her the Elders need us in Abilene, where they can watch over us, that he knows it will be difficult to leave her home, but it really is very important. Ava doesn't even blink. She absorbs every piece of information and when Tsam has finished she only has one question.

"When do we leave?"

Weary, and aching in places I didn't know existed, I'm relieved when Tsam suggests we wait one more night, before starting back in the morning.

Ava smiles around the room. "What do you want to do today?"

Tsam scratches at his shoulder blade and I can tell he wants to fly but it's impossible here. The snow comes too quickly and the air is too thin. "I think we should rest, try to gather some strength for the journey home."

Ava looks bitterly disappointed. She chews at her fingernail for a moment, then turns to Garrett. "Do you need to rest too?"

Garrett blushes violently and stutters, "I... ah..." which causes Tsam to stifle a laugh.

"I could show you the village?" she asks, wide-eyed.

Garrett's pinkness reaches all the way to his ears now. "Ah, sure. I'd like that."

When they leave, I slump down by the fire and rest my head in my hands. Tsam crouches beside me. "I find her exhausting," I tell him. "I don't know what I expected, but..."

Alyssa bobs down too, on her haunches, and prods the fire with a twisted branch. "I wouldn't worry," she says. "It looks like my brother's going to take her off your hands for a while."

Kole is standing behind us, so quiet I've almost forgotten he's here. "Why hang them like that?" he says. For the first time, there's a wash of emotion in his voice. "How can their souls pass on when their bodies are suspended?"

I remember something we saw yesterday, just before we reached the village. "We've seen the remains of animals on the mountains. That leopard's carcass – it wasn't decayed, but it had been scavenged."

Tsam and Alyssa are looking at me as if they have no idea what I'm talking about.

"It would be almost impossible to bury someone in the snow here, it's too hard. And if the body was close to the surface then—"

"The scavengers would eat them," finishes Alyssa, shuddering.

"Up there, in the coffins, nothing can reach them," I say. It is a plausible explanation. Although I have no evidence to support my theory, Kole seems placated.

Ava and Garrett are gone nearly all afternoon. It is dark and stuffy in the hut but I don't have enough energy to explore further than the doorstep. Instead, every so often, I stick my head outside and let the sun warm my face. Alyssa and Tsam spend the time reorganising their packs, while Kole sits in the corner of the room with his eyes closed, meditating. I try to sleep but feel restless, so I walk to the back of the hut and look at Ava's bookshelves. She owns volume upon volume of magickal texts. Histories, theories and practical works. I take down the one called *The Essence of the Elements* and return to the fire.

When I open the book, a map falls out from between the pages. It is hand drawn on thin leathery paper that might be an animal skin. It depicts the mountains, with notes and remarks about the most accessible routes and the locations of plants and herbs. I pass it to Tsam, thinking perhaps he can find a quicker path to the foothills, and he spreads it out between himself and Alyssa.

I am only a few paragraphs into my book when Ava returns. She is bouncy and grinning. "We had a wonderful time. Garrett is very good at climbing." Then, her face freezes. She is looking at the map on the floor, and the book in my hands.

"You took my things," she says quietly.

I close the book. "I'm sorry, Ava. I should have asked." I hold it out to her. "Here, I'm finished with it."

Ava doesn't take the book. She is trembling. "What else did you take?" she asks, hurrying to the bookshelves.

I glance at Garrett but he shrugs and shakes his head so I walk over to her. "Ava, I promise. It was just this one..."

She whirls around and grabs my hand, the one holding the book. Her touch is hot and, even through her gloves, I can feel her skin fizzing. Her eyes flash at me and she tightens her grip. But then, as quickly as it appeared, her anger is gone and she is small again, delicate. She lets go of my hand and hugs me, patting my hair. "You're my sister, Émi. You can borrow anything you like. I'm sorry I was unkind. Sisters share things but I've never had one before and I'm not used to sharing."

I hug her back and tell her it's alright, I don't mind. But when I return to the fire, I exchange a look with Tsam: *I told you. Something isn't right.*

Ava doesn't seem to notice that the mood has changed. Garrett is the only one still managing to be friendly, listening as she says how wonderful it is to have people to talk to.

"It really is lovely to have guests," she says. "My friends want to invite you for dinner tonight, in the village."

I was hoping to simply go to sleep, wake early and get off this mountain as soon as possible but it doesn't look as though we have a choice. When the sun goes down, we wrap ourselves in our cloaks and boots and follow Ava outside.

A faint mist has descended over the mountainside and it clings to the rocks and to my skin. Dinner takes place outside, in a small stone circle behind the hut of the old man with the grey beard. In the centre of the circle, a dead goat lies stripped of its hide. It has been butchered, and beside it a bloody knife lies on a rock. A handful of villagers, twenty at the most, sit beside one another. There is a fire, but it is small and produces little warmth. The goat's meat sizzles on a grill.

Ava gestures for us to sit down and when the meat is cooked through, chunks are passed around the group by a short woman with black teeth and long white hair.

Kole declines. He bows his head and puts his hands together, respectfully. "No, thank you. I do not eat meat."

The woman holding the platter frowns and shoves the meat at him, jabbing a finger at the food and then at Kole's mouth.

Once again, he says, "No, thank you," and she moves on, shaking her head.

While we eat, the mist bites down harder on the mountainside. The Watchers hug their wings closer to their shoulders to draw in some warmth but Kole and I have no protection other than our cloaks and we're beginning to shiver. The woman with black teeth joins the circle to enjoy her share of the goat, when Ava scurries over to me.

"They're going to perform, in your honour," she whispers, excitement dancing across her face. She doesn't give me a chance to respond, but hurries to a nearby hut and returns with a pile of thick furry blankets, which she hands out, one between two, around the circle.

Kole and I have to share. "What are they performing?" he whispers, leaning so close that I can feel his breath on my ice-cold earlobe.

I shake my head. "I don't know."

The performance is a silent dance. At first, it is comical – plodding and squatting, and not particularly rhythmic. But the more they move, the more entranced I become. When they finish, I almost clap and then stop myself, bowing my head and smiling instead. They don't smile, just nod at us and then quickly file back to their homes.

There is no moon here, no lanterns or torches to light our path, so we stay close to Ava and stumble our way back to her hut. Tsam tells Ava we will leave at sunrise, then we arrange ourselves into rows at the back of the hut for a few hours' sleep.

Kole says he will take the first watch. Last night, Ava persuaded us there was no need, the colony being so isolated. But tonight Kole insists, I suspect so that he can ensure we don't oversleep, and I agree to watch with him. It is too cold to stand guard outside, so we take a rug and a blanket and huddle by the doorway. Ava sleeps facing the wall so I can't tell whether she is awake or not.

"What do you think of her?" I ask Kole, as quietly as possible.

He shifts and stretches out his legs, rubbing his calf.

"She seems very..." he searches for the right word, "child-like. She clearly understands why we're here, but I'm not sure she appreciates the magnitude of it all."

For a man of few words, Kole has phrased exactly what I was thinking. I pick at a splinter in the floorboard beneath my thigh and I'm about to say that maybe she will be different away from here, when a flash of jumbled thoughts that aren't mine cloud my vision.

Trust – don't trust – Mahg – father – lonely – so lonely – friends – happy – sister – mine.

I shudder and Kole nudges me. "Émi?"

I'm seeing Ava's thoughts. They're here in my head, but I can't bring myself to share them with him. Instead, I tell him I'm feeling sleepy and wake Tsam to take my shift. Kole looks over at Ava, as though he senses something, but greets Tsam with a silent nod when he takes my place.

I want to sleep but the words haunt me, repeating themselves over and over on a loop until I begin to wonder whether they really were Ava's... or mine.

NINETEEN

The following morning, I feel more stiff and achey than I did the night before but Ava looks as though she has been awake for hours. Alyssa – who took the final watch – confirms that Ava woke before sunrise and has been pottering about ever since, filling a backpack with clothing, books and trinkets.

"She's packing," says Alyssa, with a raised eyebrow.

Tsam sighs and ruffles his feathers. "Let her bring it," he says. "But if she can't manage the weight of it once we get going, she'll have to ditch it."

We waste no time wrapping ourselves up in our travelling clothes and we are at the door, ready to leave, when Ava rushes back inside. She returns with *The Essence of the Elements* and tells me she would like me to keep it. I thank her, flipping through the pages for the map of the mountains, but it's no longer there. Tsam doesn't have it either, so he and Alyssa have to try and conjure the route they planned from memory.

Leaving the village, light bounces off the snow. Although the ground is still frozen, sunlight warms my face. The sky is clear and blue, allowing us to make the most of the calm and move as quickly as we can.

We have stopped for some water, when Ava says to Kole, "Do you have an elephant?"

He blinks at her. "Maya is not mine. We are each other's."

"Maya's a pretty name. Do you ride her? I'd like to ride an elephant... I've never seen one. Only pictures in my books."

Kole stiffens. "The elephants allow us to ride them in battle. *Only* in battle."

"Do you think she'd let me—"

"No."

"That's a shame," she says, shrugging.

While the rest of us find Ava's childishness unnerving, Garrett is drawn to her. He walks by her side and helps her over rocks, even though she doesn't need assistance. He chatters to her about life in Abilene, telling her about the things we will show her when we return and answering her questions. And all the while, Ava's eyes sparkle.

We walk as close to sundown as we dare, then find an enclave to shelter in. I am using the last inches of daylight to finish a sketch, when Ava sees what I'm doing.

"Oh," she breathes, "you draw beautiful pictures."

She takes the sketchbook from me, without asking, and starts to leaf through it. I tell myself not to be annoyed. After all, I took one of her books without permission. I try to be flattered by her interest. She flips from back to front, so it is a while before she comes across the drawings of my second night in Abilene, when I saw her in the mist.

Ava runs her fingertips over the sketch. "Is that me?"

"Yes," I tell her. "I dreamed about you before, too. Back when I lived in Nhatu. I didn't know about you then. But I saw you."

Ava's face creases. "Why didn't you know about me?"

I glance at Tsam then back at my sister. "Ava, I thought Søyen told you that I was hidden in Nhatu. So Mahg couldn't find me?"

She frowns at me, as if she has no recollection of ever knowing this, but then she nods hurriedly. "Oh yes, of course. Yes, I remember."

"I didn't know who I was until Tsam came to fetch me. Just over a week ago."

Ava takes my hand and squeezes it. "But it's alright, Émi. You know now. And they'll never part us again. Ever."

That night, I dream. Not pictures, nothing solid or fully formed. Just shapes, darkness and words. On waking, dread throbs in my stomach. Dread that solidifies every time I look at Ava. I tell myself I'm being ridiculous, that I'm just struggling to accept she's different from me. But I'm not sure I believe it.

It has snowed overnight, and when we emerge from our hiding spot Ava claps her hands.

"Fresh snow!" she cries.

I catch Alyssa rolling her eyes and muttering, "Yes, because she's never seen snow before."

"Émi, Émi," says Ava, swirling round. "Can I show you a game?"

I adjust my pack on my shoulder and say, "Not really Ava, we need to—"

"It will only take one minute." Her eyes beg. "I promise."

I shrug at the others, and rest my pack on the ground. Ava puts hers beside mine and pulls me to her, then tells me to lie down. When I hesitate, she laughs.

"Go on..." she says, tugging me down.

I lie down. She lies beside me, but leaves a large space between us and stretches out her arms. I do the same. "Like this," she says, moving her arms up and down in the snow. I copy her and, when we stand, she hugs me to her side and says, "See? We made Watchers, from the snow!"

She's right, our bodies and arms have carved Watcher-shaped silhouettes.

"You know what would be fun?" Ava says, to Garrett. "If you do it, too! Then it will be really a Watcher!"

"I'm sorry," Kole interrupts. "Enough, now. We need to go."

Ava's smile hardens. "Okay," she mutters, making a scene of struggling with her pack. Garrett helps her, telling her it's a bit too heavy for such a trek. She blinks back at him. "I know, I was silly bringing so much. Maybe, would you...?"

Garrett blushes, then fumbles with the pack, trying to figure out how to carry two at once. "Of course, I'll take it for a bit."

Alyssa loses her temper. "No. Absolutely not. This is ridiculous." She snatches Ava's pack. "Garrett has his own things to carry. If you can't manage it, you'll have to take some things out."

Ava pouts. "But I can't. I need them."

"Right then," says Alyssa, marching towards the edge of the rock face. "Your choice." And she throws Ava's pack over the edge.

Ava cries out and rushes over. "No, no, no, no." She is crying. Her pack is gone.

Garrett rushes to Ava to try and calm her, but she pushes him off and rounds on Alyssa. "My things!"

Ava's eyes are full of fury. She is shaking. Then, she screams. She holds her hands out and, for the first time, I realise how terrified the Cadets must have been when they saw me attack Falk. Sparks stream from her fingers, forming a fireball, bigger and brighter than anything I could conjure. Tsam pulls Alyssa back and I start to reach for Ava but she raises the fireball in the air, aiming it at Alyssa.

Garrett and I shout, "Ava, no!"

At the last moment, she swivels round and hurls it at the mountainside. It speeds through the air, burning orange, until we can't see it any more. I release my breath, but I'm shaking. Then I see Tsam's face drain of colour.

"We have to fly," he whispers.

Alyssa says, "We can't, Tsam. The air's too thin..."

But he's not listening. He points. "We have to fly."

Alyssa's hand flies to her mouth. And then I hear it. The distant rumbling.

An avalanche.

We can't move quickly enough. Tsam shouts at us all to leave our packs, then tells Alyssa to take me. He wraps his arms around Kole's waist.

"I'm too heavy," protests Kole but Tsam shakes his head and braces himself to fly.

Ava is still trembling, her limbs stiff, her lips thin and pinched. Garrett gently tells her he's going to fly her to safety and she lets him take hold of her but she's rigid and uncooperative.

The snow is hurtling towards us, like a violent, fast-moving cloud. Tsam manages to take flight but he's struggling to hold on to Kole, who is bigger and heavier than he is. Gripping me tightly, Alyssa propels us up beside them. The avalanche is almost on us, but Garrett is struggling with Ava's dead weight. Just seconds before the thundering carpet of snow hits, he gives a final heave and launches himself into the air.

We are safe, but the force of the avalanche rips through the atmosphere and throws us off balance. The Watchers tumble into one another. They beat their wings ferociously, trying to right themselves, but Tsam cries out and starts falling.

As he hurtles towards the ground, he loses his grip on Kole.

The two of them tumble, and fall, and hit the snow with such force they are propelled down the mountain. They are on top of it, and beneath it, and on top of it again, faster and faster, as they travel further and further away from us. I am screaming, Alyssa is holding on to me, flying after them, I can't see Garrett and Ava.

———

We land awkwardly at the bottom of a ravine and Alyssa releases me. The avalanche has come to a halt, but we can't see Tsam and Kole. I am frantic, my heart is pounding.

Alyssa is trying not to cry, muttering to herself, "Where are they? Where are they?"

When Garrett and Ava lands behind us, I think Alyssa is going to grab Ava and throttle her. But she doesn't – she runs to her brother and lets him embrace her.

"It's alright, Lyss," I hear him whisper.

She straightens herself. "Where are they? Did you see? Where did they go?"

Garrett shakes his head. Ava still isn't speaking. Then I hear something.

"Shush," I tell the others, holding up a hand.

There it is again.

I follow the sound, wading through the snow, and when I see them I don't even try to hold back my tears. They are staggering towards us, holding each other up. I can't get to them quick enough and, when I do, I don't know who to check first. My fingers flutter over Kole's arm but he steps away as Tsam hugs me to him.

"You're alright?" I ask.

"I'm alright," he says. "A bit battered, but alive."

Kole is rubbing his thigh. Something has sliced an angry

gaping wound across it but we have no medical supplies – they were in his pack.

"On the bright side," says Garrett, puncturing our panic, "we've reached the bottom quicker than we expected." He pauses and looks around, unsure whether he's overstepped the mark, whether it's too soon for jokes, but Tsam thumps him on the shoulder and grins. "Always find the silver lining, don't you?"

They hug and all five of us laugh, not heartily, but with the exhilaration of having nearly died and managing not to.

There is no time to rest, and no way the Watchers can carry us any further, so we begin to trudge in the direction of the foothills, hoping to reach the horses by nightfall. Just as the sun is beginning to dip under the horizon, we see the tree where we left them. Except, they're not there. Tsam checks his compass and tells us this was definitely the spot, but they must have wandered off, and any elation we felt at surviving the avalanche quickly fades with the knowledge that our trek back to Tarynne will take twice as long without them.

Alyssa and I gather firewood, while Kole and Tsam rest, and Garrett fusses around Ava. She is still silent, staring into the distance as if she's vanished from herself.

We having nothing to eat, just water and a handful of oats Garrett had been storing in his pocket. We have no medicine either, and the gash on Kole's leg is beginning to worry me. Noticing me looking at it, he beckons me over and asks if I'll help him dress it.

"There are some dark green weeds by the stream," he says. "They're not as strong as lilac weed but they're from the same family."

I nod. "I'll fetch them, wait there."

When I return, Kole has torn two pieces of fabric from his cloak. I soak one piece with water from the fire and use it to clean the wound. Then I crush the green weeds as best I can and smear them onto his skin, binding them with the second piece of cloth.

"Thank you," he says, meeting my eyes and keeping them a little longer than usual.

When I return to the others, I realise Tsam has been watching me and it makes me blush. Feeling guilty, and not sure why, I ask him if he needs any cuts attending to. He tells me he's alright, but gestures to Ava.

"I'm not sure she is, though. She hasn't said a word since—"

"Since she nearly killed us," Alyssa finishes for him.

Garrett looks over then, from his spot next to Ava, and strides across to us. He crouches down in front of Alyssa and takes her hands in his.

"Now, you listen to me, Alyssa Minik. What you did – throwing away her things. It wasn't right."

Alyssa flinches.

"It was unkind, and unnecessary and you nearly got us all killed."

There's a sharp intake of breath from Alyssa and her eyes burn. "Me?"

"Yes. You. She's different from what we expected, but perhaps we could try and have a little empathy." He's looking at me now. "Émi, your life in Nhatu wasn't easy but at least you had people. Ava had no one up there. We don't know how long Søyen's been dead. She could have been alone for years."

"You don't know that," says Alyssa.

"No," says Garrett, "but I know it's not my place to judge her because she's different from us." Then he stands up. "You need to apologise to her, Alyssa." And he walks away.

When we settle down for the night, Ava is the first to fall

asleep but I'm not far behind her. I don't know how long I've been sleeping, or how close to morning it is, when her scream wakes me. She is crouched with her knees tucked under her chin, rocking backwards and forwards. Garrett is trying to get her to look at him, but she keeps pushing him away, so I try. "Ava," I say, gently, stroking the only bit of skin on her arm that isn't covered by either glove or tunic. "It's alright. We're all okay. No one was hurt."

When I say that, she lifts her head, tears streaming down her thin cheeks. She pulls me close, with such urgency that I almost topple over.

"He tried to kill me," she whispers, looking past me at Tsam. "He doesn't want me here. He hates me. He thinks I'm dangerous."

"Ava, what do you mean? What happened?"

Gripping my arm, she hisses. "He tried to kill me. Smother me in my sleep."

I look back at Tsam, who shakes his head at me, eyes wide and alarmed.

"Ava," I say, "Tsam wouldn't hurt you, he's our friend. You must have had a bad dream."

Quivering, Ava looks down at her hands, then at Tsam, then me. I sit down beside her and let her rest her head on my shoulder, patting her oily hair.

"Shhhh now," I tell her. "No one's going to hurt you. We're here to look after you."

Ava stiffens, then lets out a sob, and collapses into me. I hold her, whispering *shhhh, it's alright* and humming the melody Ma used to hum when I was small and unwell. It seems to soothe her and, eventually, she curls back into sleep. Afraid to move for fear of waking her, I beckon Tsam over and he crouches beside me.

"Ém," he whispers, "I have no idea..."

"It's fine," I say, shaking my head because it's ridiculous that he'd think for even one second I'd believe he would hurt Ava. "I just think we need to be careful with her. Gentle, like Garrett said."

Tsam nods, squeezes my arm, then retreats before Ava wakes.

TWENTY

The next morning, Alyssa's embarrassment at being told off by her brother still burns in her face.

"I've never seen him like that," I say to her, as we stomp out the fire and drink the last of our water.

She lowers her head. "He's right. I shouldn't have done that. The way she was last night. She's fragile."

I nod.

"Something must have happened to her to make her like this," says Alyssa.

"Maybe the things in her pack were all she had of her father's," I offer, thinking of the notebook that I still carry.

Alyssa nods and I watch from a distance as she goes to apologise to Ava. Then it's time to leave.

Back when we were travelling with the horses, we crossed the plains between Tarynne and the mountains in no more than ten hours. But without them our journey takes much longer, and we are forced to continue walking into the night. There is nowhere to shelter and once the sun dips below the horizon, it turns bitterly cold.

Ava is huddled at the back of the group beside Garrett, shivering despite the fact that she should be more used to the cold. She worries endlessly with the scarf at her face – patting it, pulling it and retying it. And she won't look at Tsam. When he speaks, she turns away as if she can't bear to be reminded he exists. Tsam takes this deeply personally. I tell him she's just confused but I can see that my words don't help.

Kole is struggling too. My nursing has done little to fix his wounded leg and he is limping badly. It is strange to see him injured. He looks vulnerable. I haven't forgotten the unease I felt when we first met, but when he stumbles and I catch him, allowing him to lean on my shoulder, I feel the tension shrink.

We have been walking through the plains without a rest for almost two whole days, when we reach a collection of rocky caves and decide to stop. The caves obscure our view of the horizon but the sky above is heavy and grey. It looks as though a rainstorm is brewing but Kole says that's impossible – this is the dry season. We peer up at the sky, shielding our eyes. The darkness is unnatural, and we still can't agree what is causing it, so Garrett offers to fly ahead and find out.

At first, his movements are slow, leisurely almost. Then, he turns back. He seems to be flying more quickly now and I exchange a worried glance with Alyssa. Within moments, Garrett is hurtling towards the ground beside us.

Alyssa grabs my arm. "He's coming down too fast."

We move to catch him but Garrett tumbles, rolling over and over and wrapping himself in his wings to shield his body from the jagged ground.

Alyssa stoops over him. "What happened? Are you alright?" She checks him frantically from head to toe, looking for wounds, but he sits up and takes hold of her arms. "I'm fine, Lyss." Then he looks at Kole.

Kole's eyes flicker from Garrett up towards the horizon and back again. I watch him take a deep breath and straighten his shoulders.

"Kole, I'm sorry." Garrett shakes his head.

"What have you seen?"

"It's smoke... so much smoke. I think Tarynne is burning."

Kole wavers for a moment, then starts running. I call after him and when he doesn't reply I follow him. Ava shouts at me to wait but I ignore her. Beyond the caves, the entire skyline has turned black and the milky limestone of the Second City is barely visible. Kole stands, feet apart, hands stretched out, his palms pressed together as if he is praying. As I approach, he buckles onto the ground. I kneel beside him and slip an arm around his shoulders. I want to tell him that it might not be as bad as it looks but there is so much smoke, more than there was in Abilene, much more.

Kole leans in to me, almost imperceptibly, but when we hear the others approaching he stands and brushes himself down. "We need to move," he says. "Quickly."

Alyssa bites her lip. "Kole, I don't think we can. It's almost sunset."

"We kept walking last night, why not tonight?" I ask, urgently.

"There are jackyls here, Émi. They're nocturnal. If we're out there, exposed—"

Kole doesn't wait for Alyssa to finish. "Then you stay," he says, striding on. It's clear he has no intention of waiting for a group decision.

No one else moves. Alyssa turns to Tsam. "Tsam, we can't."

Tsam looks at me, then nods slowly. "Alyssa's right."

Speechless, I rub my temples. Tsam puts his hand on me but I shake him off. "You're serious? You're going to bunk down and get a good night's sleep whilst his home burns to the ground? What if it was Abilene? Would we be having the same conversation?"

Calmly, Tsam says, "Yes, we would. Sometimes it's necessary to put logic above emotion."

He sounds like a different person, someone I don't recognise. In the distance, Kole's silhouette is fading and I can't wait any longer. "Fine. You stay, but I'm not."

When I catch up with him, Kole is walking as quickly as he can but his face is etched with pain. We walk past sunset and into the night, where the light of the moon stretches our shadows into elongated desperate versions of ourselves. As we draw closer to Tarynne, it looks as if the sun is starting to rise, but it can't be, it's too early. I shudder as I realise that the glow comes from the city, engulfed in flames. I daren't look at Kole but, more than once, I have to steady him when he stumbles.

Just before sunrise, a breeze drifts over the plains, carrying the unmistakable sound of the elephants. Icy fingers creep up my body. "They sound like they're..."

"Crying," Kole finishes. "They're crying."

We follow the sound all the way to the bathing pool. Here, every bush, tree and blade of grass is scorched or flickering with orange flames – it looks as though the worst of the fire has raged through here already, but still the flames don't die.

Inside their caves, the elephants are calling. Kole dives into the pool and swims to the other side where men, women and children are running frantically to and from the water's edge, filling up their buckets and hopelessly trying to drench flames that refuse to go out. By the water, a boy of ten or eleven is nursing a young elephant, whispering gently in its ear and smearing a thick brown paste into a burn on its flank. Kole and I each grab an empty bucket and take a place in the line to fill them, but the flames do not abate.

An hour later, the fire towers over our heads. My eyes are watering and my throat constricts with every breath of smoke that I inhale. The anguished noises from inside the caves are dying down, and the beads of sweat and tears on Kole's face bleed together as he calls out to Maya, desperate for a reply. Our faces are black with smoke and my arms feel like they are made of lead. When I stop to pour a jug of cold water over my head, someone taps me on the shoulder.

"I have an idea," says a voice.

It is Ava.

Garrett, Alyssa and Tsam are standing behind her. They must have carried Ava all the way here to catch up with us. "We can both make fire, can't we, Émi?" she says.

"Yes, but—"

"Then maybe we can put fire out, too."

I shake my head, too tired to understand what she's saying. "Put it out? How?"

"Follow me," she says, unwinding her scarf from around her face and slipping her hand into mine.

Ava and I walk towards the flames at the entrance to the cave, where they are at their fiercest. Kole spots us and pulls at a neighbour to stand back. Soon, everyone is lowering their buckets and staring at us.

Now, Ava is different. She's not the monster on the mountain, or the scared little girl who needed me to hold her. Even her voice is more measured. She turns to me and takes both of my hands in hers. "When Father first taught me, he told me to use my emotions. Anger makes fire. Sadness can stop it. Understand?"

I think so. I tell her I'll try, even though I'm shaking, and the two of us step forwards, bringing ourselves as close to the flames as we dare. The heat licks our faces. I feel the sparks bubbling inside me and I try to make them cooler, bluer, like ice, like water. Ava takes my hand and together we breathe deeply. I think of the day my father was taken away, I think of Ma, of Nor and of Kole's face when he saw the smoke, then suddenly my memories merge with Ava's and I see Søyen reading her a bedtime story. I see his body at the bottom of the ravine, a shadowy figure standing over her, embracing her, then waving goodbye. We open our eyes and reach our intertwined hands towards the flames. I pull the melancholy out of myself and channel it into the fire. I imagine it as a pale blue light, sweeping over the flames, pushing them back down into the ground... and it works. The flames sputter and begin to fade.

"They're putting them out!" a voice cries. I hear Kole order whoever it is to be quiet and everything becomes still. The world slides away. There's nothing but me, Ava and waves of despair. Soon, the fire is nothing more than flickering embers, and the Taman are able to pick their way across them into the caves. From the limestone steps, Healers appear with baskets of bottles, creams and plants.

Our work is done and we lower our hands, unlinking our fingers. Tsam herds Ava and I away from the caves. We are both shaking. He tries to make me sit down, but I shrug him off and go to find Kole. Inside the caves, a scene of quiet chaos is unfolding. Healers and Taman kneel before elephants, smothering them with remedies whilst they chant.

I find Kole and Maya somewhere towards the back. Maya looks unharmed but she is bucking from foot to foot and her eyes are darting from Kole to the entrance. Kole is speaking smoothly, trying to calm her, but when I approach he stops.

"She's lost Niri," he explains. "He was by the pool when the fire started."

I step forward and Kole reaches out to stop me. "Careful."

I approach more slowly. "Maya? I saw a calf outside, his leg was injured. It could have been Niri but I'm not sure."

Maya's eyelashes flutter. She looks at Kole and he tells her, "Okay, we'll go and see."

He walks beside her out of the cave, stroking the tip of her trunk, but when we are outside and she sees the calf, Maya releases an ear-splitting cry and charges towards him. Niri tries to stand and stumbles, unsteady on his injured back leg.

"Steady, Niri," says the boy guarding him. "Let her come to you."

The calf stops, swaying his trunk from side to side as his mother approaches. When Maya reaches him, she sweeps her trunk over his body from head to foot, then sniffs at the injured leg, before pulling him close and rocking him against her.

Tears prick the corners of my eyes but before I can let myself cry Tsam calls me to where he and Alyssa are standing. A short distance away, Ava is sitting with Garrett. He has his arm around her as she wipes away tears.

"Is she okay?" I ask Alyssa.

Alyssa looks over at her brother and my sister. "Garrett will look after her," she says. "Don't worry."

Tsam smiles at me and rests his hand on my arm. "Well done. You were amazing."

I smile back but I'm finding it hard to forgive his unwillingness to walk through the night. Tsam scuffs his foot and asks me to fetch Kole. "We need him to gather his Elders. We need to know if this was Mahg."

Kole is reluctant to leave Maya but, eventually, I pry him

away. We pass clusters of Taman and Healers tending to the elephants but the rest of Tarynne is unscathed by the fire; it looks as though the elephants were the target. The thought hurls a knot of nausea up into my mouth. It was deliberate. Calculated. Trapping them there. Leaving them to burn.

The Tarynnese council chambers are halfway up the pinnacle. A circular pool has been carved into the floor, in the centre of which a fountain bubbles gently. The northern side of the room is completely open, as if someone forgot to build a wall there, and remnants of smoke give the view a hazy greyish tint that is dizzying to look at.

Ava has re-wrapped her face in her scarf and is picking at the singed edge of her left glove. Garrett sits beside her and Alyssa lingers by the back wall.

The oldest of Tarynne's Elders, a woman less youthful than Hitra but with a similar smoothness to her voice, thanks Ava and I. She has tears in her eyes as she grips our hands.

"The girls made of stone," she whispers. "Thank you. Thank you..."

"Can you tell us what happened?" I ask.

The woman shakes her head. "The first we knew of the trouble was when the elephants started calling. We didn't see who started it. They didn't come inside the pinnacle. It was the elephants they were trying to hurt."

"Maybe it was just a show of force," says a man with a birthmark on his collarbone. "As in Abilene?"

"No," says Kole. "This was designed to hurt."

No one speaks, until Alyssa steps forward and says, "If this was Mahg, surely he wouldn't stop at the elephants. It doesn't make sense."

Garrett agrees. "And if there were others he was trying to hurt..." He glances around at me, Alyssa and the rest of our group. He means us. "Even if someone told him we'd passed through here, we were long gone. If he was hoping we'd return, wouldn't he have waited in the shadows until we were here?"

"Unless he wanted to draw us here," I say, remembering how we chased the smoke. "Perhaps this is exactly what Mahg wanted us to do."

The woman bristles and pats at her crop of silver hair. "There's not a living soul in Tarynne who would betray your visit. Not a single one."

Alyssa mutters, "Apart from Mahg's mother..." Kole bangs his fist on the edge of the pool so hard that the ripples are almost waves, rounding on her.

"Wait," I whisper, and then, louder, "Wait!" Everyone stares at me. "His mother...?"

Kole glares at me.

"No," I tell him. "Silvana, where is she? Has anyone checked on her? There's only one reason Mahg would come here..."

Kole is already rising to his feet. "... to get information from her."

"No, surely not..." stutters the woman with grey hair. But I can't respond. I don't have time. The weight in my stomach tells me she's wrong.

TWENTY-ONE

Silvana's door chimes but doesn't open when we press the symbol, so we are forced to go through Kole's dwelling and out onto his veranda. Her archway is dark and silent. Kole pauses. I tell him I'll go first and he doesn't object.

The living room is empty. In the kitchen, an empty mug sits alone in the basin. We pause at the entrance to Silvana's bedroom, then I push open the door.

Silvana is lying on the bed, her milky eyes staring at the ceiling. A sandal hangs from her right foot, suspended by a strap that has caught on her big toe. A chain of fingerprint-sized bruises circle her throat. She is not breathing.

Wordlessly, Kole stands above her. He puts her shoe back on her foot and folds her arms across her chest. Something falls from her hands – the pendant with the cobalt blue amulet, the one that carried Søyen's message. Kole picks it up and gives it to me. I shake my head but he says, "She would want you to have it."

Neither of us wants to leave her but Kole says he must tell the Elders what has happened. I return to his dwelling without him. Below, at the bathing pool, the cleansing ritual should be taking place but the plains are empty. Inside, Tsam is stalking up and down, chewing his bottom lip.

"Silvana?" he asks as soon as he sees me.

I shake my head. "Dead. Strangled." There's nothing more to be said.

He lets out a sigh and sits down, hard, on the cushions by the fireplace. Ava makes a small mewing sound and Alyssa punches the wall in frustration. Only Garrett makes no sound. He lingers in the middle of the room, shaking his head.

When Kole returns, he tells us Hitra is here, Sayah too. "They want to see you, Émi, and Ava."

"Now?" I ask, feeling so exhausted I don't even know how I will stand upright.

"In the morning. There will be a burial for the ones we lost. After that."

I don't ask how many elephants are gone. I can't. In fact, I can barely move. My limbs ache and there's a throbbing in my temples, as if a chunk of me died with the flames I put out. Taking in my appearance, Tsam says we should all try to get some sleep. It's been a long time since we last closed our eyes and our bodies are on the verge of collapse.

Kole is the only one who doesn't pretend to bed down. All through the night, I hear him pacing from the veranda to the kitchen to the living room. At first light, I wrap a blanket around my shoulders and find him down by the lake. He is tinged with sooty residue and an angry burn is emerging from his tattered vest, just below his collarbone.

I sit down beside him and he starts to talk. "Without you, I could have lost Maya," he murmurs. "We could have lost all of them. I owe you—"

"Kole..." My hand hovers over his, not quite touching. "You don't owe me anything."

"The burials will begin soon," he whispers, shifting closer.

The movement and the closeness of his hand make my skin prickle. I find myself wishing I could fold into him. But then I tell myself it is only because I'm exhausted and upset and I pull away.

Back at Kole's apartment, Tsam is waiting for us on the veranda. When he greets us, I feel as if he can see inside my thoughts and a clot of guilt lodges in my belly.

Before we go inside, Tsam says, "I think you need to talk to Ava, she's... Well, you'll see."

In the living room, I do see. Ava is pacing up and down, pulling at her gloves as if she can't get them to reach high enough up her arms and clutching her scarf so it covers her mouth and nose. I take a deep, calming breath. Her behaviour is starting to remind me of my mother and I know I don't have a lot of patience for it.

When I ask what's happened, Garrett confesses. "I suggested she take off the gloves, change her scarf..." he says apologetically. In truth, I'd have done the same. They're dirty and frayed, completely unnecessary now we are past the cold of the mountains.

When Ava was beside me yesterday, teaching me, holding my hand, she was a different person – calm, knowledgeable, impressive. But now she is a child again, troubled and erratic. I don't try to reason with her, just tell her Garrett is sorry and that she doesn't have to remove her scarf or gloves if she doesn't want to.

She looks at me like a rabbit in a snare. "You promise, Émi?" she whispers. "You promise you won't make me?"

I glance around at the others, disturbed by her fear. Then I take hold of her shoulders. "I promise."

"Thank you," she says, sighing. "Thank you..."

After that, Ava changes her clothes but keeps her grubby accessories. I change too, and so do the others. Then we wait for the bell that will start the burials. Ava still can't bring herself to look at Tsam and I'm standing self-consciously between them when Silvana's pendant begins to glow. It hangs just beneath the necklace Nor gave me, heavier and colder, and I'm stroking it absent-mindedly when Ava gasps and points to my throat. The instant she does, the pendant becomes too hot to bear and I fumble to unclasp it. It is so hot that I drop it and, when it hits the ground, beams of brilliant white light spurt from its surface. I stagger back, holding on to Ava as a moving image is projected onto the wall in front of us.

We are watching Silvana. She is in her room. She walks slowly backwards, retreating from something or someone. Her eyes are wide and her face is pale. When she bumps into the side of her bed, trapped, she holds out her arms.

"My love," she whispers. "It's not too late to end this. You can stop. You can come home."

Despite years of imagining him for my posters, despite knowing he has feathers as black as coal and sharp burning eyes, when Mahg speaks my blood runs cold.

"Mother..." he says, as though the word is an obscenity. Silvana does not waver. She stands still, keeping her arms outstretched as if she believes that at any moment, her son might fall into them and beg forgiveness.

"Please..." she says.

Mahg stops beside her, taller, sharper, harder. He laughs. The sound is guttural and hacking. He sits on the bed and pats the mattress, inviting his mother to sit beside him. Silvana does as he suggests and clasps her hands in her lap. They are trembling.

For a fractured, quivering moment neither of them speaks. Then Mahg sighs and shakes his head. His hair is long, as slick as tar, pulled into a knot that stretches his skin tight over his jagged cheekbones.

"I know you have been keeping something from me," he says. "I know the Watchers didn't divide the stone into four. I know there was a fifth piece, and I know what it became."

Silvana's face remains impossibly still, her eyes fixed ahead.

Mahg leans closer, so close to her ear that her hair shivers when he whispers.

"I know Søyen told you where he took his girls."

Silvana turns to him and starts to protest but Mahg puts his long dirty fingers over her mouth. His nails are like talons. They scratch her cheek.

"Ah, ah... I'm talking," he scolds. "It was really very clever to send them to my islands – to hide them in plain sight. Risky, but clever. And I never would have known..."

His islands? The Spectre must have told him Kole's story... I look at Kole but his gaze is fixed on Mahg, his jaw set. I find myself praying that Silvana holds her nerve – that she doesn't betray what she knows.

"I'd like to tell you I figured it out on my own, but it was pure luck." He laughs again. "They were in the orphanage, of all places! One of them escaped. But she has been captured and will soon be returned to me." He pauses, and takes his hand away to rub at his chin. "I still need to weed out the other one though..."

Silvana's eyes dart across Mahg's face. "Why?" she asks.

Mahg doesn't answer. He is enjoying telling his story. "My overseers are rounding up the orphans – just the girls. When the runaway is returned, I will use her to lure out her sister."

Trying to deter him now, Silvana says, "What if she won't give herself up? What if she doesn't reveal herself? Mahg, this will not—"

Mahg suddenly stands and turns his back on Silvana. "If the

second girl doesn't reveal herself, I will extinguish them all. The sister, too. I'd prefer them to fight with me rather than defy me, but..."

Silvana's fingers are interlocked so tightly that her knuckles are turning white. She can no longer look at her son. She knows there is no runaway. No special orphan who will be tricked into confessing.

"All the girls?" she whispers. "You'll kill all..."

Mahg turns back around. He is smiling but it hardens into a grimace. "That's enough now, Mother. I'm not here to be pleaded with. I'm here to tie up my one remaining loose end. The very last thing that chains me to a life I want to forget." He moves closer to her. "To a time when I was weak and undervalued..." His hands settle around his mother's throat. Silvana closes her eyes. Her face reddens. She gasps for air and Mahg leans in. "There is just one more thing you should know," he whispers. "My father's death? It wasn't an accident."

Silvana's eyes spring open and she begins to struggle.

"I cut off his wings. Thrust a blade into his heart. Watched him die..."

She grabs at his fingers, trying to pry them from her neck but he towers over her, his hands tightening.

"He thought he could save me, too. But he was wrong. You were both wrong. So sanctimonious, so naive. You didn't believe I could be great. You didn't nurture my talents."

Silvana is twitching. Her mouth gapes.

"But I am great, Mother, and when I have the stone – all of it – I will rule The Four Cities. There will be fire and smoke! Abilene will fall! They will all fall!" Mahg is shouting now. He presses down on Silvana's throat, and spreads his wings until the room is engulfed by his blackness.

I look away. The sound of Silvana's last choking breath seeps into my bones and I fold onto the floor. Ava places her hand on my shoulder. The others lower their gazes and stare at the ground. Kole has turned his back.

"It's over," Ava whispers.

When I look up, the wall has gone back to being a wall. Kole is so still that I can barely see him breathing.

Alyssa flicks a finger across her cheek, wiping away a tear. "She was very brave."

"And clever," says Ava. "She recorded the message for us, didn't she?"

Tsam nods. "Yes. So we can't waste it."

"Waste what?" I ask, throbbing with a sickening mixture of anger and despair.

"The opportunity," he replies. "Mahg thinks you and Ava are on the Islands. So we know we can make it safely back to Abilene. We know we have time..."

"Back to Abilene?" I say, looking from him to Alyssa.

Tsam tenses his muscles. "Yes."

"But he's going to kill those girls. There is no overseer, no runaway. No one to use as leverage, no one to come forward and reveal themselves. They'll die – all of them – if we don't help."

"It isn't our place to help," says Tsam.

Ava helps me to my feet and slots her arm through mine.

"But we have to," she tells the others. Her words are thin and meek, as if she isn't really sure whether she's saying them out loud, but knowing she is on my side gives me strength.

"We. Are. Not. Leaving them," I hiss.

"The Elders will help them," says Alyssa. "If we tell them—"

"Alyssa, don't. Just don't." I turn back to Tsam, trying to soften my voice, to reason with him. "The Elders will say it's too big a risk. They'll leave those girls just like they left everyone in Nhatu to fester and die. You know they will, Tsam."

"I'm sorry, Émi. The answer is no."

I bring my face closer to his. "You don't control me. You don't tell me what I can and can't do. I'm going, with or without your help." We stare into each other's faces, neither of us willing to back down.

Finally, Garrett pulls at my shoulder. "Vote," he says, "we should vote."

"Fine," snarls Tsam, stepping back. "Those in favour of going to the Islands..."

I raise my hand instantly, Ava is slower but once she has voted Garrett does too.

"And in favour of going back to Abilene..."

Tsam and Alyssa lift their arms. Kole stands in the archway, silhouetted against the brightening dawn sky. "It is my lie that led to this. No more lives can be lost because of it. I am going to the Islands."

Tsam lowers his hand, juts his wings out, and back, and out again.

"Alright," he says eventually. "We'll go."

The first toll of the bell shifts us into motion. Tsam may have conceded, but he is certainly not a willing team member. It feels as though a chasm has opened up between us. I don't know how to cross it or how to pull him back to my side, so I try to focus on what needs to be done. We have no supplies. Our packs were lost in the avalanche, so all we have are the things in our pockets or on our belts. But there is no time to plot, or plan or even study our map. Kole says we must slip away straight after the burials because Hitra and Sayah will try to stop us if they discover what we're doing.

So by the twelfth toll of the bell we are already descending the steps to the bathing pool.

There are no graves – the deceased are laid out on the earth so that they can be kissed by the sun's warmth and by the grass and the wind. Ten elephants, Silvana and... my breath falters... and Bael. Tiny, smiling Bael who tussled with Niri and called me 'Miss'. He looks like a doll. It's as though he's playing a game. Surely at any moment, he'll open his eyes and jump to his feet, laughing. But he doesn't.

As the elephants emerge from the caves and form a circle around their dead, I feel myself wavering. I sense Kole moving a little closer to my side, almost as though he knows. But then he leaves me. He walks to Silvana and kneels beside her. Niri folds himself down beside Bael. Ten Taman join their ten absent friends, and someone starts to sing. It is not like the singing I'm used to hearing. It's not joyful. It is like grief has been given a voice of its own. The solemn notes vibrate off the limestone walls, filling the sky and our hearts.

Each body is washed. Gently, delicately. Kole strokes Silvana's arms and face with a square of damp white fabric. When he's finished, he rests it on her face. Niri is trying to do the same, but he's struggling. He is too small, too uncoordinated, and Maya looks like she is breaking with sadness for him. Kole helps him, in the end. He takes the cloth from the elephant's trunk and wipes Bael's hands, feet and cheeks. The singing continues and I feel like I am fracturing at my edges. I'm not sure I can stand to be here a moment longer; it hurts too much.

Then the ceremony ends. The Taman rise. Niri retreats to Maya's side, and the elephants lift their trunks into the air. The singing reaches its crescendo then fades away. The silence it leaves behind feels louder than any song. We stand for a long time, some praying, some crying. Then the bell rings again and the crowd melts away.

I find Hitra and Sayah. They are on the veranda with Tarynne's Elders, waiting for us to bring Ava to them. Before they can see us, we disappear into the sea of Taman and Healers at the steps and, instead of ascending them, we go west, quickly, past the caves.

We travel along the underside of the pinnacle under the cover of trees and shrubbery, heading north, away from Tarynne, away from Abilene. And towards Mahg.

TWENTY-TWO

We have stopped in a cluster of trees. There are still some hours left before sunset but we are exhausted and, with Tarynne and the Elders safely behind us, we agree to rest and get our bearings.

I am arranging some kindling to make a fire when I hear a shout from Kole: "What are you doing?"

I turn and see Maya lolloping towards us, swinging her trunk in Kole's direction. He runs to her and strokes her just beneath her shoulder.

"You shouldn't be here," he tells her, "it's dangerous."

Maya huffs.

"Alright, I won't argue with you," Kole replies. Then he notices Niri. "Maya, no. He can't..."

I walk over and crouch beside Niri. He looks terrified.

"Kole," I whisper, "he has no one else."

Kole breaks his eyes away from Maya and looks down at Niri. Bael died saving him from the fire. Niri still has his mother, but in a lot of ways he's an orphan. Just like Kole.

"Alright," Kole whispers, as though he's read my thoughts. "He can stay."

Lighting the fire and helping Garrett hollow out a chunk of wood to use as a pot, I feel like our group has splintered in half. Alyssa and Tsam are on one side of the fire, sitting next to each other and muttering over the map. Ava, Kole and I are on the other. Garrett is in the middle, trying to lighten the mood but, for the first time, failing miserably.

When Alyssa stalks off to try and find some plants we're able to eat, I follow her.

"I'm sorry. I know you didn't want to do this," I begin.

She shakes her head. "It's not you," she says. "I mean, it's not this. I'm—" She stops, as if she's not sure whether she can trust me. She looks around, then lowers her voice. "It's Ava."

"Ava?" Her behaviour has been troubling me too, but since we left the mountains it has slipped further and further from my mind.

Alyssa leans back against the nearest tree trunk. "Émi, what I'm about to say – it's going to sound... Well, mad. Like I've got something against her, but I'm just..." She looks at me, her eyes pleading. "He's my brother."

I move closer and put my hand on her shoulder, hoping she knows that I won't judge whatever it is she's about to tell me.

Alyssa smooths back her hair, looking suddenly vulnerable. "Garrett's so under her spell. He thinks she's acting the way she is because she's troubled. I've tried to see her the way he does. But I think it's more than that." She pauses, trying to read whether I'm going to defend my sister. "And I think, deep down, you feel it to."

I shift from one foot to the other. I should stick up for Ava, and yet...

"Go on," I tell her.

"There's a drug used by people on the Islands: Wrack. I've never seen it, just heard about it. Some years ago, the Watchers had awful trouble keeping it out of the outlying villages nearest the Islands. It's made from the seaweed on the black beaches, thick like tar. They drop it onto their palms and it dissolves into the skin, into the blood..."

I tilt my head at her. What does this have to do with Ava?

Even quieter now, so quietly I can barely hear her, Alyssa says, "When people have been using it a lot, their skin starts to turn black. First their hands, then everywhere." Alyssa waves her hands in my face. "The gloves, Émi. She won't take them off. Even out here, where it's swelteringly hot. She won't stop wearing the scarf either. And the way she was when I ditched her pack... as if she really needed whatever was in there." Alyssa shakes her head. "I don't know. Maybe I'm seeing things because I don't like her."

I look over my shoulder, half expecting Ava to jump out of the trees and accuse me of betraying her. It doesn't make sense, and yet... it does.

I take a deep breath. "Let's assume you're right. How would Ava have access to this stuff, if it's only found on the Islands?"

Alyssa shrugs. "I don't know. I hope I'm wrong. But if I'm not... Garrett can't see it, won't see it, even if it's right there in front of him. I can't let him get hurt, Émi."

She is frantic now, her hands clenching and unclenching. I promise her I'll keep an eye on Ava.

"And you'll try to see beneath the gloves?" she prompts. "Because that's the only way we'll know for sure."

"I'll try," I promise, giving her a hug even though I know she hates it.

Later, around the campfire, I reel back through my memories of Ava. I can see why Alyssa thinks Ava is hiding something, but an addiction to something only found on the Islands, when she hasn't left the mountains or spoken to a soul other than Søyen for nearly seventeen years? It's not possible.

I'm staring at Ava from across the fire, watching her fidget with her gloves, trying to think of a way to see what lies beneath them, but Tsam's sullen mood is distracting me. He has barely spoken to me since we left Tarynne and seems to be doing everything he can to avoid me. Now, he is sitting next to me but his body is stiff and unfriendly.

I nudge him in the ribs. "Cheer up, we're not dead yet," I say, waiting for him to smile, but instead he stands and prods a stick in the fire.

I'm still trying to understand exactly when Tsam got so very far away from me, when Alyssa catches my eye and nods at the other side of the campfire. I follow her gaze and notice that Ava is slipping away from us, into the undergrowth. Seconds later, Garrett follows her. Alyssa moves as though she's about to go after them but I hold her back.

"Let me."

Beyond the fire, the space between the trees is almost pitch black but the hum of Garrett's voice guides me through. Just beyond the trees, out in the open, Garrett and Ava have stopped. He is holding her hands..

"Ava, you can trust me," I hear him say. "I want to help."

There are tears in her eyes. A tightness tugs at my stomach and I feel guilty for thinking the worst of her. Alyssa is wrong. Ava is simply nervous, fragile, like my mother after my father was taken away. Garrett is the right person to help her; he is kind and good and happy. All the things she needs.

I'm about to turn away when Ava starts sobbing, loudly. Garrett rubs her shoulders and stoops, trying to encourage her to look at him but this only makes her sob even louder. Eventually, she pushes him away.

"You can't help me!" she cries.

A smile dances across Garrett's lips. "Of course I can. Nothing can be that bad..."

Ava stares wildly at him for a moment, then grabs at her scarf and pulls it from her face, ripping her gloves from her hands and throwing them to the ground too. She holds her palms out, shaking them at Garrett as if there's something stuck to them.

"Look at me!"

Garrett's smile collapses. He seems rooted to the spot, unable to move. Ava's hair is much darker than I remember, longer and greasier. But it isn't her hair that disturbs me, it's her hands. They are black, gnarled and wizened as if they belong to a person who is long dead. The blackness stretches up past her wrists, almost to her elbows.

Ava steps a little closer to Garrett. I think she's going to pick up the scarf, but instead she scoops her hair back and exposes her neck. The blackness is there too, creeping up towards her mouth and wrapping itself around her throat. The whites have disappeared from her eyes, so that they seem like nothing more than two deep round holes in her face, as if I'd see right through to her skull if I looked long enough.

Garrett gulps and lowers his eyes to the ground. Ava's face contorts with shame. Tears are streaming down her cheeks and her hands are trembling. Garrett looks up then and rushes towards her, wrapping her in his wings.

"It's alright, everything will be alright," I hear him murmur. "I'll help you. We all will." He is facing me now. For a brief moment, I think that his eyes lock on mine so I duck back into the shadow.

I am planning to run to Alyssa, tell her she's right and ask her what to do, when Garrett makes a gurgling sound. His wings droop and he stumbles backwards. His pupils are unnaturally wide. He slumps forward. A trickle of deep red blood escapes from the corner of his mouth and runs down his chin.

I feel myself swaying and bite down hard on the scream that's trying to escape, slamming my hands over my mouth and forcing myself not to look away.

Ava pushes herself free from Garrett's slumped embrace and he falls to the ground. As he does, someone appears behind him. My eyes are so blurred with tears that I can't see who it is. But then I blink. And there he is, just as he was in Silvana's vision. Tall. Taller even than Kole. And angular. His movements are slow and controlled, as if he's floating above the ground. His black wings are folded flat against his back and his lips are twisted into a smile that's almost a growl. Ava steps back and lowers her head. She doesn't look afraid. Mahg doesn't acknowledge her, just stoops down and kicks Garrett over onto his stomach.

In the middle of his back, the hilt of Mahg's dagger is barely visible between his snow-white feathers. Mahg pulls his weapon free. He raises it up to his face, slides his finger across the blood-stained blade and licks its tip. My stomach lurches up into my chest. Garrett's wings are red now. Blood red. Dead red.

Mahg moves closer to Ava. "Well done, my little flower," he drawls. "I know that was hard for you."

Shaking from head to toe, Ava scrambles to kneel at his feet, holding out her hands. "Please..."

Mahg takes a small brown bottle from a strap around his neck and tips it upside down, squeezing two drops of thick oily liquid onto each of her palms. It sizzles as it meets her skin and the dark veins on her neck begin to fade.

"Thank you, thank you," she whispers, her eyes closed, swaying slightly, no longer shaking. When Mahg pats her head and tucks the bottle and its strap out of reach, Ava tugs at his knees, "Just two? You said..."

"Be patient, my love. There will be more when we get home. Now, come. You've been brave but there is one more thing we need to do. Will you do this for me? This one last thing?" He tucks a finger under her chin as he talks to her, smoothing her hair with his other hand as he blinks slowly.

Ava nods, her eyes fixed on the brown bottle.

"Good girl, now give me your hand..."

I manage to hold down the stream of hot violent nausea until I'm just a few metres from our camp. Then, finally, I allow myself to retch into a bush. When I straighten up, my legs are quivering so badly I'm not sure I'll be able to walk, but I can hear the crackle of our campfire and I know I'm almost there.

Alyssa sees me first and rushes to my side. "Émi, what's happened? You're shaking." She glances past me, expecting to see her brother.

I try to speak but nothing comes out.

Alyssa's eyes flash. "Émi," she says. "Where's Garrett?"

I feel the nausea rising again and force a slow deep breath. I make myself meet her eyes. "Garrett... he's..."

"What, Émi?"

The words come out before I can stop them. "He's dead, Lyss."

Alyssa jolts backwards. Tsam has arrived beside us and asks what I'm talking about. Kole asks where Ava is. Maya and Niri shrink back into the trees. My ears are ringing and I feel like my head is being pushed under water. Just as think I'm going to pass out, Kole tells everyone to be quiet and makes me sit down.

"Émi, what happened?" He's holding my hand but I can't feel it. All I can see is Garrett's face and that trickle of blood.

I inhale and beg myself to hold it together. "Ava was crying.

Garrett was comforting her. Mahg came out of the shadows. He stabbed him. From behind. Garrett didn't have the chance to defend himself." I pause. I don't want to tell them about Ava but I know I have to. I tell them that Ava's skin was black and scaly, that the inky thick veins in her neck had been hidden by her scarf, that Mahg dropped black liquid in her palm and she begged him for more, that he must have been following us all along, that Ava must have lead us here on purpose. That she is on his side.

Alyssa's lips are so narrow they have almost disappeared. She was right about Ava.

My voice cracks. "She let Mahg..."

"Let him what?" Tsam asks me.

"He cut off her finger," I say quickly, so I don't have to absorb it. "So it would look like there was a struggle, like she was taken and Garrett died trying to save her."

Alyssa hugs herself with her wings, rocking as she stands, looking as if she might fall down.

"Did you check...?" She can't get the words out. "Are you sure he's..."

I think of Garrett's face, the blood. I remember turning his body over and holding my cheek next to his lips. Not a single breath. I wish I'd managed to comfort him. I wish he'd said a few last words that I could repeat to Alyssa. But, just like that, he was no longer there.

I expect Alyssa to bombard me with questions, to scream and kick and break things, but she becomes very quiet. She stands in front of me, mute, as though she has caved inwards. After a long, vibrating silence, Tsam takes her hands and guides her to a spot by the fire. She stares at it. She isn't crying but Tsam is. They stare together and don't move. I am with Kole, still trying to remember how to breathe and, now, there's no Garrett to sew us all back together.

"Where did they go?" Kole asks me.

"North, I think. He said they were going 'home'..."

Kole frowns and it looks almost painful. "I don't understand..." he says, under his breath. "Mahg thought you and Ava were among the orphans."

I shake my head. I can't line up the pieces, either. They don't fit.

"He knew her. She knew him. What we saw – everything he told Silvana. It must have just been for show." I remember how readily Ava agreed that we should go to the Islands and save the girls... "I thought she was on my side. But she tricked me."

Tsam looks up from the fire. His eyes flash and I can't tell if it's the reflection of the flames or his anger finding its way to the surface. "And you fell for it."

"I..."

"The gloves..." Alyssa whispers, covering her face with her hands and starting to sob.

"If you'd listened to me, Émi..." Tsam is shouting now. He is incensed, grief channelling itself into anger and seeping from his pores, burning me like acid. I haven't seen him like this before and normally I'd shout back but he's right.

I did this.

I pushed for us to go to the Islands, to save the girls. And now Tsam's best friend is dead. Alyssa's brother is dead. Garrett is dead. So, I let him shout at me. I let Tsam tell me we should have left Ava in the mountains, that she probably killed Søyen, her own father, that she's evil and all is lost. I let him say that he wishes he'd never laid eyes on me, that he should have left me to rot in Nhatu, that I probably don't feel any of this because...

"You're not even human!" he spits.

Finally, the fight goes from his eyes. He knows he has gone too far.

I'm not crying any more. I'm beginning to feel like the old me. The me who let Falk leer and humiliate. The me who said 'yes, sir' and 'no, sir' and pretended it was normal to be treated like an insignificance.

Yesterday, saving the elephants with my magick, I felt as though I could do anything. I believed I was made for something greater. I believed Ava and I could storm the Islands, rescue the orphans, defeat Mahg and free the people of Nhatu. Just like that. I was naive. I underestimated Mahg and overestimated myself.

I feel undone, but I can't show it.

I straighten my shoulders and calmly, as if he is merely an acquaintance, ask Tsam if he would like me to stay with Alyssa whilst he and Kole fetch Garrett's body.

I don't know whether Tsam can tell that he has broken us, whether he knows he has sliced through whatever was there and cast it aside. I don't look into his eyes long enough to find out. Instead, I go and sit beside Alyssa, and smother myself in her grief.

It doesn't take long for the boys to fetch Garrett back to us. They lower his body quickly to the ground, trying to stop Alyssa from seeing that his feathers are clotted with blood. But it's too late.

She walks over to him and reaches into her pocket, taking out something small and red. It's Garrett's harmonica. "I found it in the snow, after the avalanche. I was saving it for..." Her voice fractures. "I don't know what I was saving it for."

Kole and I stand beside Niri and Maya while Tsam and Alyssa stretch out their wings and kneel beside Garrett's body. Without making a sound, they reach their hands up to the sky then down to rest on Garrett's chest. They do this four times, then they fold his arms across his body and Alyssa tucks the harmonica into his left hand. Tsam sits quietly while Alyssa strokes her brother's pale cheek. The air is so still that when she finally speaks, her words echo through the air.

"What am I supposed to do, Garrett? You're my big brother. You..."

Tsam takes Alyssa's hand. He tries to speak but nothing comes out. Alyssa looks up at the sky, where dawn is preparing to break.

"We should fly him back to Tarynne," she says. "Hitra and Sayah may still be there. They need to know what's happened. They need to know Ava is with Mahg."

Tsam nods in agreement, but Alyssa doesn't look at him – she looks at me.

"Émi, you're not coming back with us, are you?" There's no anger or judgement in her voice. She's guessed what my plans are.

Tsam stiffens but doesn't turn to me. I feel Kole by my side and I know he'll carry on if I do.

"I don't understand any of this," I tell her. "But if it's all because of me, I have to put it right. I have to go on. I have to stop Mahg. And Ava."

TWENTY-THREE

Tsam and Alyssa are still crafting a stretcher from branches when Kole and I set off. He tries to send Maya and Niri back to Tarynne but they won't go and, secretly, I'm glad.

When I first left Nhatu, there were five of us, then six, now two: me and Kole. The one person I thought I'd distrust for the rest of my days is the only person who will help me. And Tsam, who was supposed to always be here, isn't.

Before we leave, Alyssa slips the map into my pocket. She can't quite bring herself to meet my eyes but her hand lingers on mine before she takes it away. I had expected her to despise me, but perhaps Tsam despises me enough for the both of them; he doesn't even look up to say goodbye.

Kole and I continue north, towards the Islands. I know this is what Mahg wants. Everything that's happened – the Spectre, Silvana's vision, the staging of Garrett's death... All of this was designed to propel me towards him.

What I still don't know is why. If he was following us all along, why wouldn't he have just attacked us? Why use Ava?

Perhaps Mahg's plan is just as he said – to lure out the second girl using the first. It's just that we got them the wrong way around. Ava is the first. We walk beneath the midday sun, across ragged brown landscape until we reach a pass that leads through a cluster of rocky hills. The hills are blocking the sky and the air turns cool. I shiver. Kole does too, but I'm not sure it's because he's cold. Maya has placed her trunk on his shoulder and she nuzzles his ear gently when he touches her hide.

He closes his eyes, then takes a deep breath. "We need to be quick. No stopping once we're in there. Just keep going until we're out the other side of the ravine." I try to ask why we shouldn't stop, but Kole is already striding ahead of me.

We are only a few paces into the pass when the clatter of falling rocks shatters my thoughts. A boulder smashes onto the ground in front of us, sending up a billow of dust. If we'd been any further along... I shudder and Maya stomps her feet. Her eyes are fixed on a detail in the rock face, up ahead. Niri instinctively shrinks back behind his mother.

"What is it?" I ask Kole. We can glimpse the route out of the pass, so I start walking again but Kole catches my arm. Maya is still watching something. She makes a huffing sound. She moves a few paces back, her ears twitching. I squint against the sun. It looks as though the rocks up ahead are moving. Kole reaches for his belt and, as he draws his weapon, I remember Garrett's stories about the Taman and how they fight, that Kole is the best of them...

Kole adopts a half-crouched position, holding his baton out in front, his other arm tensed. Maya is shaking her head. I want to ask Kole what's happening but, before I can speak, the shifting rocks change colour and morph into something larger. It's a creature, about half the size of Maya, with huge muscular shoulders and a jutting lower jaw, with teeth that protrude up towards its nose. Its eyes flash a brilliant shade of green and it dips its head in line with its neck, as it charges towards us

I want to inch towards Niri but I daren't move. It is a changeling. I drew them for my posters, roaming the ruins of The Four Cities beyond Nhatu. I didn't draw them like this, though. I didn't capture their bulk or their salivating jaws.

It is nearly upon us when, suddenly, it freezes on the spot and tilts its head to one side, examining us. Maya breaks ranks. She charges forward and stops inches away from the changeling's chomping mouth. Towering over it, Maya releases a cry so loud I think it will shake the entire hillside loose. The sound sends a shiver down my body but the changeling doesn't flinch. It simply tilts its head the other way, snarls and pounces right over Maya's head, hurling itself at Kole. Too late, Kole attempts to spring sideways and his baton flies from his hand.

The changeling claws at him, gnashing its teeth. The two of them are tumbling over one another and Kole tries to wrestle himself free – grabbing at its neck and chunks of its fur. Maya charges forwards but Kole and the changeling are tussling too fast and there's nothing she can do. She turns to me, her eyes pleading.

I look down at my hands. I hear Tsam telling me I'm not even human and I shake it off. *No. I'm not. I can do this!*

Even without Ava. Especially without Ava.

I stare at the changeling. I fix my eyes on its face and don't let go. Almost instantly, the fire shoots straight into my fingertips and the same tiny ball of energy that I conjured in the mountains springs into life. I don't hesitate. I lift my hand, palm out, as though I'm opening a door – and then I push.

The ball hurtles forwards, spinning, sparks flying. It strikes the changeling square in the side of its face. It releases an anguished roar and leaps backwards. Then its eyes are on me. I hold a ball of light in each of my hands now and, when the creature coils itself, ready to attack, I don't hesitate – I hurl them straight at its chest. It roars and keeps coming for me, so I hurl another. Now the changeling is on me, but it's not fighting me.

Its muscles slump. It stops moving. It's dead.

Its weight has knocked me to the ground, pressing on my chest and making it hard to breathe. I want to push it off but my arms are pinned at my sides.

Finally, Maya and Niri come to my rescue. Using their trunks, they roll the changeling off and help me to my feet.

Kole is covered in scratches. Brushing himself down, he tucks his weapon back into his belt and beckons for us to leave, quickly. I follow him but, inside, a whirlpool of emotion is gathering speed. At first, I feel giddy with pride – I conjured the sparks to save Kole's life. But I also killed. I took away a life, and I meant it.

I wait until we have exited the pass before I let the whirlpool drag me under, then I lean against a tree and try to anchor myself. Kole doesn't try to comfort me like Tsam would have, or ask if I'm alright. He just waits beside me until I'm able to look at him.

"I knew it was going to kill you. I had to..." I can't finish the sentence. "But what I did – using magick to hurt. How am I any different from...?"

Kole's eyes flicker across my face. He moves closer. "You are nothing like Mahg. Nothing."

I try to believe him but I think of the changeling lying in the dust and it makes my head swim. Solemnly, Kole finds my eyes and brings me back to him. "The first life is the hardest, Émi. But as long as you keep feeling it here..." He takes my hand and clasps it against my chest, "you'll be alright."

I feel like I've forgotten how to breathe, but for an entirely new reason. I step back, looking up at the branches of the tree, at the sky, at anything but his eyes. I'm blushing and knowing that I'm blushing makes me blush more.

This is not the time, Émi. Not even nearly the time.

Thankfully, Maya comes to my rescue. She snuffles Kole's cheek with her trunk and flaps her ears at him until he releases me from his stare.

Before I've really had chance to recover, we continue north. Kole is still having to bite through the pain from his avalanche injury, and we're both covered in scratches, burns and bruises that seem to multiply of their own accord.

I don't need to look at the map to know that if we kept on the same course we would come to Nhatu, but Kole says we should camp for the night. Eventually, we will start veering west, towards the Islands. It makes sense – the Islands are Mahg's home, and isn't that what he told Ava? That they were going home? But something in the back of my consciousness niggles at me. I'm not quite sure we're making the right decision.

Together, we have managed to make a fire and we're sitting side by side, too awake to sleep, when I ask Kole about his parents. It's a question I wouldn't have dared to ask before. But out here alone, in the dark, it feels easier somehow.

"Garrett told me they were killed when you were a boy," I prompt, "by a changeling?"

I expect Kole to offer me a one-word answer, or perhaps even none, but he starts to speak.

"They were looking for livitt flowers," he tells me. "There was a sick child. They were both Healers and they often took me with them when they went foraging. They felt it was important I learn healing as well as fighting. The changeling took us by surprise..." He pauses, looks at me then down at the blade of grass he's been twirling between his fingers. "I didn't try to help them. I hid."

"You were a boy, you couldn't have fought it," I say softly.

Kole nods, as if he knows I'm right. But I'm sure that knowledge doesn't make the memories any easier to live with.

"They weren't dead," he continues. "My father told me to take my mother back to Tarynne, so I carried her. I left her with the Healers and led a group of Taman and elephants to fetch my father. When we reached him, he was no longer alive. When we returned to Tarynne, my mother had joined him."

I blink fast and try not to let Kole see that my eyes are glistening with tears, but the image of him as a small boy – trekking through the desert with his mother in his arms, too late to save his father – breaks my heart. And it's how I feel; praying that I get back to my mother in time, that she won't already be dead when I reach her.

Kole's eyes meet mine, still dark but swimming with a rawness that grips my soul and shakes it loose. He slips an arm around my waist, pulling me into his warmth. I know I should break away. I know this isn't the right time. But it is. So when he presses his lips against mine, I let myself forget where we are and why we're here and I kiss him back.

Eventually, we pull apart. I trace the outline of his birthmark with the back of my fingers and Kole closes his eyes. Then he looks up at the stars and says we should try to sleep. I thought I would feel embarrassed, but I don't. Without asking, he lays down behind me and wraps me in his arms.

I am asleep within minutes.

It is not yet morning when I wake with Søyen's message to me ringing in my mind.

Just a piece of it... as long as they remain connected.

As long as the pieces of the Fire Stone remain connected... Why? Why this bit of the message and nothing else? Shifting gently in Kole's arms so that I don't wake him, I pull the map from my pocket and spread it out in front of me. The embers of the fire and the beginnings of a sunrise give me just enough light to see by. I place my index finger on the lake in Abilene, where the Fire Stone began, where Ava and I began. I stare at it, my eyes darting between the four cities, playing the words over and over.

As long as they remain connected...

I sit up, straight and quick. Behind me, Kole stirs, suddenly alert. When he sees that we're still alone, he relaxes and looks down at the map. I am looking at it too. I can't take my eyes away from it.

"I need something to draw with," I whisper.

Kole doesn't ask why, just reaches into the embers and finds me a charred piece of wood. When he hands it to me I lean over the map and start sketching – a dotted line between Abilene and Esyllt and one between Nhatu and Tarynne. They form an off-beat cross, like the arms of a crooked compass.

I look up at Kole. "The pieces of the Fire Stone had to remain connected, so it didn't lose its power," I say.

Kole nods. "If the connection is broken, everything the stone feeds – air, water, fire, life... They'll all start to fade. It's why each city had to have a piece of it."

I direct his eyes to the map and trace the lines I've drawn. "Right. And these are the connections, see?"

Kole nods again, still unsure what I'm trying to tell him. "They're called fire lines, Émi. Lines of magickal energy..."

"It doesn't matter what they're called. Just look at where we are – where we're heading."

Kole shifts closer, his shoulder leaning against mine. His eyes widen.

"We're heading right for the middle," I tell him. "The spot where the lines meet. That can't be a coincidence, can it?"

Kole looks at me, then the map, then me again.

"What if this was Mahg's plan from the beginning? To lead Ava and I to this place," I put my finger on the spot right in the middle of the map, "to where the fire lines converge. Think about it – the Spectre told us Mahg was searching for an orphan from the Islands, the attack on the Fledgling Ceremony made us leave without the Elders and, after the fire, Silvana's death led us away from Abilene because we thought we could save the orphans. Then, finally, Garrett's death in the woods was supposed make us believe that Ava had been kidnapped, to ensure we'd stay on track." I point once more at the centre of the fire lines. "Heading here."

Kole spins me around so he's facing me but before he can speak we're interrupted by Maya. She is holding her trunk up to the sky, pointing at something blurry and white. Two some-things: Tsam and Alyssa. They land in front of us. Tsam's eyes immediately graze over Kole and I, closer than normal, too close, and then down to his feet. I stand, awkwardly.

"What are you doing here?"

Alyssa looks at Tsam but he doesn't speak so she says, "Émi, we think you're walking into a trap."

"You're right," I say, gesturing to the map.

Alyssa looks down, sees my workings and frowns at me.

"Everything that's happened has to have been leading to this," I tell her. "Getting Ava and I to the place where the fire lines meet. The question is why?"

Alyssa shakes her head, crouching over the map and biting her lip. "The fire lines... Abilene used to be the heart of the stone's energy. That's why the Watchers were there, to guard it. When it was divided, they gave a piece to each city so that it would remain connected, so the energy could still flow." She looks up at Kole and Tsam. "Maybe Abilene's no longer the place where the stone's energy is strongest. Maybe it's here."

She points to the centre of my hand-drawn cross. "All this time we thought Mahg would want to attack Abilene again, but perhaps he's got something bigger in mind."

My head is spinning. "Like another spell? More dark magick?"

Alyssa shrugs. "I don't know, but I don't think we have a choice now."

I frown at her, expecting her to say that this means we have to return to Abilene.

"Mahg has Ava. Whatever he's planning, he can still use her, even if he doesn't have you. We don't have time to fetch the Elders. We have to try and stop him."

Tsam sighs and I feel like they've already disagreed over this.

"In all likelihood, we're walking straight into a trap," he says, "doing exactly what he wants us to do. How can we possibly stop him?"

"Because he doesn't know that we've figured it out," I say. "That's the one advantage we have. Mahg doesn't know that I saw him..." I pause, but Alyssa blinks at me to continue. "He doesn't know I saw him kill Garrett. He doesn't know we've found the fire lines. He thinks we're running blindly towards the Islands, trying to save Ava."

"But instead we're running blindly towards Mahg, trying to stop him from what exactly?" Even though Tsam is arguing the case, I can see he knows he's not going to win.

"Tsam," I say, trying to reach him, remind him of how things used to be. "I know you want to protect me. But Alyssa's right. There's no time to fetch the Elders. Whatever he's planning, we're the only chance of stopping it." Even as the words leave my mouth, I know how this sounds. Two Watchers, a Taman and a girl made of stone.

What chance is that?

TWENTY-FOUR

We are agreed. We keep going. Into the centre of the storm. We are two days' walk away. On the map, Kole indicates a village where he thinks we may be able to gather supplies and persuade someone to send word back to Abilene. It is the middle of the afternoon when the sky up ahead darkens. The clouds are thick and grey but I don't feel as though it's going to rain.

"Storm?" Kole asks Tsam, who is walking with us while Alyssa scouts ahead in the sky. Tsam squints at the distance then stops dead.

"I think it's smoke," he says. I'm about to dismiss him, assuming he is seeing smoke instead of clouds because of what happened back in Tarynne, but as I look at the horizon, I begin to think he's right. Without speaking, he takes flight and disappears above the clouds.

Kole and I wait with the elephants and, a few minutes later, Tsam returns with Alyssa. Their faces are ashen.

"It's a village," Alyssa says, forcing the words out as though they are scalding her throat. "I don't think anyone's alive."

We walk together to the village. Where once there were

houses, there are now only simmering piles of ash. Not one structure has been spared. There are bodies everywhere. For a moment, no one speaks. I cough from smoke that scours the back of my throat.

"We should check," I splutter. "Someone might still be alive."

I have checked the pulse of four women and two men when I finally find someone who has a heartbeat. It's a boy the same age as Bael, his face blackened with smoke. I hold my cheek close to his mouth, bracing myself for the sting of feeling nothing but, as I lean closer, he groans and his breath tickles my skin.

"Here!" I shout, waving my arms at the others. "He's alive!"

Kole is the first by my side. He kneels beside the boy and hesitates for a second. Then he pulls the boy's head gently onto his lap.

"It's alright," he whispers. "You'll be alright." He turns to me, tells me to find some water and he takes a handful of dark orange leaves from his pocket. "This was all I could carry. I should have brought more..."

I find an ash-coated trough and use a nearby bucket to scoop out some water. I take it to Kole and he dips in the leaves, wetting them so he can squeeze them into mulch and smear them on the boy's skin. Maya and Niri are watching him. When Niri steps forward, Maya puts her trunk in front of him but he wriggles away from her grip and picks his way over to Kole. He looks at the boy as if he knows him. He sniffs at him and I put my hand on his flank.

"It's not Bael," I say gently.

Niri looks at me, then back at the boy, and waves his trunk at Kole's hand.

"You want to help?" Kole asks. Niri blinks. Kole nudges over the bucket. "His arms and legs are the worst. I'll do those.

You wash his face. Alright?" Then he rips a square of fabric from his shirt and holds it up to the elephant's trunk, so he can take it.

Determined to be able this time, Niri dips the fabric into the bucket and starts to pat at the boy's cheeks. I want to stay and help, but Tsam and Alyssa have stopped searching and are standing in the centre of what would have been the village square, speaking in solemn whispers. When I walk over to them, Alyssa says, "There's no one else. Just the boy."

I sigh and scrunch my face into my hands. "Why would Mahg do this? These people were harmless. They have no weapons, nothing he could possibly want."

"Perhaps there wasn't a reason," Tsam says. "It's not just burns, the bodies have other wounds too. These people were slaughtered. Perhaps it was just for fun."

Alyssa glances at the horizon. It will be dark soon.

"We should bury them," she says. Her eyes are moist and, as she wipes at them with the back of her hand, it makes me wonder where she and Tsam left Garrett.

When he's finished with the boy, Kole agrees with Alyssa and with Maya's help, we move the bodies of twenty-eight villagers into rows and bury them beside a cluster of birch trees that used to be white but are now tainted with grey. By the time we have finished, the moon is high in the sky and our foreheads are glistening with sweat. My breath billows in clouds as we move the last of the soil back into place and, when the final grave is finished, Tsam and Alyssa stretch their wings out and lift their hands up towards the sky, as they did for Garrett. Kole and I follow suit. Maya lifts her trunk.

Niri is still with the boy and it feels wrong to light a fire, so we huddle in the shadow of one of the smouldering buildings. Every now and then, the wind whips through the decimated village and the flames ignite a little more. Each time they do, I lean towards their warmth and feel instantly guilty for appreciating it.

Kole and Tsam take the first watch while Alyssa and I sleep. After an hour or so, we swap. Then, just before sunrise, the boy wakes up. Opening his eyes to find a baby elephant mopping his brow, he frowns as if he is dreaming.

I touch the boy's arm and ask his name.

"Jamiyl," he croaks.

"Jamiyl, I'm Émi. Do you remember what happened?"

Jamiyl coughs, then winces. "I was playing with my sister," he says. "They came from nowhere. Shouting, with torches."

"Who did, Jamiyl?" Alyssa steps in. I frown at her not to be too pushy but she continues, "Do you know who they were?"

"They said they were soldiers of Mahg. They said we had a choice – join them, or..." The boy begins to sob and the tears sting his cheeks, which makes him sob more. "My Pa said 'No, I won't go with you. None of us will.' So they chased us. They had swords, and the houses were on fire. I lost my sister, and my Ma and Pa fell down..." Jamiyl's words are jumbling together and he is breathing so fast he looks as though he might faint.

"It's okay," I tell him. "You're safe now, try to breathe."

Jamiyl manages to calm himself. "A couple of people said yes, so they took them. But everyone else..."

"Jamiyl, you've been a big help, so you just rest now. My friend, Niri, will look after you." Jamiyl looks at Niri, and moves his hand to touch the calf's foot. Then he closes his eyes. He is sleeping again.

"It doesn't sound like Mahg was here. Just the soldiers, trying to force the villagers to join them," says Alyssa.

The three of us mumble our agreement. Then there's the sound of someone else's voice. A fifth voice. From the remains of the building just behind us.

"We missed someone!" I cry, charging towards the sound.

"Émi, be careful," Tsam warns, using my full name as if to indicate he's still not friends with me.

The charred wooden beams are still hot so I pull my jacket off and wrap it around my hands. Tsam and Kole do the same and we tug at the wreckage until, eventually, we see a booted foot.

"There's someone here," I call.

Gently, we pull the figure out into the open. He is groaning and clutching his upper arm with his opposite hand. He doesn't look badly burned, but he has a bloody wound on the side of his face and scratches on his hands.

"Is his arm broken?" Alyssa asks.

"Let me see," says Kole, reaching for the man's arm. Whoever it is groans loudly and wriggles away, hugging his arm to his body. Kole frowns. "Don't be afraid. Show me." His tone has sharpened.

"Kole, go easy," Tsam says. "He may not have seen a Taman before."

But Kole doesn't go easy. He grabs the man's hand and jerks it away from the arm that it's cradling. He holds it there, hovering midway between the man's chest and his chin, then launches himself forwards, wrapping his fingers around the man's throat and squeezing. Tsam and I grab for him, trying to pull him off.

"He's one of them," Kole growls, releasing his grip and stepping back, panting, unused to losing control. "Look at his arm."

I lean over. The man doesn't try to resist this time. Kole is right – emblazoned just beneath his shoulder is a tattoo. It's a black pair of wings, wrapped in thorns. From his position on the ground, the man spits in Kole's face, then grins at him. Kole slowly wipes the spittle from his cheek and I see his hand hover next to the baton on his belt, but he doesn't draw it.

I put my hand on Kole's arm. "We can't kill him, he's unarmed."

Kole nods at me. "Find something to tie him up," he says. "We'll take him with us."

Leaving the village, we continue north. Every now and then, I'm certain I see the flint walls of Nhatu glinting on the horizon. But I know I'm mistaken. There is too much distance between here and there and, even if there weren't, the Alder Woods would obscure the city from view. It has been twenty days since I left. Twenty days since the Cadets captured my mother. She may not be alive. She may have been sent to the camps, like my father. Perhaps I will never find out. Perhaps we are walking to our deaths.

As if he can sense my despair, Kole nudges me to look at Niri. Jamiyl is on Maya's back and, beside them, Niri is watching Jamiyl intently, as if for fear he will disappear.

"I'm worried that Niri is bonding too much with the boy," Kole says.

"Is that a bad thing?"

"It is unusual for a calf to lose their Taman so early. If he becomes close to the boy and the boy dies, or leaves..."

"Niri's heart will be broken twice," I finish.

Kole nods, looking at the calf as if he'd do anything to prevent that from happening.

"Maybe it's fate we found Jamiyl," I murmur, more to myself than to Kole. "The boy has no one. Maybe they need one another."

Kole looks at me, his dark eyes tracing the lines of my face. When we met, I wished he wouldn't look at me because I thought he wanted to kill me. Now, I wish he wouldn't look because it makes me want to kiss him.

Mahg's soldier makes a choking sound that brings me back to myself and I turn around. We don't know the man's name. So far, he's refused to speak to us. His wrists are bound with a rope that is also tied to Tsam. He coughs again and scratches out his first word.

"Water?"

Back in the village, we found some charred travelling flasks that we filled with water from the ashen trough, but our supplies are already running out and we're entering more and more sparse terrain.

"None to spare," says Tsam, tugging on the rope so that the soldier trips over his own feet. Alyssa narrows her eyes, as if she's unsure whether it's right to withhold water, but Tsam ignores her and continues walking. His face set and wings stiff, he is almost unrecognisable from the boy I grew up with. The person who came to fetch me from Nhatu was sensitive and charming. He glistened with cheerful confidence, and smothered me with concern. I hated that he faffed over me so much but I'd put up with any of that now, if it brought the old Tsam back to me.

The terrain between the cities is a savannah that floods with one season and crumbles with the next. This is the crumbling season – dry, arid and brown – and we are walking along the cracked remains of a riverbed. Tsam and Alyssa have been taking it in turns to scout ahead, looking for signs of more soldiers, but the heat and the limited water supply mean they both need to rest. When we stop, we look at the map.

"Not far to go," says Tsam, darkly. "If Mahg's there, we should see them soon."

"I think you should stop flying," I tell him. "Mahg will be watching the skies."

Tsam looks like he wants to argue with me, but he knows I'm right. Tsam and Alyssa are our best chance of stopping ourselves from walking straight into a trap, but they're also our biggest giveaway.

"We'll walk a bit further," says Kole, "then I'll go ahead while you all stay out of sight." I want to tell him no but when he sees the expression on my face he adds, "I'll be careful."

We continue along the riverbed until it begins to curve and dip down. We can't see clearly what lies around the bend, so Kole tells us to wait. He jogs ahead, quietly, biting through the pain in his leg. Soon, he's out of sight. He seems to take an eternity to return and Maya is starting to get anxious. When he does, he is breathless. "It's him. Mahg. Ahead."

My heart flips over in my chest. "Did you see Ava?"

Kole shakes his head. "I daren't get any closer. In the wet season there must be a waterfall. It's dry now but it dips down into a canyon. There are tents, lots of them. He's there, I can feel it."

The soldier, who is now tied to a tree, tips his head back and bares his yellow teeth in a guffaw. Spittle drips down his chin as he shouts, "Master, I'm here!"

His voice is too scratched by smoke damage to reach an intimidating volume, but Tsam wrestles to keep him quiet, reaching to cover his mouth. As he does, the soldier bites down on Tsam's forearm, drawing blood. His hands spring free of the rope and, too late, we realise he has worked loose the knot. He pushes Tsam back and starts to run but Alyssa swoops down on his back like a bird clawing its prey. She kicks him to the ground and Kole grabs him, forcing his arms behind his back and knotting them tightly with the rope. He ties his feet too and yanks hard. There will be no more escaping.

"Leave him here," says Alyssa, tending to Tsam's arm. "We can't take him any further."

Kole agrees, then turns to Maya. "We can't take you any further either, Maya." The elephant flaps her ears but Kole continues. "If this was a battle, you'd be at my side. But we need to be quick and quiet here. I love you, but quiet... It isn't your strong point, is it?" Maya blinks as if she is truly considering the question, then nudges Niri with her trunk. "Yes, Niri too. Take Jamiyl back to Tarynne. Émi, where's the map?"

I hand it to him and he asks for my charcoal, scribbling a note onto the back. "Give this to the Elders, alright?"

Maya flaps her ears and kneels down so that Kole can secure the map in Jamiyl's pocket. I hug her leg and she ruffles my hair with her trunk. I hug Niri too and can't stand the thought of the two of them journeying back all that way, alone, but I make myself pull away.

Instead of following Kole's path through the exposed riverbed, we dip into the spiky undergrowth surrounding it. Even so, the feeling we are being watched grows stronger with every step.

I try to think of Ava, to ask myself where she is and what she's doing. I feel that I should know, that I should be able to conjure a vision to help us prepare for what we're walking towards. But there is nothing. She is gone from me. Not even a whisper.

Eventually, Kole suggests we stop. "The canyon's up ahead, but there aren't many places to hide."

"We should wait until dark," I say, thinking of the Cadets, raiding when we least expected it. The others agree, so we crouch in the bushes and wait. The sun seems to take an eternity to set. Gradually, the sky turns orange, then grey, then navy blue, then black, and, before the moon even has a chance to rise, clouds sweep in to obscure its glow. As quietly as we can, we creep closer to the rim of the canyon.

On our bellies, flat in the dirt, we peer down at the tents.

There are, perhaps, fifty of them with thorny black wings emblazoned on their canvases. The same symbol we saw on the soldier's arm. They have been pitched in a ring surrounding a large black tent with a black flag raised at its main pole. Next to it is a smaller but identical tent, also of black canvas.

At regular intervals between the tents, fires have been lit and soldiers with loud crackling laughs sit drinking and playing the stone-throwing game that Tsam and Garrett showed me in the Alder Woods. These games are less friendly. Every now and then they erupt into a flurry of punches and profanities, until the soldiers calm down and start all over again.

"Mahg must be in there." Kole points to the large black tent.

"You think Ava's with him?" I ask.

"Maybe. Maybe in the smaller one," Kole says.

"So what's our plan?" asks Alyssa.

They're all looking at me. I take a deep breath. Try to think. "The four of us can't defeat Mahg on our own. I think we should just get Ava out of there. If we're right – if Mahg wanted the two of us here, at this spot, then the best we can do to stop him is make sure neither of us is here. Right?"

The others nod. Tsam wriggles closer. "We need to go down there. Figure out where she is."

"Tsam," I say, touching his arm and trying to make him look at me, "you and Alyssa are going to have to stay here."

Tsam blinks at me.

I gesture to their feathers. "Your wings. They're too bright, too easy to spot."

They know I'm right and exchange a worried glance. "Alright," Alyssa says. "We'll watch from here. Go down there, see if you can find Ava. If you can grab her easily, do it. If not, come straight back here and we'll figure out what to do."

I nod. "Alright."

"Ém," says Tsam, "if you get in trouble, you send up a spark.

We'll come get you out." I tell him I will and he smiles. For a moment, just one brief moment, he forgets that he's angry with me. Then he remembers. "Okay, then. Good luck."

I haven't really thought about how Kole and I are going to descend the rocks into Mahg's camp. Keeping low to the ground, we trace the rim of the canyon until we find a spot that slopes down less violently than the other sides. Then we start our descent. There's nothing to hold on to and we have to walk sideways on, to stop ourselves from breaking out into an uncontrollable run. Beneath our feet, the rocks and shingle keep shifting, sending cascades of dirt down towards the canyon floor. Each time a stone dislodges, we pause and flatten ourselves back against the rock, certain we've given ourselves away. By some miracle, we don't.

We make it to the bottom of the canyon in one piece and linger in the shadows for a moment to catch our breath. Then, one at a time, we dart forwards and hide ourselves behind a tent in the outer circle. We choose our path carefully, weaving through the shadows and moving only when the soldiers are shouting raucously at one another, certain they are distracted.

Eventually, we reach the small black tent. I lean closer to the canopy and strain my ears to hear noises from inside – nothing. Then, my fingers tingle and a firefly-sized dot of light ignites and sizzles in the centre of my palm. I squash it before it grows. That energy can only have come from one person. Ava.

"She's in there," I tell Kole. "I can feel her."

We move to the back of the tent and find a place where the canvas overlaps, knotted together with a length of twine running between eyelets. Then we crouch down and, with shaking hands, part the walls of the tent, just the tiniest amount, so we can see inside.

We were right. She's there.

The floor of the tent is covered in a deep red carpet that reminds me of the blood on Garrett's chin. In the centre, there is a wooden bed draped with blankets. Ava paces in front of it. Her hands are naked, gloveless. She is trembling and beads of sweat glisten on her worried forehead. Her hair is damp with it, and the black veins bulge at her throat. She is muttering something to herself, over and over, as she paces. But I can't hear what she's saying. Occasionally, she looks up, as if she's heard something, but then looks away and continues to mutter to herself.

"Right, she's alone," Kole whispers. "What are we waiting for?"

TWENTY-FIVE

Before I can answer, Ava swivels towards the tent's entrance and hurriedly drops to one knee. The door flap twitches to one side and Mahg strolls in, smiling. Ava doesn't dare look up until Mahg is stood in front of her, his wings spread and his shoulders tensed.

"Ava," he says, his voice thick and slimy.

She lifts her head. "Master," she says. "I've been lonely."

Mahg's neck twitches, irritation flashes into his eyes but he swallows it down and reassures her. "I'm here now," he says, tweaking a finger under Ava's chin and guiding her to her feet.

Ava's top lip begins to quiver. A tear rolls down her cheek. The black veins on her neck throb and Mahg's ebony feathers bristle.

"Come now," he soothes, stroking the side of her face. "You're not still upset about yesterday, are you?"

Ava sniffles and her breath catches as she speaks. "You told the soldiers to... the... village. They didn't do anything wrong."

Any pretense at sympathy is dropped. Mahg rounds on her. "They were heathens!" he snarls. "Enemies! They refused to join our noble cause so they were punished." Ava flinches and takes a step backwards. Mahg throws out his arms in disgust. "You think they were innocent?"

"You said—"

Mahg doesn't allow her to finish. He knocks her off her feet so that she cowers on the ground and he is standing above her. Slowly, he reaches down and wraps a hand around her neck. He squeezes. Ava pulls at his hand but he lifts her whole body by the throat, until her feet are dangling in the air. Then he releases her and she falls to her knees, crying quietly.

"Never challenge me again. Do you understand?"

She nods fervently, rubbing the skin at her throat.

Mahg turns and sweeps back towards the entrance. With his back to her he says, "No treats until after. I need you to behave."

Ava stretches out her hand as though she's about to beg him not to leave. Then, once he's gone, she rocks back on her heels and collapses into a heap of sobs.

"After what?" I whisper to Kole.

He shakes his head. "I don't know. But if there's an after, then this is the before. We won't have another chance to get her out of here."

I don't hesitate. I climb through the fold in the fabric, and tiptoe up to Ava. In her ear, I whisper, "Ava, it's Émi. Shhhhh."

When I place my hand on her shoulder, a tiny spark jolts into the air but she doesn't flinch. I kneel down in front of her and she raises her head, looking at me through half-focused eyes.

"Am I dreaming you?" she asks, her voice barely above a whisper.

"No, I'm here. We're here to bring you home."

Ava throws her arms around my neck and squeezes me tight. "I did a bad thing, Émi."

"I know," I tell her. "I saw."

"He said..."

"It doesn't matter, not now. We need to get you out of here. Then we'll talk. Alright?"

Ava nods and I help her to her feet.

"He'll find us," she whispers.

"Not if we move quickly," I say, waving towards the spot in the tent's lining where I know Kole is waiting.

Ava moves slowly, like she has lead in her toes. I push her through the gap first, then follow. Kole examines her closely.

"That was a little too easy," he whispers to me but I don't have time to think about whether he's right.

Kole leads the way, then me, then Ava, hanging on to the back of my shirt like a toddler who doesn't want to lose her mother. We are almost at the edge of the camp when I feel her grip loosen. I turn. She has stopped. Kole and I are concealed in the shadow of a tent in the second to last ring. But Ava stands frozen to the spot, out in the open, staring down at her hands. Kole meets my eyes and his expression is close to panic.

"Ava," I whisper, as loudly as I dare. "Ava, come on."

Ava is scratching at her neck. She lets out a gasp and begins to rock back and forth. She looks over at me and I hear her voice even though she isn't saying anything.

I need it, she begs.

I have no choice. I step out of the shadow and grab her arm. "We don't have time. We have to move."

Ava digs her heels in and refuses to shift. "I can't!" she wails. "He's the only one. The only one who has it." She waves her hands at me and I realise she's talking about the liquid he gave her. Time is running out.

"We'll get you some," I promise. "But we have to go. Now!"

Ava's eyes light up. For a second, she believes me. Then her face crumples. "You're lying," she says. "I can see in your heart and you're lying."

I look back at Kole and finally he gives in and charges

forwards. He grabs Ava and throws her over his shoulder. He plants his hand firmly over her mouth but she bites it.

And then, Ava screams.

Kole wrestles her to the ground and pins her to the floor. She is bucking against him, kicking and struggling. Torches spring up around the edge of the camp. Soldiers are shouting.

"What was that?"

"Who is that?"

"Intruders! Where are they?"

Ava stops kicking. I lean down and plead with her. "Ava, we have to run. They're going to find us."

Gingerly, Kole removes his hand from her mouth.

"It's too late," Ava whispers.

The back of my head throbs, like someone inside my brain is cracking a hammer against my skull. My eyelids are heavy. I force them open. I tug at my hands but they are tied behind my back. My feet are bound too, and I am strapped to a post. I realise I'm outside, high up. Sharp talons of wind slice my bare arms and feet. My boots are gone. So is my jacket. Beside me, Ava cowers, her body rolled in a ball. I can't see Kole.

From behind me, Mahg's voice drawls. "You're much prettier than your sister."

Then he steps into view. Up close, his wings send shivers through me. They are far broader than Tsam's, with coal-coloured feathers that taper like daggers.

"I'm glad you made it, Émi. I was worried you wouldn't be on time."

My mouth isn't gagged, but I don't speak.

"Now," he says, "I suppose the most sensible place to start would be to offer you a choice. I like offering people choices."

I think of the burned villagers. They had a choice, join him or...

He laughs a little. "In a perfect world, I would like you and your sister to fight alongside me. We could be great, the three of us. We really could..." He tails off, wistfully. Then suddenly, he snaps round and pinches my face between the fingers and thumb of his left hand. His nails dig into my skin. His breath is acrid and sour.

"Never," I spit.

Mahg sighs and releases his grip, as if he didn't expect anything different. Above, a crack of thunder ripples through the night sky. A drop of rain falls on my cheek.

"Ahhh," says Mahg. "It is almost time."

Turning his back to me, he steps forwards. We're on a ledge, sticking out from the side of the canyon. A cacophony of growls, whoops and cheers bursts up from below in an explosion of sound. "Soldiers," he calls, spreading out his wings. "The night has finally come!"

They cheer again. "It has been seventeen years since the Watchers of Abilene stopped us from taking what we deserved!"

Boos, this time.

"And at midnight tonight, it will be seventeen years since the Fire Stone was divided, buried and hidden from us."

Midnight, seventeen years... tomorrow is mine and Ava's birthday.

"But I have a surprise for you all." Mahg turns around and grabs Ava, pulling her to her feet and shoving her to the rim of the ledge. He leaves her there, swaying. Then he returns for me. As he lines me up beside her, his fingers grip my arm so tightly that his talons leave grooves in my skin. A whip of lightning flashes across the sky and illuminates the basin below.

There are hundreds of them. Soldiers, looking up at us.

When they see Ava and I, they bay and bark as if they want to drain our blood. Their hatred simmers like a volcano, waiting for its chance to erupt and destroy.

"We have the fire girls! We have them!" Mahg shouts, his voice echoing, getting louder, bouncing off the rocks. "And tonight, at midnight, at the place where the fire lines meet, we will harness their power." He draws a knife, holds up Ava's arm, and slices her palm. She cries and tries to hold her hand to her chest to stop the blood. It's no use; it drips down her arm, off the point of her elbow and onto the ground.

I try to move back but with my ankles tied I stumble. Mahg grabs my hands, unties them, and stabs my right palm. The pain is sharp and I watch as my blood converges with Ava's in the dirt.

"Their blood will mix with mine!" Mahg shouts, lifting up his own hand, raising the blade to meet it. I look down. An icy shiver grips my spine, forcing me to hold my breath. At the front of the crowd, a pair of salivating soldiers are holding Kole's limp figure between them; he is unconscious, his hair hanging down over his face. They throw him to the ground and one of them spits on him. Beside me, Ava lets out a cry of anguish. I try to meet her eyes but she is shaking her head and rocking back and forth.

Mahg slices his hand open and grabs Ava to him, pressing her wound against his and squeezing it. He sighs, his eyes rolling back as if he can feel her energy seeping into him.

"Their blood will create the most savage army The Four Cities has ever seen! You will have wings – you will fly, fight and destroy all who try to stop us!"

The basin shudders with the weight of the cheers. Then Mahg comes for me. The thunder groans, the lightning cracks and the rain gathers speed. My blade is gone. My feet are tied. I have nothing to fight him with. I can conjure a ball of sparks, but what will they do? They won't be strong enough, they won't be big enough, and Ava can't help me. My mind is racing. There must be something. Suddenly, I remember Falk. I remember spreading my fingers. Poof! An explosion. Too much fluid in the lantern.

I look at Ava; I need a moment to think. There's something, it's there, I can feel it but I need time and he is almost on me. Ava's eyes meet mine. *Please,* I beg, silently. *Please hear me, Ava. Please help me.*

A wave of realisation washes across her face. Mahg is still glowering at me, so he doesn't see it. But I do. She knows. Finally, she sees that he has manipulated her. She looks down at her hands and it is as though she is seeing herself for the first time. She exhales quickly, like someone is punching the air from her lungs.

Mahg's wings flex in and out, and his black eyes glint viciously. He grabs my wrist but I fix onto Ava's eyes and don't let go. As I stare at her, I feel the sparks ignite in my belly. The potion. Rhea's potion. *Burns like acid.* It's still there, buried against my skin on the inside of my shirt.

In an instant, before I know what she's doing, Ava conjures a fireball into her hand and launches it at Mahg. It misses him, perhaps on purpose, and collides with the side of the canyon. Rocks explode out. The crowd below roars. Mahg whirls around and grabs Ava's arm, dragging her towards him.

"How dare you?" he screams.

As Mahg takes hold of Ava, I summon the sparks into my hands. I stare at them and keep them hovering in front of me, a swirling hot ball of energy. Then I reach for Rhea's vial. With my thumb, I flick the lid to the ground. I pour the liquid into the flames that I'm holding. The fireball doubles in size, then trebles, swirling with the green of the liquid and the bright hot white of the flames, spinning round and round.

The crackling heat causes Mahg to turn. He releases Ava, smashing the back of his hand across her face so that she tumbles to the floor. He reaches for me, miniature black lightning bolts pulsating in his hands. Magick like mine, yet not like mine.

I pull my hand back over my shoulder, then hurl the acid fire towards him. With every muscle, every fibre, I will it forwards. He raises his hand and releases a bolt of his own but my fire rips through it, straight for him.

The instant it touches his flesh, the fireball explodes. The skin on the side of Mahg's face starts to slide off his cheekbone, melting. The flames engulf him. He screams. The soldiers roar.

I can't get to Ava, she's on the ground. Mahg's arms and wings are flailing; he's close to the edge of the canyon. I cast another ball, and another, each one sending him closer to the edge.

I try to step forwards, to hit him again and send him over. But I forget that my feet are still tied and I fall to the ground. From the floor, I manage to release one last bolt of flames that hits Mahg square in the chest. And he is gone. Still screaming as he plummets into the canyon.

I scramble towards Ava and reach for her. My fingers brush against hers. Her eyes widen. They are dark, and then something flickers. A reflection. Orange. Flames.

I turn around, too late. Mahg is back, his face contorted, fire lashing his skin. He's grabbing my ankles and pulls me over the edge with him.

We are falling.

Below, his army screams his name.

I wait for them to swallow me up.

TWENTY-SIX

Above me, green leaves rustle against a powder blue sky. Occasionally, sunlight drips in through the window beside the bed. My eyelids sting. I reach for the bedside table and find a glass of water. When I drink, my throat burns.

Slowly, I sit up and swing my legs out of the bed and onto the wooden floor. On a stool at the foot of the bed, a fresh set of clothes has been neatly folded. I pull them on and, instinctively, reach up to pin my hair. Raising my right arm causes a sharp flash of pain to travel down through my elbow and into my fingertips. I push back the strap of my vest and peer into the mirror; my shoulder is bandaged. The side of my face is grazed and a few strands of hair behind my ear are singed. I try to remember what happened but the only image I see is Mahg being engulfed by flames, reflected in Ava's eyes...

I recognise where I am – Rumah's house. It's quiet. As I pad down the hall towards the living area, I can't tell whether anyone is home. I push the door open and my heart sinks. Rumah is sitting at the kitchen table with her head in her hands. Her wings droop down towards the floor. There is no sign of Tsam.

"Rumah?" My voice splinters.

She looks up and quickly wipes the tears from her face. "Émi, you're awake!" Gently, she ushers me into a chair and brings me a cup of tea with brown leaves floating on the surface. "How are you feeling?" she asks, her eyes moving from my cheek to my shoulder.

"Rumah, what happened? How did I get here? Where's Tsam? Ava?"

Her face falls. "You don't remember?"

"Tsam wasn't there when... he and Alyssa were..." I hang my head and rub my forehead. "I don't know."

Rumah rests her hand on mine. "He's alright. They both are." Then she shivers. "They have gone to fetch Garrett's body."

I sigh and close my eyes. That's why Rumah was crying. "I'm sorry," I tell her, although the words are nowhere near enough. "What about the others?" I can't say their names. The knot in my stomach is telling me Kole and Ava are dead too.

Rumah kneels in front of me. "It's alright, Émi. Breathe. Kole and Ava are going to be alright."

Tears spring to my eyes. "Really?" I whisper.

"Ava is in the hospital. Physically she's fine but emotionally she's in a bad way."

"The drugs?"

Rumah nods. "She's fragile but she's in the best place."

"And Kole?"

"Battered and bruised, but he's alright. He'll be here soon." Rumah glances at the clock. "He's been here every day."

I frown and pain shoots through my temples. "How many days?"

"Three," says Rumah solemnly.

"What about Mahg? I don't remember—"

A knock on the door makes me jump and sit bolt upright in

my chair. But when it opens and I see Kole, I feel as though I'm going to cry again. His eyes widen to see me out of bed but he doesn't hurry over. He walks slowly and with a slight limp. Noticing my alarm, he wiggles his leg at me. "It's nearly healed," he says. "I'm fine."

Rumah pulls out a chair so that Kole can sit down. "Now that you're here," she says, "I'll go and tell the Elders Émi's awake."

After Rumah leaves, neither of us speaks. Kole's hair is tied back, as usual, but the side of his face sports an angry graze and his arms are covered in bruises.

"How did you...?" I don't know how to ask all the questions that fill my head. "I saw you, with the soldiers, I thought..."

"When you attacked Mahg, there was chaos. I stayed on the ground, got trampled on a fair bit." He winces. "Tsam and Alyssa saw everything. Mahg tried to drag you down with him but he couldn't keep hold of you. Tsam fought him off and then caught you as you fell. Alyssa rescued Ava and, when you were both safely out of the camp, Tsam came back for me. He flew me to the riverbed then told me to run. He couldn't carry both of us..."

Kole starts to reach for my hand, then changes his mind and just rests his palm on the table between us. "He flew you back here, then went straight to Hitra. She sent Watchers to raid the camp, but it was all gone by the time they got there. No sign of Mahg or the soldiers."

"What about you?"

"I didn't make it far. The Watchers found me."

I shake my head and lean back in my chair. "And Mahg?"

"I saw you burn him, but he flew. He's hurt, but we don't think he's dead, Émi."

My heart flutters with panic. "But if he's not dead... our blood. He tried to..."

Kole moves closer, touches the side of my face, tells me *shhh*. I lean into him. I feel his lips brush my forehead and I want to stay like this forever. But then I hear myself whispering, "Kole, I can't."

Instantly, he pulls away. His muscles tense. "I see."

I search his face, but the softness has gone. "It's just – not now."

He looks away. "I understand."

"Kole, please..."

We are interrupted by footsteps on the boardwalk. Tsam appears without Alyssa. His feathers are charred and his complexion is grey but when he sees me his face brightens. He hurries over to wrap his arms around me. He squeezes and squeezes and I'm not sure he's going to let go.

"I'm sorry," he whispers, "I was angry and childish. I should never have behaved the way I did."

He glances at Kole and I shake my head quickly. "None of that matters now."

"We need to go to the Elders," Kole says, pushing his chair back and moving towards the door.

Tsam nods. "Émi, are you up to it?"

Tsam insists on flying me to the Academy.

When we reach the Elders' chambers, Alyssa is waiting for us. I hug her and, at first, she stiffens, but then she relaxes into it and hugs me back.

"You're alright?" she asks. I tell her I am, although I'm not sure I know what alright means anymore.

Inside, Hitra is alone. Brock, Roan and Sayah are nowhere to be seen. When everyone is seated, Hitra sighs and gazes wistfully at the empty chair where Garrett should be sitting.

"I am so sorry to be meeting under these circumstances," she says, looking at Alyssa. "Garrett was..." She doesn't finish her sentence. Instead, she asks each of us in turn to tell her our version of events. Everything tallies with what Kole told me and the way Hitra reacts suggests she has heard all of it already.

"Well, despite our horrible loss, I must say well done to all of you." She pauses to glance at Alyssa. "You brought Ava back to us, and more – Mahg is significantly injured. This buys us time to gather the remaining pieces of the stone and should stall the growth of his army. This is more than we could have hoped for. Now, go home and rest. We will talk more tomorrow."

We stand to leave and we're almost at the door when she says, "Tsam, may I speak with you for a moment?"

Out in the corridor, I tell the others to go ahead. I need to talk to Hitra, too. Before anything else happens, I need to know that my mother is alright. I need Hitra to keep to our agreement. I push open the door, just a little, and then stop. Hitra is spreading out her wings, strutting towards Tsam like a bird circling its prey.

"You were told to exterminate the girls if they became a danger," she hisses. "What do you have to say for yourself?"

Tsam's expression remains calm but his feathers are quivering. "I tried. There was an incident in the mountains, with Ava. I tried to do it after that but she woke and I—"

Hitra rounds on him. "There are no excuses. Your failure could have cost us everything."

Tsam swallows hard and tries to smile. "Perhaps it was for the best? Now we have Émi and Ava back safely. We can help Ava, we can—"

Hitra's eyes are so full of anger they make me shudder. Slowly, she says, "We don't know whether Mahg is alive or dead. If he's alive, he is going to be very angry. And we have no idea the kind of hold he still has over Ava. How much of her blood merged with his. He could be on his way here as we speak. She could still be dangerous – volatile."

Tsam clears his throat. "I'm sorry, Ma'am, but I don't believe Mahg would come here. Now he knows we have both girls and he's seen Émi's power, he won't attack us."

Hitra sits down and fixes her steely gaze on him. "Perhaps not us. But he's going to be more desperate than ever to take a share of the stone from one of the other cities. So you'd better pray we can stop him."

Tsam hangs his head, as if the weight of his mistake is physically painful.

"And Tsam? From now on, you watch those girls. If you think for one second that they're not on our side, you destroy them. Because it's better they're dead than fighting for Mahg. Do you understand?"

Tsam is almost at the door and doesn't look back, just says, "Yes, Ma'am. I understand."

My mind is whirring. I didn't see it. At first, it was Kole I was wary of. Not Tsam. Not my Tsam. I don't know who to talk to. Suddenly, I feel as though maybe they're all in league together, just waiting for me to put a foot wrong, to become a little too powerful – a little too unpredictable.

I am still desperate to ask Hitra about my mother, but I can't bear to be near her. I feel so nauseous I don't even remember the walk from the Academy down to the lake but by the time I reach the water, the sun is setting and the air is cool. I'm shivering but I can't bring myself to be around the others. I don't want to go back to Rumah's house. I don't want to see Tsam. Because everything he ever said to me was a lie.

A hand on my shoulder jolts me back to reality – Alyssa.

"Émi," she says, "are you alright?"

"I should be asking you that," I tell her.

Alyssa sits down beside me, picks up a pebble and turns it over.

I hesitate. I don't want to burden her with what I know, but I can't keep it inside either.

"Ava wasn't lying about Tsam," I say, blurting it out quickly so it's not quite as painful.

At first Alyssa hardens at the mention of Ava, but then she frowns. "What do you mean?"

"He tried to kill her after she caused the avalanche. I heard him with Hitra."

Alyssa shakes her head, as if she can't absorb what I'm saying.

"Apparently, Tsam was supposed to exterminate Ava and I if we became dangerous or – unpredictable."

"He wouldn't," Alyssa says.

I pick at a pin-sized hole in my jodhpurs and look across the lake. I'm trying not to cry because my grief at losing Tsam is nothing compared to Alyssa's grief. But the tears come anyway.

Alyssa takes my hand and squeezes it. "Have you talked to him about it?"

"I can't. I can't even be near him."

"How about..." She pauses, bracing herself to utter the name of the person who caused her brother's death. "Ava? Have you seen her?"

I shake my head and brush the tears from my cheek. "I don't know what to say to her. To either of them. When I left Nhatu, I had to rebuild everything. Relearn who I was, who to trust. Tsam was my one constant. The one who had been there, in the before and the after. I thought he'd always be mine. My person. The one who I could fight with and disagree with and it wouldn't matter." I lower my voice. "I pushed Kole away because I felt guilty. Because I thought Tsam..."

"Oh," says Alyssa. "I didn't know."

"And Ava? I believed her. I thought she was innocent, troubled…"

Alyssa gives a deep sigh, as though she's been contemplating what she's about to say for a long time. "Garrett would say she was innocent. That Mahg manipulated her, that the drugs made her someone she's not. He'd say we should forgive her…" Alyssa's voice falters and she takes back her hand. "I don't think I can do that. But Ava's your sister, Émi. You should try. Just talk to her. And to Tsam."

Unexpectedly, she hugs me, then she stands and tells me she has to go. I don't follow her. Instead, I stay by the lake, steeling myself for taking her advice.

TWENTY-SEVEN

I sit until I'm blue with cold. I welcome the discomfort. When I return to Rumah's, the house is in darkness and I'm able to sneak back to my room.

The next morning, as soon as the sun rises, I go to visit Ava. She is in Abilene's hospital wing, a room carved into the rock next to the waterfall.

"They say the power of the stone helps people to heal," the nurse says as she leads me to Ava's room, blushing when she remembers who I am. "She's not saying much, but I'm sure she will appreciate your visit."

Ava sits by a window that looks out across the lake. She doesn't turn around when she hears me enter, or when I sit down beside her. Her hands are in her lap, wrapped in white padded mittens. Her hair seems a little lighter and the black veins have faded to blueish grey, but her eyes are set deep in her face and her lips are thin.

"Ava?" I ask, resting my hand on her knee. "Can you hear me?"

She doesn't move but, slowly, she whispers, "I'm sorry."

After that, no matter what I say, she doesn't respond. I tell her everyone is alright. I tell her no one is angry with her, that we're going to help her get better. But she just blinks at the window, silently. Eventually, I stand up to leave and I'm almost at the door, when I change my mind. I stride back to her and kneel down, then I unhook Nor's pendant from my throat and refasten it around Ava's. I kiss her forehead, and whisper, "Everything will be alright. We have each other."

Leaving the hospital, I return to Rumah's house to change my clothes. She has leant me a white shirt and now she uses a small delicate brush to paint silver swirls at the corners of my eyes. Tsam is also wearing white, with silver markings on his hands and forearms. When he speaks to me, I answer politely, but I can't look into his eyes. I don't want to see the betrayal.

At the lake, Watchers, all dressed in white, stand on the cliffs. More have gathered on the bridge, but the beach is reserved for friends and family. Rumah, Tsam and I descend the steps and join a line of Watchers with silver decorations on their hands or faces. Alyssa and her parents are in the centre of the line. Alyssa is holding hands with a young Fledgling who can't be more than twelve years old. I ask Rumah who it is, and when she tells me it is Alyssa and Garrett's younger sister, sorrow knots my insides.

From behind the Academy, the Elders fly into view. They are carrying a wooden stretcher. Upon it, Garrett's body is covered with a long white cloth. The Elders rest the stretcher on the surface of the lake, then fly back to the eastern tower where they stand with their arms outstretched in prayer.

Everyone copies them, humming gently, then Alyssa's parents hold hands and wade out towards their son's body. They place their hands on top of him, the way Tsam and Alyssa did in the woods, and the Watchers beside the lake dip their heads in respect.

When I look up, Alyssa has dropped her little sister's hand

and is calling me to her. "Émi," she says, "are you ready?" I nod and slide off my sandals. "Are you sure? You don't have to."

"I want to. For Garrett."

I walk out into the water. I let the ripples lap gently at my thighs, and keep striding out until they reach my chest. I have to paddle to stay afloat. Garrett's father and mother kiss me on the cheek, then swim back to the shore. When they are back on the beach, standing beside their daughters, I raise my hands up into the air and press them together. Whispers pass quietly through the crowd. I open my palms, revealing a tiny ball of flames. Tears are falling from my eyes and I'm struggling to see.

"You are safe," I whisper to Garrett, "and you are loved." Then, I lower the flames and allow the fabric to catch light. Gently, I push him towards the spot where I know the Fire Stone glows.

All around the lake, the Watchers of Abilene spread out their wings and lift their hands to the sky. "You are safe," they call, "and you are loved."

The chant is repeated in soft, poetic whispers until the flames die down and Garrett is no more. Then everyone gathers on the beach to solemnly and quietly celebrate Garrett – his kindness, his humour, his strength. I speak with Alyssa and her family for a while, then slip away to check on Ava. She'll have been watching the funeral from her room and I daren't think about how she is feeling.

I am crossing the entrance hall of the Academy, towards the stairs that lead to the hospital wing, when Tsam catches up with me.

"Émi, wait." I keep walking and if his strides weren't so big he would have to trot to catch up with me. "Are you alright? You've barely spoken to me..."

I bite my lip. If I speak, the words will tumble out and I

won't be able to stop them until they're all dried up. I keep walking, staring at the ground.

"Émi, what's wrong?" he asks.

I wonder whether he knows, deep down. Whether he's been waiting for the moment when I would discover the truth.

Slowly, I force out the words. "I heard you with Hitra."

Tsam's face tightens. "You..." His wings droop and he sweeps a hand over his forehead.

"If you're about to tell me it isn't how it sounded," I spit, "don't bother. There is nothing you can say."

"Please," he says. That's all, just please.

"You were my friend," I say, tears biting at the back of my throat.

Tsam softens his voice so that it's barely a whisper. "I'm still your friend, Émi..."

"How can you say that?" I am shouting now, my voice bouncing off the Academy walls and taunting me. "Everything that ever happened between us – every conversation, every look. You had an ulterior motive. You were watching me." My voice cracks. "You were waiting for me to slip up, to become a threat. And then what? You would have smothered me in my sleep? A dagger? An arrow? Poison? What? How would you have killed me, Tsam? The same way you tried to kill Ava? In the dead of night when I couldn't protect myself?"

Tsam opens his mouth but no sound comes out.

"You made me feel so guilty for liking Kole. And all the time you were manipulating me. Like Mahg manipulated Ava."

"Émi, no, that's not—" He puts his hand on my shoulder. His touch burns. I can't bear it. I push him away. A spark flies from my palm and sizzles as it meets his chest. He doesn't flinch.

I'm exhausted. The fight inside me has gone. "I will never be able to trust you again."

Tsam jolts back as though I have slapped him in the face. "I wouldn't hurt you."

"That's not what you told Hitra. I heard you, Tsam. I heard you promise to do it properly next time."

"If I'd said no she would have asked someone else. But I'd never do it, Émi. I couldn't."

I hold up my hand. The tears have stopped. "I. Don't. Believe. You."

We are staring at one another, silence hanging between us like a dagger, when the door at the end of the corridor bursts open. It flies back on its hinges and clatters against the wall.

My knees tremble. I grin so wide it hurts my cheeks. "Amin?"

I fling myself forwards and throw my arms around his neck. He embraces me, then gently pushes me away. His hair is wild and his skin is dirty. My grin collapses.

"Émi," he croaks, "You must come back to Nhatu. The Council... They're going to execute your mother."

Thank you so much for joining Émi at the start of her journey. There is so much more to come and I can't wait to share the second and third instalments with you.

If you loved *Fire Lines*, I would really appreciate a short review wherever you bought the book from. Your help in spreading the word is invaluable and means the world to me.

You can also sign up for the *Fire Lines* mailing list and be the first to read exclusive excerpts from book two. Just visit:

WWW.FIRELINES.CO.UK

Cara x

ACKNOWLEDGEMENTS

Writing a book is all-consuming, terrifying, exhilarating and hard. And this book, my very first novel, would never have happened if it wasn't for the support and belief of some very important people.

Firstly, I must thank my editor Karen Ball. Her advice was invaluable and helped my manuscript to shine.

I'd also like to thank the brilliant and wonderful Helen Crawford-White, who designed a cover beyond my wildest dreams, along with all those who proofread, beta-read and generally enthused about *Fire Lines* in the run up to publication day.

To my friends – I am so grateful that you stuck around while I spent eighteen months living like a hermit and declining far too many social invitations in favour of sitting in front of my laptop. You know who you are and you're the best.

To my husband, who believed in me and encouraged me from the beginning – in so many ways, I would not have achieved my dream without you. I love you.

To my dog, Molly, who provided cuddles, laughter, a calm presence when I felt like I was going mad and the excuse to get out into the fresh air when I was in danger of moulding into my chair – if only you could understand how instrumental you are to my existence. Toast and Dentastix will be your rewards.

To Mum and Dad – I don't even know where to start. From the word 'look' you made me believe I could do anything I set my mind to. And, as always, you were right. You fed my imagination and gave me a house full of books. We coloured-in, listened to books on tape, read stories at bedtime, went to the theatre and explored the world. You showed me that running a business is hard but entirely within reach if you work for it. You are my heroes.

To my sister, Petra, who was the first person I trusted with so-early-they're-embarrassing-to-even-remember drafts – your ideas and input helped to shape Émi's story. Without your help, my characters would have all had names like Bob or John, and there would still be passages of text labelled things like 'think of word for plant'. One day we will co-write and it will be amazing.

To my grandparents, whose spirits will be with me for as long as I am breathing – I miss you. I wish you could have seen this book, held it in your hands and run around telling everyone you met that your granddaughter became an author. Perhaps, up in the clouds somewhere, you're doing just that. I hope so.

To Uncle Eric, who is still trying to train the business side of my brain to cope with accounting – thank you for your time and patience, I'll get there eventually!

And finally, to all those who have bought a copy of *Fire Lines*, read it and got to this little page at the back – there simply aren't enough words to explain how grateful I am. I hope you enjoyed the story and I hope book two will be even better.

ABOUT THE AUTHOR

Cara Thurlbourn writes children's and young adult fiction. *Fire Lines* is her first novel and it's a story she's been planning since she was fifteen years old.

Cara has a degree in English from the University of Nottingham and an MA in Publishing from Oxford Brookes University.

She lives in a tiny village in Suffolk and has worked in academic and educational publishing for nearly ten years. Cara blogs about her author journey and in November 2016 she crowd-funded her first children's book. 10% of its profits are donated to animal rehoming charities.

Cara plans to write at least two more books in the Fire Lines series, as well as a young adult mystery series, and has lots more children's stories waiting in the wings.

You can sign up for Cara's newsletter, for give-aways, updates and latest releases, here: www.carathurlbourn.com/contact